Praise for

COOLEST AMERICAN STORIES 2023

"An unforgettable, diverse, and lively collection of tales that go above and beyond cool. Once I cracked this open, I was hooked."

—Alex Segura, bestselling author of *Secret Identity*

"*Coolest American Stories 2023* will remind you why you fell in love with the short story in the first place: unforgettable characters, memorable plots, and crackling prose. The tension hums on every page. This is a collection you won't want to miss."

—PEN/Hemingway Award finalist Rebecca Johns, author of *The Countess*

"Quirky, surprising—and yes, cool—these stories mirror the heartaches (and occasional joys) of the human experience with humor, poignancy, and grace. The anthology is a showcase of the latest and greatest talent writing in the short form today."

—Tara Laskowski, winner of Agatha and Anthony Awards, author of *The Mother Next Door* and *One Night Gone*

"Read these edgy and exceptional stories for inspiration, entertainment, and to take in the drumbeat of the zeitgeist. *Coolest American Stories 2023* is a rewarding and panoramic selection."

—Elizabeth McKenzie, author of *The Portable Veblen*, longlisted for the National Book Award

COOLEST AMERICAN STORIES 2023

MARK WISH
& ELIZABETH COFFEY

EDITORS

coolest stories press
new york

www.coolestamericanstories.com
@JustCoolStories

ISBN 978-1-7375739-2-0
ISBN 978-1-7375739-3-7 (ebook)

PRINTED IN THE UNITED STATES OF AMERICA
10 9 8 7 6 5 4 3 2 1

CONTENTS

WARNING

Our goals at *Coolest American Stories* are 1) to create a national love of the short story and 2) to decrease division in the United States by providing a common ground of enjoyment for *all* people, from *all* walks of life and backgrounds—by publishing the most interesting and compelling stories with the widest appeal. Interesting, compelling, and appealing storytelling, however, can at times prove disturbing to some, so please, by all means, do enjoy the stories that follow, but be prepared to be surprised, startled, and maybe, here and there, shocked.

INTRODUCTION

Roughly a year ago, while drafting the intro to *Coolest American Stories 2022*, I looked for support of *Coolest*'s philosophy—that interesting storytelling could help make a divided America cool again—and found some in the advice Salman Rushdie offered in his recent book *Languages of Truth*: "Unless what you know is really interesting, don't write about it."

This morning, as I draft this introduction to *Coolest 2023*, Mr. Rushdie lies in an intensive care unit with stab wounds in his neck and abdomen and an eye that might never see again, a ventilator keeping him alive.

So what am I supposed to say now, America? *Thank you for embracing the interesting work of Mr. Rushdie—and of the authors of the stories in* Coolest 2022*—and thereby becoming cool again?* I cannot say that. I cannot say that because, clearly, much of America continues to be the opposite of cool. After all, for a good number of people, anger seems to be the default mode; headlines everywhere I look this morning remind me that, in addition to the terror that has visited Mr. Rushdie, U.S. citizens are now threatening to attack their country's top law enforcement agency with physical violence because that agency merely did what taxpayers paid it to do.

Still, as Elizabeth just mentioned as she sits across our apartment reading this morning's news, I really should write "*something* positive" in this intro. Because, as she's pointed out, countering anger with anger would not be cool.

So in Mr. Rushdie's honor, and in the spirit his life has reflected—that of pressing on with one's storytelling come what may—let me highlight the recent success stories of the thirteen authors in *Coolest 2022.*

Coolest 2022 author S. A. Cosby's success of late has been uplifting to say the least. For quite a few years before 2021, Shawn kept doing what he believed in—writing interesting, candid, and, for some readers, even startling fiction—and since 2021, his persistence has been paying off. His novel *Blacktop Wasteland* won even more major awards in 2022, and his novel *Razorblade Tears* rose quickly to bestseller status, widespread critical acclaim, and, just weeks ago, inclusion on Barack Obama's 2022 Summer Reading List. Shawn is clearly the superstar of *Coolest 2022*, but the literary success of the other twelve authors in that volume have sparkled in 2022 as well. Frances Park's novel *The Summer My Sister Was Cleopatra Moon* was recently accepted by Heliotrope Books in NYC (she tells us the appearance of her story in *Coolest 2022* "spurred on" this success), on the heels of the publication of her memoir *That Lonely Spell.* Lee Martin's novel *The Glassmaker's Wife* will be released soon by Dzanc Books. The German publisher Schüren-Verlag will publish a translation of D.Z. Stone's book about Dieter Vaupel, *A Fairy Tale Unmasked: The Teacher and the Nazi Slaves.* Megan Ritchie is, as I write this, in Edinburgh to draft her first novel thanks to a University of Miami Dean's Summer Award she won this spring.

On top of that, the thirteen authors published in the inaugural volume of *Coolest* have had so many short stories accepted or published in 2022 that to list all of them here might be considered boastful on my part and—well, uncool.

But maybe the best news about these thirteen authors, as Elizabeth and I see things, is that their stories in *Coolest 2022* have led readers from across the United States (and even readers from around the world) to reach out through email or social media to let us know they've found these stories immensely engaging and enjoyable. We've been gratified and, frankly, blown away by the overwhelmingly positive reader reviews on Amazon, one of them by a person who posted this:

> *This is the best curated story collection I've read in years (well decades, if I'm being honest). I had intended to read a story here and there, in between a novel I had started, but found I couldn't stop. I read cover to cover and was sad when I got to the 13th story. There are no tedious parts and pages, just a powerful ride.*
>
> *Each story is a gem on its own with layered and nuanced characters who will stay with you well after your read. Filled with people you know and people you want to know more. There are laugh-out-loud moments, as well as thought-provoking and poignant ones. I can't wait for the 2023 edition and it's only January!*

And no, we didn't pay for that review or any other; even if we would've wanted to (and we *never* would have wanted to), our tiny marketing budget never could have allowed it. The success we've had so far, then, seems to be thanks to word of mouth among readers. Readers from all walks of life who, like us, believe that, when it comes to storytelling, "cool" equals "interesting."

If you ask me, the writer-reader connection, emotionally and viscerally, is what storytelling and certainly what *Coolest* is all about. And at the risk of overreaching, I'll also go ahead and say this: If, in 2023, any short story will touch your heart enough to cause you to reconsider your beliefs, recalibrate your anger, or alter the current lot of your relationships for the better, that short story very well might appear here, in the pages that follow.

I hope you'll find some of Salman Rushdie's fearless spirit in the bold and heartfelt thirteen stories here in *Coolest 2023*. In any case, on behalf of Elizabeth and me, I dedicate this second annual volume of *Coolest* to Mr. Rushdie, thank him for his generosity over the years, and wish him Godspeed toward days and nights infinitely better than these.

—Mark Wish

COOLEST AMERICAN STORIES 2023

MEET AND GREET

GEORGIA SMITH

My mom didn't believe in being hungry. I don't think she was hungry for a single second. I would come home from softball practice to a box of Oreos open on the counter, six greasy bags of Hardee's takeout on the kitchen table, discount Halloween candy in every drawer. What was I supposed to do, stare at it? Spring of my freshman year, when I went to live with my aunt Allison, all that changed. We rotated between three dinners: grilled chicken and corn with nothing but salt, scrambled eggs on an English muffin, and bow tie pasta with red sauce and some spinach thrown in. The first couple weeks, I was starving. I missed sugar so much I'd sneak handfuls of my aunt's gummy vitamins after she went to bed. I saved up change at the bottom of my backpack to buy as many snacks from the vending machine in the cafeteria as I could and ate them in the bathroom stall between classes. But when I came back to school in the fall, they had redesigned the cafeteria and moved the vending machine to the middle of the room, and with everyone watching I couldn't work up the courage to get anything but a Diet Coke. Eventually I got used to being hungry all the time, but I haven't quite gotten used to being skinny (if I can call myself that). I lost sixty pounds between my freshman and sophomore years, if anyone's counting.

It was pretty much just after the truck incident in the middle of my freshman year, when I was still big, that I started watching *Shadowcrossed*. The truck incident is a nice way of saying my mother was either trying to kill me with her pickup truck or was so negligent driving it into me that, well, long story short, a judge decided it was "in the best interest of the child" that I live with my aunt Allison. Anyway it was while I was lying there in my aunt's guest room with the blinds shut, doped up on hydrocodone, waiting for my leg to go numb, that I started watching *Shadowcrossed* and first fell in love.

Funny enough, I didn't care for Dr. Rory McNeil at the very start. He was a brilliant scientist, and in the first few episodes his only purpose was to explain the chemistry behind the mutation and the only possible weaknesses the Shadow-Walkers might have. He was arrogant, rolling his eyes when Matty and Liana asked how the throat-burning curse could be reversed, and even locking Nell out of the lab after she tried to steal a sample of the Sludgecrawler's DNA. But near the end of season one, when the barricades collapsed and half the world was set on fire, he joined the survivors in the bunker and became a crucial player in the fight against the apocalypse. It was in the bunker that everyone learned that his mother, who also had been a scientist, died giving birth to him, and that his father made him promise to carry on her legacy (just before he, the father, succumbed to his wounds from a bear attack on a camping trip ten-year-old Rory had begged him to go on). That's when my heart went out to Rory. Rory as a boy, Rory as a man—all of him.

In short, Rory amazed me. In a world of flesh-eating zombies and supernatural monsters and every imaginable opportunity for cliché, he was incredibly human, a careful web of contradictions—flawed but courageous, arrogant but self-deprecating, witty and vulnerable and powerful all at once. He was attractive, but not in the cookie-cutter way you'd imagine. He was smaller in stature than the other male leads and had a jagged, off-kilter smile. But what I liked most about him was his eyes. They were impossibly dark—brown circles stark against his pale face—and they had their own language. Rory's eyes could say so much. I mean *really.* They were just killer.

I knew of course that Dr. Rory McNeil was not real, but Daniel Fitzpatrick was. Daniel was Irish and put on a foolproof American accent as Rory. He hadn't always planned to become an actor; he'd grown up in a working-class family in Dublin and joked that if he hadn't gotten his lucky break, he'd be pouring pints at his father's pub. When he was fourteen his mother made him audition for a local production of *The Secret Garden.* He got the role of Colin and unexpectedly fell in love with live theater: "It was absolutely terrifying, but I adored it." After finishing secondary school he earned a scholarship to the prestigious Gaiety School of Acting, where he trained in Shakespeare and became serious about pursuing acting as a career. He was practically unknown for his first eight years in the industry, mostly in UK-based indie films and minor roles on crime dramas. I watched them all, of course, but just found myself frustrated at how they wasted his talent.

After *Shadowcrossed* shot up in popularity, Rory's status as a breakout fan-favorite character catapulted Daniel to a ridiculous amount of attention and scrutiny in the public eye. There was little known about his private life. He'd been photographed getting breakfast with Gemma Crawford, aspiring model and daughter of some aging Australian actress. He was once spotted in his car with what looked like a joint in his hand, which quickly became a controversial topic among fans.

In interviews, he talked at length about how grateful he was to play such a complex character and to be a part of the epic world of *Shadowcrossed*. He was articulate and thoughtful, only occasionally stumbling over his words. I began to notice he had a habit of zoning out, getting a bit lost in the interviewers' questions, and then snapping back to reality in an instant—big brown eyes sparking with life as he answered politely. Of course there was more to him than the soft-spoken, courteous exterior—I knew there was, but I didn't want to see it. I was content to imagine that the Daniel I saw in interviews was a complete and perfect picture of him. I loved him so much it hurt.

But I didn't tell anyone how much I loved him, not even Aunt Allison, who sometimes watched *Shadowcrossed* with me. I guess some part of me was ashamed. Other girls were going on dates with their lab partners and making out in the backs of cars in the school parking lot, and I was sick in love with an image of a man on another continent. This was stupid, and I knew it. Still, it was *love*, and it was pure, and I was able to keep the Kat who loved Daniel separate from the Kat who went to school and pitched for the softball team and washed dishes with my aunt. Everyone else could understand that Kat, but they wouldn't understand the Kat who loved

Daniel. It was Daniel I talked to when I lay in bed at night listening to nothing but the pipes and the ice maker, thinking things I couldn't say to any real person I knew.

The fact that Daniel was coming to Knoxville to do a meet and greet in April was astounding. I could hardly even make sense of it. Daniel Fitzpatrick, at the A&E Conference Center just six miles from my school? I didn't have money for a ticket, and I couldn't ask my aunt. *Eighty* dollars for a one-day pass to the convention, and another *two hundred* for a photo with Daniel? I was staring at those numbers on my phone late at night when I got the idea to do something pretty terrible.

My aunt was asleep—I could tell by her snoring. I called Colton, who I'd had a history with. I didn't have to say much for him to drive over in thirty minutes, and that was because of the history. And the history was this: The night Colton turned eighteen, meaning old enough to commit statutory rape, he got drunk with a bunch of guys on his football team at a party, got a classmate of mine drunk, took off her clothes, and, well, had his way with her. He also was drunk or mean enough (he later told me he was merely drunk enough) to give his phone to a teammate of his and ask him to take photos of him attempting to have his way with her again, and then, drunk or not, he was stupid enough to send the photos, six of them, to a whole bunch of his football-player friends, as well as to me. He told me later he'd sent them to me by accident, and usually I believe him about that. And usually I believe it was right not to report him to the police after the girl he had his way with begged me not to because she wouldn't be able to handle the embarrassment.

Anyway now, with my aunt asleep, I met him outside in the driveway. It was cold out and I was just wearing my sweatpants and a YMCA T-shirt. He was leaning against his ugly white Silverado like he thought he was in a movie. He seemed bigger at night, more grown-up than he looked in those photos. He'd cut his hair oddly and it made his face look square.

"You got skinny," he said.

"Shut up," I said.

"It's not a bad thing."

"I didn't ask you, did I?"

"I meant it in a good way."

"I need a favor," I said.

"What."

I didn't have to answer. Everyone knew he worked evening shifts as a busboy at Big Zack's Rib Shack—he wasn't rich by any means, but he always had wads of cash.

"How much?" he said.

I decided to round up a little.

"Four hundred."

"What for?"

"I can't tell you. But if you give it to me, I'll delete the pictures."

"You'll delete them in front of me?"

"Yes," I said.

"How do I know you don't have copies?"

"Cause I don't, dipshit."

He squinted a little, trying to look like he had a single goddamn thought. His eyes were like an animal's, hardly perceiving. He promptly drove home, then came back with the cash. I still couldn't look at the pictures without wanting to vomit, and with Colton standing so close when I pulled them up on my phone, I also felt more than a little shaky. I deleted them once, then again from my trash folder. It actually felt nice, seeing them just evaporate like that.

"Oh, I missed one," I said, a total lie.

"So delete it then."

"Not unless you let me borrow your truck for a couple hours."

"Now?"

"No. In a few weeks. I'll let you know."

"How am I gonna get to work?"

I held up my phone. "You'll figure something out."

"Fine then."

"Thank you."

"Thank *you*," he had the nerve to say as he handed me the bills.

"Fuck off."

"You're not gonna tell me what the money's for?" he asked.

"Not any of your business."

"I just want to make sure . . . that you're, you know, not in any trouble."

His eyes turned silver and murky, reflecting the glare of the streetlight two doors down.

"I'm not," I said.

"I've wanted to talk to you," he said. "I've thought a lot since the last time we talked, about how fucked up things were. About what I did."

"Yeah," I said.

"Maybe I could come to one of your games, give you a ride home or something."

"I don't think so," I said. "Good night."

I turned around. The windows of the house were completely dark, like no one lived there. I counted the cash one more time as I heard the Silverado's door slam and noticed the headlights making a stretched-out shadow of me on the driveway.

• • •

The convention was on a Saturday. I felt a little lonely going by myself, but I only had about two friends anyway, and I didn't like either of them all that much, and neither of them watched *Shadowcrossed.* I wore my most stylish outfit, one of the few that fit me these days—a blue floral dress with a white button-down on top. I curled the ends of my hair and drew on thick strokes of eyeliner. I took the bus there. A weird old man sat next to me even though the thing was nearly empty.

They checked my ticket what felt like twelve different times, but I finally made it inside. The lobby was packed. Some people were wearing *Shadowcrossed* T-shirts; others were dressed up like characters—I saw plenty of Rorys, his ripped blue sweater and ammo vest the most recognizable outfit of season three. The scene was pure chaos: giant herds of teenage girls, children running around, nerds pretending to duel one another in the corner of the lobby. The overlapping voices and bright lights made the headache I always have these days worse.

My time slot to meet Daniel was 12:45, and I had arrived at noon. I decided to buy a six-dollar bottle of water, take my time drinking it, then make my way over to the line. I stood in line behind a girl twice my size, who was filming the whole thing on her phone and talking to the camera like someone was actually listening. "I am at Geek Con day two, in line to meet—STOP, I'M GOING TO HYPERVENTILATE—meet Daniel FUCKING Fitzpatrick. I'm not going to be able to speak. I just KNOW I'm not gonna be able to speak. Say a prayer for me, guys. Say a prayer for your bitch."

She went on like this for God knows how long. I wanted to deck her in the face and do whatever it took to keep her hands off Daniel. When I thought about him standing behind the thin wall I was leaning against, I calmed down a little. He wouldn't want me to get angry.

Girls were leaving the meet-and-greet room in clumps, some of them filming themselves giggling hysterically, some of them speechless.

"Next in line," the attendant in a green Geek Con T-shirt called. The big girl stepped forward.

"One autograph, three photos, sixty seconds," he said in a flat voice, looking down at his watch.

The girl nodded solemnly. The door opened and she disappeared.

Sixty seconds later, the attendant repeated the rules to me. I didn't say anything back. The door opened up and the big girl walked out, her phone just inches from her face, which was contorted into something between a scream and a sob. "HE IS A GODDAMN ANGEL," she screeched as she was swallowed by the crowd.

I stepped inside. There were two other people there, a photographer with a sour look on his face and another attendant in the green shirt. And in the middle, sitting on a small stool in front of a backdrop of the *Shadowcrossed* logo, was Daniel.

I knew him so well. I knew every molecule of his face and body. But somehow it was like seeing him for the first time. He was a real person. He was not a tiny figure on my iPhone screen.

"Hello," he said.

"Hello," I said back. My American accent sounded dull in the echo of his warm Irish one.

He was wearing a black T-shirt, grey jeans, black boots. He looked impossibly cool.

"What's your name?" he asked.

"Kat," I said. I took a few steps closer to him.

"Nice to meet you, Kat. I take it you're a fan of the show?"

"Yes," I said. "I like your character."

"Thank you very much, Kat," he said. "Would you like to get a photo?"

"Yes," I said.

I stepped closer to him. There were maybe just four inches between us. I hadn't been this close to a guy since I'd been in my aunt 's driveway with Colton, who always smelled like dry sweat and barbecue. Daniel smelled like a fireplace and no food whatsoever. He stood up, tentatively lifted his arm and put it around me.

The photographer took three photos, *FLASH FLASH FLASH*—I tried to smile but I could hardly look at the camera with Daniel so close. With his face next to mine, I could see he was tired. There were faint lines on his forehead that hadn't shown on camera. He was so thin it seemed like anything could break him. I never wanted to leave him. I could feel the time dwindling, each second evaporating right out of my hands. We only had a few left.

He looked me in the eyes. "Thank you for coming out," he said. "It's really humbling, getting to meet each and every one of you."

I didn't know what to say.

"I still can't believe any of this is real, to be quite honest," he continued. He had become deft, I imagined, at filling silences left by dumbstruck fans.

I just nodded. A small, awkward twitch of the chin.

He gave a tired smile and then looked down at his hands. I could hear my heartbeat. I had failed completely, been unable to convey even an iota of the love I had for him, a love so great it had displaced every other feeling I'd ever known.

I dropped my phone and it fell with a flat thud. He bent down to pick it up and handed it back to me, our fingers not quite touching, and just after that, I noticed, on a calling card beside a bottle of mineral water on the floor near the stool he'd sat on, the word *Porter's* handwritten and underlined twice.

"Time's up," an unenthusiastic voice called.

• • •

Nobody went to Porter's Pizza and Wings for pizza or wings. It was a dive bar through and through, and if you didn't know that to begin with, you had no business being there. I had heard of some of the popular kids using their fakes at Porter's; Mary Helen on the softball team had gotten kicked out for throwing up on the bouncer. I hoped not to see any of them there, but the good news was the popular kids usually went downtown on Saturday nights, and Porter's was in the suburbs.

Seeing as I didn't have a fake, getting in could be tricky. Then I realized I maybe didn't have to get in through the front door. Porter's was in the middle of a strip mall, flanked by a hair salon and an Italian deli. If you walked all the way to the supermarket at the end of the mall, you could get behind the stores, where they keep the dumpsters and loading zones. I crept through the narrow gap between the very back of the supermarket and a wire fence to get to that rear area, where it was pitch-black and a little spooky. But from over the middle of the roof of the mall, you could see the yellow glow from the patio in front of Porter's.

And so it was through the back entrance at Porter's that I saw him again—my love, Daniel—crossing from the bar to the corner of the room, where a man he seemed to know stood holding a beer. Daniel's hair was a bit messy, and he wore a loose plaid button-down over the same black shirt from earlier.

And just like that, I was one of them, a partygoer in a bar, a grown-up doing grown-up things, a lonely soul on the hunt for booze and human connection.

And suddenly, Daniel began toward me, though he wasn't looking at me. Then, as if he'd thought better of where he'd been going, he headed out the open front door, so I did too. He quickly found a quiet spot in a corner of the patio, set his drink on the railing, and lit a cigarette. At the meet and greet he'd seemed tired, but now he looked downright gloomy. I considered, for the first time, that he sometimes felt the way I did. That he could feel loneliness, anger, even profound disappointment at the path his life had taken. This only made me love him more.

I also began to realize I couldn't just follow him and lurk. He was *Daniel*. I walked up to him.

"I know you probably come to places like these to get *away* from fans," I said. It came out a little shaky but otherwise fine.

He looked right at me and blinked a few times.

"Sorry?" he said, all earnestness.

"You're Daniel Fitzpatrick," I said.

He smiled softly. "I am," he said. Then: "Wait a minute! I recognize you from earlier! You were at the convention!"

I had considered that he might recognize me but hadn't exactly planned for it.

"Nice memory," I said, attempting to play it cool.

"I'm good with faces, that's all."

"My name's Katherine," I said.

"Lovely to meet you again, Katherine. I don't blame you for needing a drink after that shitshow," he said. And then the same sort of weariness came back into his eyes, and I was afraid he just wanted to be left alone but was too polite to say it.

"How'd you hear about Porter's?" I asked.

"My mate—well, my publicist—Terry, he heard about it from one of his internet friends here in the States. They're meeting tonight, late night business talks, I guess you could say. I'm just along for the ride."

"It's a good spot," I said.

"Is it?"

I nodded.

"How old are you, Katherine?"

"I'm twenty-one," I said.

"Aye, are you now?"

"Yes. People always tell me I look young for my age."

"Most of the girls who go to those conventions are no older than sixteen. Makes me feel a bit weird, to be honest."

"It's all innocent," I said. "They just love the show."

He smiled and scoffed a little.

"Who are you here with?" he asked.

"My friend Julia," I said. "She's inside, trying her best to score free drinks."

"And how's that going?"

"A long process, apparently."

"Right," he said.

I was eager to change the subject. When he lifted his glass to take a sip of his drink, I noticed his knuckles were red and scraped.

"You get that fighting zombies?" I asked.

"Huh?"

"Your hand."

"Oh. That's a tricky story."

"What happened?"

"You won't want to hear it."

"Nothing shocks me much," I said.

"Right. Well, try not to take this too personally. But it gets to be a bit much for me sometimes, those conventions. The greets and meets, the sobbing, the tattoos of my face and the death grip hugs, being ushered and carted around like a prize cattle. It can get me feeling nauseated, literally. Last night I had something of a tantrum and tried to end the press tour early."

"And?"

"And my manager didn't take kindly to it. He gave me a good slap and a shove against the wall. And, well, the poor kid from Dublin in me took over."

"This was just yesterday?"

"Yeah," he said. His eyes shifted downward, and I almost got the sense he was embarrassed to have told me this. "He's fine, my manager. Don't fret."

"But what about you? Are you okay?"

"Oh, they stuffed me with Zoloft and a couple of caffeine pills. I'm grand."

"They drugged you?" I asked.

He laughed. "Oh, that's nothing. It's not all bad. Listen to me . . . don't I sound like a tool, whining about my miserable life of fame and riches?"

"No, you don't."

"Yeah? I really did mean it, by the way. Whatever I said today about being grateful for you and everybody who watches the show. I really am. Grateful, that is. I just think sometimes I'm not cut out for this kind of thing."

The hand holding his cigarette, I noticed, was trembling.

"Would you take it all back?" I asked. "The fame? Playing Rory?"

"Right now, yes. But I suppose then I'd be bored off my ass. And I'd be at some other bar, bitching and moaning about that instead."

"Danny!" a voice called, and I looked over to see the man Daniel was with earlier poking his head out the door. "Quit pretending you're in some emo music video and get your ass back in here!" The man, who I figured must be Terry, then noticed me and looked quickly at Daniel. It was such a subtle look he probably thought I didn't catch it.

"This is my friend Katherine," Daniel called. "We were just chatting."

"Hello, Katherine!" Terry said.

Terry joined us, and we talked for a while. Terry was friendly enough, but he wouldn't stop mentioning Arthur, the Instagram influencer who had a brilliant idea for a livestream interview with Daniel and was allegedly arriving later in the night. When Terry asked me questions about myself, answers just started bubbling out of me, answers and stories I didn't think I was capable of inventing. I told them I was the captain of my college's dance team. I told them I worked part-time at my mom's grocery store. I told them I'd just broken up with my boyfriend of three years. All the while, Daniel nodded politely and laughed at Terry's wry comments, but his gaze at me was unfocused.

Then Terry's phone rang. "It's Arthur," he said, and he stepped off to the side.

Daniel and I just looked at each other for a moment. He seemed unsure of what to say without Terry there.

"Do you ever miss being a kid?" I asked.

"Sorry?"

"It's just . . . when you were a kid you cared about things, real things. Like your schoolwork and your sports, or, like, animals you'd meet on the street. And once you get older, it's like you're just sort of drifting along watching everything happen around you and not really caring about anything but TV shows."

He took a drag of his cigarette. He was facing the inside of Porter's, and the moon, which was low, cast little white reflections onto his eyes.

"Are you all right, Katherine?" he asked.

"*Yes*, I'm all right," I said. "I'm just talking."

The night air had chilled a little. He kept glancing into Porter's like he was keeping an eye out for someone.

"You didn't come here with your friend Julia, did you," he said.

"She went home," I said. "She just texted me. She's not feeling good."

"One too many free drinks?" he quipped. His eyes were glassy and, for the first time, illegible.

"Something like that," I said.

Terry hung up the phone and interrupted to let us know Arthur would be on his way soon. Daniel excused himself to the bathroom and left his drink to bleed through its napkin on the railing.

There are a lot of things that I'm not good at explaining. I couldn't explain why *Warning: Nicotine is an addictive chemical* has never made anybody think twice before buying vape juice. Or why I miss living with my mom, who once, long before the truck incident, put a centipede on my face to wake me up for school and told me onion rings count as a vegetable. Or why I crushed up my leftover hydrocodone pills to bring to Porter's, then poured the powder into Daniel's drink while he was off in the bathroom. The best way I can try is this: There are some things that you are compelled to do without ever *really* getting the chance to consult yourself on whether or not they're a good idea. In my own experience, it seems like there are these invisible shapes and patterns and happenings around you that give you no choice but to do the things you do. That's the best explanation I can give for it, anyway.

Terry and I then had a bland conversation about Instagram follower ratios, but I couldn't focus on much else other than why Daniel was taking so long on his way back to the patio. Terry took another call and left me just standing there pretending to text someone. When I finally saw Daniel walking back toward me, the music had gotten louder and people had started dancing, bumping into one another and dodging drinks both on the patio and inside. Daniel grabbed his drink as soon as he stood next to me, sipping from it as if it were all he cared about. Then Terry pointed inside, indicating Daniel and I should go in, so we did. Daniel was soon leaning against a wall while Terry stood on the other side of him, texting. The thumping beat of Guns N' Roses faded out and was replaced by a bass-heavy remix of Whitney Houston's "How Will I Know."

"I fuckin' love this song!" Daniel slurred.

"Get out there and give us a show, Danny boy," Terry said, giving Daniel a nudge on the shoulder.

Daniel stumbled forward.

Terry noticed me. "Katherine! You're still here! Go dance with Danny!"

As if to steady Daniel, I took his hands. They felt cold and bony. I danced the only way I knew, swaying back and forth and stepping my feet in and out of a little imaginary box. Daniel was looser, enthusiastic but clumsy and disoriented. He twirled me around. Whitney's voice swelled and rippled, and the neon signs on the wall lit us in and out of blue flashes, and I felt alive and real and knew that every single thing I'd done or seen or given up to be here had been worth it.

Then a new song began, and Terry grabbed Daniel by the shoulders, a show of brotherly affection, but stepped back when he realized Daniel had all but collapsed against him.

"Jesus," he said. "I leave you alone for a few minutes and you somehow manage to get plastered. You can take the man out of Ireland but you can't—"

Daniel was lurching suddenly to the side. "Catch him!" I yelled, and Terry grabbed his arm to keep him upright.

"Christ," Terry muttered.

Daniel's eyes were open but cast downward at the floor. Terry snapped his hands in front of his face. "You with me?" he asked, but Daniel just blinked. "Danny?" Terry said cautiously. He was supporting all of Daniel's weight now. "Don't zonk out on me now, Danny. Arthur's on his way. I can't fuck this one up. Danny?"

Terry shook him, but Daniel gave no sign of understanding.

"Jesus," Terry repeated. "What the hell were you drinking?"

"Just a gin and tonic, I think," I said. "Where are you guys staying?"

"The Hilton downtown. Less than twenty minutes away."

"I can get him back," I said. "I drove here, and I haven't had a drink in hours."

Daniel seemed to hear this, and he looked up at me with his shiny brown eyes. Terry and he exchanged glances; Daniel's chin dipped, possibly a nod.

I held the door as Terry dragged him out to the parking lot. Colton's Silverado, which was parked far away from all the other cars, glowed a brilliant white under a gray light from one of the tall poles. Terry helped Daniel into the passenger seat—"In you go, big guy"—then gave me the hotel's address and room number, and thanked me for my kindness.

"Give me a call when you've made it to the room," he

told Daniel, who was slumped over with his hair flopped down onto his face. "And don't forget, we leave for Tampa at nine. Set your alarm, kiddo."

Daniel let out a groan, which Terry seemed to accept as an answer. Terry told me again, "1107," then slammed the passenger door shut, and the noise jolted Daniel back to awareness. He sat up and raised an unsteady hand to try the handle. When the door didn't open, he pounded on the window and screamed "TERRY!" but Terry was already heading inside.

Seeing Daniel like that made my heart ache. It struck me that he looked like Rory McNeil, not Daniel Fitzpatrick. And if there ever was anything Rory had shown me, it was that it's never too late to do a good thing, no matter who you are or what you've already screwed up.

"You're gonna be okay, Daniel," I said, but he was still facing the window and didn't seem to hear me.

The radio was set to the country station Colton apparently listened to. I didn't know what to tap to change the channel, so men sang tributes to biscuits and fallen soldiers while I cruised toward the highway. I had never driven this late at night, and I found myself getting spooked whenever cars whipped past. A couple times Daniel sat up and clutched at the dashboard and murmured something about an airport, then leaned back and drifted off again.

We crossed over the flat black river and reached downtown. I got the strange sense that I didn't live in this city at all. In the distance I saw the tall reflective face of the hotel. I turned onto the driveway and parked out front. Daniel was asleep, but when I unlocked the doors he opened his eyes, blinked, and sat up.

I went around to his side, opened the door, and took hold of him by his hands. To my surprise, he could stand but he didn't seem to know who I was. I helped him shuffle along toward the entrance, which took a while, but no one in the lobby said anything as we walked past the check-in desk and made it to the elevators.

On our way up, I took the room key from his wallet. By the time we stepped off on the eleventh floor, he was pretty much dead weight, but I was able to lug him down the hallway.

As soon as we got inside the room, he staggered into the bathroom. I wandered toward the giant frameless windows to give him some privacy. To me then, the skyline looked like a phony backdrop. His clothes were strewn across his suitcase; I folded them and zipped the suitcase closed. I checked my phone. It was two in the morning. I had eleven missed calls from my aunt and three from Colton. I turned off my phone and sat down on the bed and looked out at the blinking city.

"Daniel?" I called out, but he said nothing.

I walked over to the bathroom where he lay on the floor, his head leaning against the base of the toilet. His eyes were closed and he'd turned shockingly pale. I doubted I had the strength to drag him into the bed, but I couldn't leave him alone like that either. I sat down on the edge of the bathtub. He said something so faint I couldn't make it out.

"What was that?" I asked, and I leaned closer.

"Tizzit the end?"

"The end?"

"Is it?"

"The end of what?"

"This. The tour. Is this the last of it?"

"Yes," I said. "It is. You go back home to Dublin tomorrow."

"Right," he said.

I pulled him away from the toilet so he could lie flat on the floor, then let myself lie down beside him. The floor was big enough for us easily, and it was clean, but the tile under us was cold. After a while the lights switched themselves off, turning all the glossy white surfaces gray. I took his hand and held it until his clammy fingers curled around mine. The refrain of his breathing softened and steadied, and as I listened, I thought about the past, about Rory going back in time to save his father from the bear and me going back in time to the fall of my freshman year, when I'd still lived with my mom. I thought about forgiveness, about who gets to decide what wrongs could and couldn't be righted. About what a person sitting at home would think while watching my life unfold in ten episodes on their TV screen. For a long time I wondered about that classmate of mine who'd chosen to trust the wrong man. I did not think at all about tomorrow for us, for any of us. There would be tomorrow for that.

ATTACHMENT

DAVID BOROFKA

I'm not going to sugarcoat it or try to explain it away. I acted badly. In this era of the Pandemic and Social Distancing, she was cleaning as a way to keep busy and be productive at home, but I should mention that nearly every bad thing I've ever done happened when Francie was cleaning, even in the best of times, because for her cleaning means disposal rather than washing or scrubbing or dusting. Sometimes the frenzy becomes too much for her. And me. This is a fact that must be acknowledged and in my case accommodated. Over the years she has thrown or given away many, many things, but the items she wanted to get rid of during this particular purge were especially telling: clothing (the plaid sport coat I wore when I received the Jablonski Prize as a high school senior); kitchen appliances (my George Foreman hamburger grill); and sports accessories (a Roto Grip bowling ball, with which I bowled my only 300 game). Don't get me wrong; she gets rid of her own things as well. These are merely the latest examples of the hundreds of items that have made their way to Goodwill, the Salvation Army, American Veterans, the hospice thrift store, not to mention our local landfills, and I name these items only because they were once mine and I remember them. Sometimes with fondness, sometimes with regret.

The fury of her cleaning and disposal makes me nervous for reasons I don't entirely understand. I'm not threatened by the loss of my material possessions alone—I hadn't worn that jacket in nearly fifty years, for example, so its time was clearly past the expiration date—but I am threatened by what that loss represents: the memory of what lives within those objects and the sense that my presence in history is being erased.

"Who could forget you?" she asked. "I mean, really. You're sixty-five years old, you're in *many* yearbooks, and you're such a drama queen. You act like the child who hasn't been chosen."

"Oh, sure," I said. "Easy for you to say, Miss Easy-Come-Easy-Go. Little Miss Sophomore Girl."

I happen to know for a fact that she has jewelry she wore when she was fifteen. It's squirreled away in a bag at the bottom of a cedar chest, and she would no more wear that jewelry now than she'd wear Mickey Mouse ears, but it would break her heart to see it go.

Maybe, though, maybe I take all of this too much to heart. We get stuff, we get rid of stuff, stuff is not us. I should be able to turn the page, right?

• • •

So, the Jablonski Prize. Named for Morton and Wilda Jablonski and endowed by their children with proceeds from their estate, this award honored the high school senior deemed to have the most promise. The Jablonskis performed together for forty-five years in our local community theater scene.

They owned Morda's, half theater space, half restaurant, neither of which was very good. The prime rib was overcooked, the drinks were weak, and the theater consisted of drawing-room farces and scripts considered racy in 1936. But Morton and Wilda were a generous and warm-hearted pair. As I say, Morda's was nothing to get excited about, and it only became worse under the ownership of their children, who saw it as their own private slush fund. But it was a local institution, and its time could be dated from the speakeasies—one more reminder that longevity can make up for any number of deficiencies. This, I think, is true for individuals as well as institutions, and I am a case in point.

I know most people point to junior high and high school as a gauntlet of zits and hormones, public awkwardness, and romantic devastation, but I found a home there among the socially frightened and the intellectually callow, a home that I never quite found again. Academics came easy, student government was natural for me, and spots on the football and baseball teams seemed reserved for me. I might as well have had a key since I was there each day and for longer stretches than the janitors. At the end of each academic year, I was up and down the stairs to the stage, picking up my annual graft from the principal and the other too-eager-to-please faculty, as though the plaques, ribbons, medals, and certificates were my right. All of those ended up in a trunk in my parents' garage, and when they died, the trunk migrated to the attic, that cave where it has remained in hiding from Francie for the past fifteen years, awaiting the recycling bin and its final end.

At the end of my senior year, when I stood up at the awards assembly to accept the Jablonski from Morton and

Wilda's oldest daughter Bernadette, my plaid sport coat led the way. Pretty splashy, I was; I could have had a job at any used car lot in town at that moment, but I had bigger fish in mind. College, for one thing, and a bigger town in which to shine. That I went to college but then came back is part of the story; that Bernadette Jablonski, then in her forties, handed me my check, and kissed and kissed and kissed both my cheeks, leaving lip prints all over my face, is another. Those kisses gave me ideas that were no more sustainable, as it turned out, than they were original.

On the other hand, Francie didn't have it so easy. I have to admit that. Her parents split up when she was thirteen, and she was forced to witness all the shouting, money-grubbing, and vile adult behavior that ensued. Dishes were thrown, glasses were shattered, threats of both murder and suicide were a daily occurrence. She lived on the other side of town and on the other side of the high school from me—it might as well have been the other side of the moon—and she was the oldest of seven, so she was constantly responsible for cleaning up someone's mess. Sometimes it was one of her younger siblings who'd thrown up in bed from the stress, but sometimes it was one or the other parent who'd drunk too much the night before. She made breakfasts out of the demolished boxes in the pantry and dinners out of air. Given her circumstances, none of the teachers at school were surprised that Francie Peck didn't have her homework done, her assignments read, or her papers written; nor were they surprised when she showed up for tenth grade with her hair dyed green, black widows tattooed on each wrist, and her jaw clenched so tight that her lips didn't show. What that meant, I understand now. But then, given my own self-absorption, she was merely intriguing. As exotic and dangerous as one of those carnivorous plants.

So of *course* I asked her out that year. I was a senior and she was a sophomore, and while I might have had the edge by age, she was by far the cannier of the two of us.

"You're kidding, right?" she said when I said we should go do something together. "You think I'm dressing up for you?"

"No," I said. "What makes you think that?"

She held her arms out as though inviting inspection. "Take a guess, Mr. Hot Shot."

She was inviting me to look at her T-shirt with its baked-in-the-dryer soup stains and her paint-spattered blue jeans, all of which could have used a wash, and as oblivious as I was, I knew that the subtext was a) she had no better clothes than this; b) even if she had better clothes, she wasn't about to put on anything finer just to engage in hand-to-hand combat in the tight back seat of a Camaro; and c) what could we possibly have had in common?

I had no answers to either a) or b), so I answered c) instead: "I'd like to get to know you." Which was equal parts evasion and truth.

I convinced her to go bowling, thinking that such a neutral activity would raise no objections, but I would be wrong. We had just gotten out of the car in the parking lot of Rodeo Lanes when she stopped and crossed her arms over her fifteen-year-old, less-than-imposing chest.

"Nuh-uh," she said. "Nope."

She pointed to the bag that held my ball and shoes. The bag that I had pulled out from behind the driver's seat and now held in my right hand.

"You have your own ball, and you have your own shoes. You're going to make me wear those red-and-green clown shoes worn by Grandma Moses and Mother Jones and make me stick my fingers in holes where who knows whose boogers are packed in, while you get excellent traction and use a ball you've cleaned on every other throw? And you're going to say we had a good time? I don't think so. No thank you."

"I've been in junior leagues since I was seven," I said. "Is that my fault?"

"Take me home," she said. "I knew this was a bad idea. The last time I went bowling, it was someone else's birthday party when I was ten, and they put the bumpers beside the gutters so we wouldn't cry."

"Look," I said. "I'll rent the clown shoes, I'll use a house ball, and I'll ask for bumpers if you want. If the lanes are quiet, they might even turn on the disco ball and the strobes."

"Don't be ridiculous," she said. "Put the bag away, and we'll call it good. I mean, we're beyond bumper age, don't you think?"

I did as I was told: put the bag behind the front seat, wore the rentals, and rolled the Fred Flintstone ball with the holes made for bratwursts rather than fingers. I didn't bother to keep score since she said it wasn't important. That hurt me. But again I did as I was told, and we got along just fine, even if we weren't playing the game that I knew. We got along just fine for the rest of that year as well. Now and again we even retreated to the back seat of the used Camaro my parents had bought me.

• • •

I guess what I'm saying is that I had it easier than most, easier than my wife for sure, and that if I now have my periods of regret, it's only because I wish I'd worked a little harder to earn the respect of others. I went away to college with my five hundred dollars of Jablonski money and the blessing of my parents, who underwrote the rest.

Francie came to see me the day before I left. She brought me a handmade card that said, "Go ahead and LEAVE, you jerk!" on the front. On the inside, it said, "Many, many happy, happy returns!" And then in smaller script she'd written, "Assuming you come back at all, that is." We had talked about this, about the reality that I was going to college while she was going into her junior year of high school; we'd seen such relationships wither and die in the space of a month or two, so we'd agreed we wouldn't put ourselves under that kind of pressure. Make a clean break of it, we'd said. Use the year to start over with new friends, and maybe the next summer, when we'd caught our breath from everyone and everything new that we'd experienced, we'd see where things stood. We were very proud of ourselves for being so mature.

I went to college as a math major, but thanks to Bernadette Jablonski, I thought of myself as an actor. I had played bit parts in school productions, but that last summer before I left for college, I played Kolenkhov in Morda's production of *You Can't Take It with You*—and I discovered that graduation hadn't meant I was done with applause or attention. Oh, no. My Kolenkhov was ripe with Russian alveolars and guttural disgust, and I enjoyed the process of dying my hair as black as Raskolnikov's heart and attaching a beard with spirit gum. I bellowed my part with gusto. If anyone had asked what the play was about, I would've said that it was the life and times of a displaced Russian ballet instructor who happens to meet an everyday American family. I was that much in love with myself and prisoner to the idea. If I were honest, however, I would have admitted that I could never wrap myself inside the character no matter how much spirit gum I applied, nor how loudly I spoke. I was too worried about forgetting my lines. Francie came to see me twice, and both times she had to hedge her assessments.

"Well, that was interesting," she said the first time. "I'm not sure the beard is you." And the second time? "Your beard stayed on well again." Not exactly the heartiest of endorsements.

I didn't let this reaction bother me because Bernadette Jablonski had already cautioned me about critics, instructing me to pay them no mind, which I didn't because she said this as she was taking off my beard with dabs of rubbing alcohol and cotton balls and touching me in places where my beard had never been. Besides what would poor little Francie know about theater, she of the benighted family and unenriched life? She didn't even know how to bowl.

Bernadette had cast herself in the role of Essie Carmichael, for which she was clearly too old, while her husband, Walter, played Grandfather Vanderhof, using an accent straight from a lobster boat. At one point in Act II, I was meant to hoist Bernadette-as-Essie in a lift, but she proved to be a little too heavy and I proved not to be up to the challenge, so we played it for laughs, and night after night she fell to the stage in a whirl of silk tights, translucent panties, and a cartwheel of pancake tutu. Her legs stuck out like Raggedy Ann's, and she swore off-script, which made the laughs from our know-nothing audience all the more heartfelt.

On our closing night, Bernadette cleaned my face of beard and then delivered me from high school inexperience in the women's restroom of the middle school auditorium, where we'd put on the show to accommodate an audience too large for the restaurant. She locked the door from the inside to keep any latecomers at bay and then hopped onto the ledge of one of the sinks with a nimbleness that belied her supposed gracelessness on stage. The ups and downs of her tutu were as exhilarating as they were frightening and mysterious.

Her husband was, at that moment, on stage with the crew, and we could hear furniture and backdrops being loaded onto dollies.

When we were through, which took about as long as it took for my pants to drop, she removed her stage paint and touched up her shellacked hair.

"Honey," she said, "there will be others, but you'll never have better."

A lie wrapped in a truth, but I didn't know which was which, and that was as frightening as anything. I could replay in my mind the grand finale of the moves that she made on me, but I've never been able to say it out loud.

Was it any wonder I needed to go to college?

• • •

I didn't get my degree in math, and I didn't go on stage ever again despite my many auditions, and I could feel my star fading by the minute. College was a time of discovery, and one of my biggest discoveries was that not many people cared what happened to me, award assemblies of the past notwithstanding. My high school teachers continued to award prizes to younger and younger students, and they no longer seemed to think much of my promise if they thought about me at all. They doted on the next years' crops instead like faithless lovers. So I became an English major with a teaching credential on the side, and I returned home like Ulysses without the fanfare or the slaughter. Rather than the conquering hero, I was just another wet-behind-the-ears new hire with a less than stellar degree. My chemistry teacher from five years earlier shook his head, and his eyes bespoke confusion. "English?" he said. "When you could manipulate differential equations? You could have worked for NASA."

"Well," I said in my own defense, "these things happen."

I could have kicked myself for not having something wittier to say. He was no summer's day, of course, while my mind was now bent on understanding truths about the human condition, truths that no derivative or launch angle could ever approach. That's what I wanted to say, but I didn't because I didn't entirely believe it, even if the space program had come to the end of its golden age.

Even Bernadette Jablonski didn't seem entirely happy to see me on my return.

"You," she said. "Aren't you supposed to be making the world safe for technology?"

"I'm teaching now," I said, to which she replied, "Oh, my God. That's what they all do, isn't it?"

I'd gone to see her at Morda's since I'd heard she and Walter and company were rehearsing one of their revivals. She'd cast herself as Aunt Abby in *Arsenic and Old Lace*, a role which put her at least a little closer to her own age, even if, in my mind, she'd chosen this play so she could cast the next male high schooler she wanted to finger. I no longer fit her preferred demographic, but given the number of her former prizewinners manning the other male roles, I could see I was no longer particularly welcome.

As if that weren't enough, I'd lost touch with Francie, and she was nowhere to be found. I heard from others that she'd dropped out her senior year, then gotten her GED, and after that, left town with a bus ticket and no firm plans and barely a hint of a goodbye. Who knew?

I threw myself into teaching since I had nothing else to do. And if my students didn't learn much of value from me, I could organize them into lockstep and make them march through the curriculum like a brigade of shell-shocked survivors. I wouldn't let the adolescents in my charge horse around with *Romeo and Juliet* any more than I'd let them off the hook for the correct use of *there*, *their*, and *they're*, and if I refused the invitation to teach the seniors, that was only due to my knowledge of what disappointments lay in wait for them. I gained a reputation, just as I gained a wife, a mortgage, two sons, and Caesar, the dumbest of dumb Labradors: slowly and over the course of years, brick by brick.

But then, just as quickly, I lost it all.

• • •

For which I blame the George Foreman grill.

And, yes, as silly as it sounds, the truth remains: Without that grill, I might still be with the woman I met at church, the woman I married because it seemed like the right thing to do, and I might still be father to the sons I sired. Houses can be bought and sold, and a Labrador is befuddled on the best of its days, but I rue the loss of all that brick-and-mortar and all those swirls of loose black fur.

The grill, well, that's gone now, too, the recent victim of Francie's most aggressive purge. She had nothing against it personally, except her general principle that appliances should be useful seven days a week and not just for the occasional one-off. And, she believed, they should also work.

"But I cooked on that exclusively," I argued. "For years."

"It's dead," she said. "And you clearly needed new recipes."

"Who needs recipes?" I said. "I got you. With all apologies to gender roles."

"Huh," she said. "I'm here now, and I've been here for years, so I say the grill's gotta go. Keep this up, and *I'll* leave."

The outside of it was black and scorched, the cord frayed, the wires exposed, and it had lived in the garage with the cobwebs and mice for thirty years or more; I never intended to use it again. I had kept it as a reminder of how tenuous life can be, but I guess such a rationale is no match for spring cleaning during a quarantine.

But I need to backtrack a bit.

Not long after I started teaching, I met Tiffany at church, one of those convention-center-size monstrosities at the white north end of town. I'll spare you the name and denomination in order to protect the innocent. In my own mind I called it the Cheez Whiz and Lard Tabernacle, since that's the way the name of the Almighty sounded coming from the mouth of the pastor who'd made most of his bones in Texas; he tended to get worked up at the conclusions of his sermons, when the spit began to fly. I had gone there thinking that, in the absence of Francie, looking for love might be best fulfilled by numbers, and this church had no shortage of single women. What I hadn't expected was the kind of women I'd find. Very earnest, they were, and very quick to offer praise to the Lard. It should also be noted that the Tabernacle was something of a track meet for dating, since the most attractive of the single women got snapped up by the age of twenty-one, and they weren't shy about asking their prospective suitors for a resume and a pay stub, if not references.

I'll say this for Tiffany: She was something of an outlier within her spiritual circle. She worked for her father's advertising outfit, and she made three times my teacher's salary—this, by itself, could have disqualified me. Unlike the majority of her evangelical sisters, though, she liked wearing J.Crew to work more than she liked wearing sweatpants at home, and she wasn't interested in nesting the moment she got married. Our wedding was a destination affair in Carmel, where the décor was Martha Stewart; our honeymoon was a quick four-day trip to Cabo because she had meetings the following Wednesday in her father's office, and as she said, she had to tend to his business. So she was all the more surprised when the pregnancy test came back positive three months later. She was more surprised than I was since, one Friday night after a few too many drinks, I knew we hadn't been as careful as we might have been. I'd been fearing the result and she hadn't been, which now meant I bore the brunt of her anger.

"How—" She looked me in the eye. "Did this happen?"

"I think," I said, "that you know how. We did this, and we did that, and there you have it."

"I mean," she said, "how did *you* let this happen?"

So, it was my responsibility: Once Brandon was six weeks old, he was off to day care half an hour before my first period at school, and I picked him up each weekday afternoon at five. I learned how to carry all the equipment and baggage that infants require these days, and I became as adept as any circus juggler with bulky bags and the brevity of time.

And then it happened again, and Tiffany again accused me of irresponsibility, and we had Kyle just after Brandon turned three, and the luggage I carried became heavier and more elaborate while Tiffany's workdays became longer and longer. The school year grew complicated with its drop-offs and pickups, and I can tell you that getting work done around the corners of baths, feedings, playtimes, and bedtimes was a challenge. Tiffany and I managed, albeit barely. But when summer came, the boys and I found ways to enjoy ourselves in spite of their mother's absences—her clients were mostly agricultural interests, and she was up and down Highway 99, along with its infinite number of long-haul truckers. The food processors and pesticide manufacturers got a kick out of seeing her pull up in her father's BMW and get out wearing white while the dust swirled around her in their graveled parking lots. They were eager for her encouragement, and she prayed with them as often as she gave them new marketing strategies and advertising campaigns. Her clients swore by her; she spoke their language; she thus had been a fundamental driver of her father's overall revenue. Or so I was told. She returned home late at the end of each day and peeled off what became my next day's trip to the dry cleaner.

But we were happy. Happy enough. Or so I thought. Until that day in July when I sat down on the couch to watch the Giants lose a Wednesday afternoon game to the Reds. Brandon was playing with DUPLOs while Kyle rattled around in one of those roller contraptions with a seat and a tray and a circle of wheels that kept him upright and, as it turned out, too mobile. Caesar lay under the coffee table and drooled on the carpet. Hamburger patties were cooking in the grill for Brandon and me, and I must have fallen asleep to yet another Giant inning of anemic offense, when Brandon grabbed my nose to get my attention.

"Daddy," he said, enunciating as well as a child twice his age. "Kyle is coughing."

"Okay," I said, coming to consciousness as slowly as a boot wades through mud. "Okay."

Caesar was barking in idiotic and frantic confusion, and I couldn't hear anything else. I glanced this way and that from my place on the couch. On television, Candlestick looked like a ghost town surrounded by drizzle and fog, and I knew that on the radio Hank Greenwald would soon be making another comment about fans disguised as empty seats. I didn't see Kyle or his roll-around chair. Not until Brandon pointed to the foyer with its slick terrazzo tiles and the potted silk plants in front of the entryway window.

And Kyle was coughing all right, and his face was red, and if he was banging his tiny fists on the tray table in front of him like Ginger Baker on drums, he also didn't appear to be breathing.

I did everything a parent isn't supposed to do in such cases, but I think I might be excused if only for being under the influence of fear and adrenaline and the useless energy of panic. I picked him up, pounded his back, and stuck a finger in his mouth, the back of which was where I felt the feathered end of one of the little plastic flower stems from the fake plants near the door. I contemplated tweezers as though they might be forceps. I kneed away Caesar, whose help consisted of jumping as well as barking. I dangled Kyle upside down, hoping to dislodge the plastic flower from his airway, and then I pounded his back again until he suddenly smiled and opened his arms to be hugged and said "Da, da, da" which to my frightened and now relieved ears sounded like "God*dam*mit, Dad."

I should also mention that somewhere within that sequence of events—the feeling around inside his mouth, the dangling, the pounding, and Caesar's barking and jumping—the smoke detector in the kitchen had begun to wail, and smoke was billowing everywhere from the electric grill, and the air in the house had turned greasy and brown.

"*Jesus* and all the saints," I said. I held Kyle, who was now breathing like a yogi, while I ushered Brandon and Caesar outside. "Stay here," I told Brandon, because in those days before cellphones, I either had to pound on a neighbor's door or go back inside to call the fire department. The fear of embarrassment told me that breathing a little smoke was no big deal, and the 911 operator, after getting the street address, mentioned baking soda once she heard the words *electric grill*, *fire*, and *grease*. So with one hand, I held Kyle, who was punching my head, and with the other, I dumped the Arm & Hammer on the grill and the fire, then found a way to get the plug out of the wall. If the order in which I did things was backward, I still count it as a victory to have had the presence of mind at all.

Tiffany pulled into the garage just as the last of the fire trucks was leaving. The boys, the dog, and I were outside on the front porch waving to the firemen. She got out of the car and joined our little tableau.

"What did you burn down?"

"Fair question," I said. "But the main downside here is there won't be hamburgers tonight."

"I see," she said.

"And we need to give Kyle a heavy dose of sweet potato."

"I see," she said again, even though she didn't.

I had talked with one of the firemen who was also their EMT, and it was he who had suggested that the more mashed food we fed Kyle, the sooner we'd find the plastic flower in Kyle's diaper, so when I explained all this to Tiffany, she held her head in both hands and took a deep breath and said, "I think you need to go."

"What?" I said.

"*Go*," she said, and she pointed toward the garage and my twelve-year-old Escort. "I can't have this anymore."

"What?" I said again. "What can't you have anymore?"

"This, this *chaos*," she said, even though we'd hardly made days like this any kind of routine. "I can't have it."

"So, what am I supposed to do?" I asked. "I *live* here," I said, since stating the obvious seemed my best line of defense. "I live here, you live here, and so do the boys," I said. "But maybe that's not true anymore."

"Maybe not," she said. "And maybe if you leave, I'll be able to breathe again."

And here I'd thought Kyle and I had been the only suffocating ones.

• • •

I packed my things that night and went to a motel, and over the next couple of weeks, I moved the rest of my accumulated stuff, including the grill, which I had rescued from the trash out of some perverse notion that, if I could fix it, I might be able to restore my marriage. But I'm not especially handy, so the outside of the case remained blackened by grease and smoke and flames, and the cord remained frayed and the wires exposed and broken, and my marriage remained equally kaput. I saw the boys and Caesar on weekends until Tiffany met the owner of a plumbing supply company, who was likewise divorced. And when he decided to move his operation to Arizona, she and the boys went with him, no matter what that meant to her career in advertising at Daddy's firm. I guess the concept of Daddy was no longer that important to her, after all, and she turned her affections toward real estate. I could have fought the move, but I didn't have the heart. And you would be right to question my parental tenacity; when I attended their eventual graduations and weddings, neither boy had much memory of me except as a well-meaning stranger who showed up at appropriate moments with a card for the occasion and a check for less than they might have hoped. Kyle has no memory of plastic geraniums, and Brandon does not remember eating hamburgers night after night. I should mention they met at church, Tiffany and her plumbing mogul, just as we had done, but it seems to have been a better match; their every

Christmas card and newsletter displays a larger and newer and more featureless house in a newer and more featureless sub-urb. On the other hand, the grill moved with me from apart-ment to house, from box to garage, a charred and guilty reminder of a former and less committed life.

So if I now resist Francie's call to eradicate these objects of the past, it's only for any benefits such reminders can bring. One of those benefits being the knowledge that our imperfections and flaws have made us who we are. Which brings me to how Francie and I met. Or re-met, as the case may be.

I taught my classes through my separation and divorce from Tiffany, and since Tiffany no longer trusted my fitness as a parent, I no longer had responsibility for our boys, and my schedule had hours open that I was unused to filling on my own. I went back to the bowling lanes of my youth and signed up for three leagues a week, one of which was stocked with former pros and upstarts who were intent upon becom-ing so. Crankers, strokers, and full rollers—you name it, we saw them all. Everyone had an idea about how to get the right path to the headpin.

One night I could do little wrong. I ended the first game with a 248 and five straight strikes. The second game I strung all twelve together for my first and only 300 game, and then, in the third game, I threw three more strikes before I left a seven pin in the fourth. The feeling was otherworldly: my feet, my arm and hand, the ball, the pins—all were con-nected and in harmony with each other. *Twenty* straight strikes. When it was all over, I sat in my spot on the molded plastic seats, held my head between my knees, and wept. One of the former professionals came by and put his gloved fist on my head and said that the first one was always special but there would be more to come. And as correct as he was about the experience being special, he was wrong about the 300 games in my future. There were close calls, but no others, and I had to content myself with the one memory. The memory of a game and the memory of that apex when I'd caught perfection in the midst of losing everything else.

That night was also the first time I felt what I would call a disturbance along my right shoulder blade. A week later a lump had formed; I felt it, spongy and hard every time I rolled over in bed; and a week after that, I began to run a fever. I lasted another week by taking ibuprofen by the shovelful, but then one night at midnight, I could no longer lie on my back or stay seated in a chair because even the slightest pressure was uncomfortable. I went to the emergency room, knowing that my case would no doubt be among the lowest of priorities, since I represented neither gunshot wound nor heart attack, broken bone nor stroke.

A bored receptionist took my information and insurance, and a bored technician took my vitals, and only my temperature of 103 provoked anything beyond mild interest. That was when Francie pushed aside the curtain and stood next to my bed. She was wearing blue scrubs, her hair now orange rather than green, and there were three rings looping through her left nostril, but I immediately recognized her and then confirmed my recognition by seeing the tattooed spiders peek out at each wrist underneath her long sleeve shirt.

"*You*," she said. "Mr. Actor has returned."

"Me," I said. "Where have you been all of my life?"

"Here," she said, "working my ass off. Community college. Getting my RN and FNP."

"Where have you been?"

"Back at our old secondary education stomping grounds."

"You're kidding." She used a light to check my eyes, then pointed to where I was to look.

"Nope, no kidding. English. Grades nine, ten, and eleven."

"Small world. We're what? Ten minutes away from each other, hospital to school?"

"I guess. How many minutes is that in life experience?"

"Light years," she said.

"Look," I said, "we can call the world big or small, but I think I have a tumor or an alien life form as parasite."

"Really." She told me to roll over onto my stomach and pressed on the plum-sized lump. "Does this hurt?"

After I came down from the ceiling, I said, "Yes."

"Try having a baby," she said. "You big baby."

"You have kids?" I said.

"Are you serious?" she said. "I know what's involved—why would I do that to myself? But I've delivered my share, so I know who deserves my sympathy. Sit up."

I did as I was told. "I suppose I have back cancer," I said, "and I have two months to live. You can tell me."

"Don't be an idiot," she said. "It's no big deal, a sebaceous cyst. I see these things all the time. It's harmless, so it just needs to be cored out."

"So I need, what, like actual surgery?"

"Not even close. It's such a minor procedure I can do it myself. In fact, I have a few times, on nights as busy as this."

I looked her in the eyes, not wanting her to leave. "You want to give it a go now?"

She shrugged. "Sure." She pulled the curtain shut, allowing us solid privacy.

"I'm guessing I'll be sedated, right?"

"Don't be a weenie," she said. "All you get is a little bit of lidocaine."

Which was when she pulled out a hypodermic that looked to have been made for elephants, and then watched me faint away.

• • •

As it turned out, Francie hit me four or five times with the lidocaine in case I woke up, and then she got busy with the scalpel, opened up the lump, and squeezed until the infection and the white, waxy gunk were gone. From what I was told later, the smell was bad enough that a patient three stalls over complained. "If they didn't get some fresh air stat, they'd rather have their heart attacks at home, thank you very much." That's what they said, or so Francie swore.

From what I know for sure, I woke up while she was packing the hole in my back.

"I can't believe you fainted," she said.

"I get a little wobbly around blood," I said. "Especially my own. And pain. I'm not a fan of pain."

She shook her head. "You probably shouldn't drive yourself home then. Who can you call?"

"That's kind of too existential of a question. A cab?"

She rolled her eyes. "You're lucky things have slowed down. Stay put and get some rest."

She woke me up at six A.M., and we walked from the ER to her car, one that was even older and dirtier and more dented than my own, and in order to sit down, I had to flick the sandwich wrappers to the floor with a Diet Coke can and a Doritos bag.

"And to think," I said, "that our health care professionals are the ones advising us on diet."

"May I remind you," she said, "that walking is not out of the question?"

• • •

She took me home, we shared our contact information, and a week later she called with an invitation.

"I'll bet you haven't gotten that thing repacked yet, have you?"

She'd given me the address and phone number of a wound clinic, but I hadn't even gotten around to making an appointment.

"No," I said, "but I was planning on it."

"Right. I didn't think so."

Her invitation was this: She'd pick me up, re-dress the wound, and then we could go out.

"The two of us," she said. "Like old times."

"Sure," I said. "What do you want to do?"

"Bowling," she said, which was the second time, and certainly not the last, that I heard a glint of cruelty in her voice.

"Okay," I said, "but you know that I'm injured."

"You're scared of bowling against a *girl*," she said.

"No," I said. "I'll have you know that I bowled a 300. Recently. A month ago."

"No way," she said. "I don't believe it. Bring your ball."

It turned out that she'd begun to bowl in earnest not long

after she got her first hospital job. She did it as something of a joke, quasi in memory of our first date so long ago, but then she discovered that she had a competitive streak, one that had resided within her all this time, albeit dormant and untapped; when she let it emerge, she also discovered that she had to govern the impulse to yell, "Fucking hell, you son of a bitch!" whenever she missed a spare, or to kick the ball return when she left a 4–10 split. So, we did as she suggested—or, should I say, I did as she directed—and we were bowling at Rodeo Lanes at ten o'clock on a Friday night.

And, if I tell you now that I lost to her 212–204 because I didn't pick up a simple 4–7 spare in the tenth, would you be surprised? Or that by the time we were done, I was sweating and my back was throbbing once again? Would you be surprised if I told you that one thing had nothing to do with the other, that I will not make that particular excuse? Even though my ball, which had been so accurate only a month before, slid past the four-pin by a whisper? Even though when that had happened and she'd won, she yelled, "YES!" loud enough for everyone to hear despite the crashing and banging going on around us?

On the other hand, the wound-packing she'd done two hours earlier was leaking and not in a good way, so we visited the ER, where she pulled out yards and yards of putrescent gauze. She cleaned me up once again, but this time I did not faint, hero that I was, no matter how nauseated I might have felt from the odor of mortality I now had opportunity to smell.

We got married a week or two later because we were both in our forties with no need to wait, but we mark our anniversary from our second date at a bowling alley rather than the date of the civil ceremony with the cake. All of which is to say that I had my first adult sexual experience in the women's room of a middle school theater, and I met the wife who divorced me at church and the wife who stayed with me in an ER after she stuck a knife in my back, and all of that is a reminder to me that nothing is ever as it is first reported.

Not long after we married, Francie changed jobs when the nurse's position came open at our high school. She got it, and of course the students love her. They love her hair and nose rings, and they love her tattoos, and they love the way she can put them in their place with salt and sugar in equal measures. She makes them feel safe and special and smart, and because she was there, my stock rose, and when I retired, they pretended to love me for her sake. When she saw the job announcement, she said she was going to apply because why should I be the only one with a summer? But now I'm retired, so my summer is the rest of my life. And now we are both living and working at home, and no one knows what day of the week it is, much less the month or the season.

"Come on," Francie said just yesterday, while she was taking a break from her endless Zoom faculty meetings and chats with students who have questions about venereal disease. "Come and help me clean out the attic."

And I answered by way of following her up there, where, soon, into a plastic garbage bag went the plaid sport coat and the delusions and hormones of my high school years. *Poof!*

Along with the George Foreman grill of my ill-fated first attempt at marriage and family. *Psst!*

But I balked at the thought of the Roto Grip leaving our lives, even though we haven't been to a bowling alley in the past ten years, because of my bad knees, the evolution of our interests, and the fact that she was beating me two games out of three when I quit for good.

So I said no right then, to this second and far more interesting wife of mine—I actually said the word *No*.

And she said, "Fine. But only if we stipulate that in this house, as long as we live in it, nothing lasts forever."

A THIN LINE RISES

MORGAN TALTY

My knees ache more and more nowadays. When I feel the urge to look at the old clipped newspaper article—now yellow—I no longer kneel on the floor in front of the closet where I keep it. I have to sit back on the bed, and I like the only light to be what shines in the window through which I can see my wife tend her garden (her knees are still good this summer). If I see her rise and disappear, or if I hear the front door open and close, I hide the article away and go about my business, which is very little these days. I have no real explanation for why I conceal this from her. I just don't want her to know I do this, to know that in my mind I go off to visit a place I very rarely talk about. I'm probably afraid she'd tell me the truth: that it's not good for me, that I shouldn't keep it in, that I should talk about it with her.

I know she won't be in for a while. She's already eaten lunch, and she's planting tomatoes and radishes and green beans, peas and carrots and the zucchinis that yield more than we can eat. When she's done, when she's buried the seeds down in the dirt, she'll take her book and read down back in the woods, out past the dense thicket where there's an opening and an immense shade, where she's set up a few blue plastic chairs around a small fire pit she gets going to keep the mosquitos back. That spot's out farther than I dare to go—the ticks are ferocious this season, and she comes in covered with them, plucks them one by one and squashes them between her fingernails.

In the dim light I rest back on the bed, and while looking at the yellowed article I recall how dark my father's room was. The only light in the room came from the dull glow making its way through the layer of dust on the television. Everything in that room was dusty, even the reclining chair he used as his bed, a wide tan beast that had taken three of his men, his movers, to carry up the narrow, carpeted stairs and push into the room, splintering the door frame. The real bed, kept level with a maroon suitcase crammed between the mattress and box spring, was the only non-dusty thing, and it awaited me each summer. That was the system both he and my mother worked out, or that was the only system my mother offered him.

The room he rented in that house was square, the ceiling flat until the middle of it slanted down to meet the wall. There were two windows next to each other, and one was pried open with an air conditioner that remained there year-round. It was always cold in that room, and loud, because the TV was always kept on (our light source), so I always had to turn it down. When I'd push the button, the TV would shift on the smooth dresser surface, and I'd always have to maneuver it back in place.

My summers there with him felt like a constant tidying. One of the dresser drawers was filled with his clothes (I kept mine packed in my green duffel bag shoved under the bed), and another drawer was filled with his black appointment books, the books that at one point had been his life, way before he and my mother divorced, way before his moving company slowly died, way before this dark room was dark and the overhead light's wires were fried, way before this room was his home, way before the long oxygen tube traced the floor and led to the corner of that room where the tanks, metal painted dark green, stood and hissed with a twist of a knob. There was also a dusty, sticky shelf above the tanks where he kept his mother's Hummels, one of which was a boy in leather breeches, overalls, and a green hat, with one hand raised to carry a platter of sausages. That one was my least favorite, but I ended up with it in the end because it was the only one that wasn't ruined.

When he was gone sometimes—to the wound care clinic (he had venous ulcers) or to the casino or, on rare occasions, overseeing his men at a small moving job, usually an eviction—I'd slip his rubbery nasal cannula over my small head and ears and plug my nose with it, twist the tank knob, and breath in deep. I'd sometimes eat a yogurt or drink a Pepsi, leaving the empty container or dented can on the sticky kitchen chair he used as his table, which was covered with his empties, each one filled with soggy cigarette butts (I once drank what I thought was a half-full Pepsi). I didn't want to be my father, and I didn't want to mimic him. I still don't know for sure why I sat in that chair and used his oxygen. Maybe, during those summers with him, my spirit was sick and needed air.

I couldn't relax in his recliner because it was broken so you had to sit upright. There'd been a time it could, by remote control, lift up your feet and lay you back. Like the Hummels, it had belonged to his mother, my nana, whose name was Mary Alice. I remember going to see her when she was very ill. It was one summer when I was visiting my father. I was no more than twelve or thirteen. We drove up to Ingraham Manor (and this was also the summer my father lost his license for unpaid fines, yet he still continued to drive), and the entire time I held his heavy green oxygen tank in my lap as if it were a child. The whole trip there was dark gray, and the rain and lightning outside didn't need to tell me—I knew what was coming. Her room was bare: a dresser, a nightstand, a painting of Jesus. In some ways its bareness reminded me of my father's room. She lay in her bed under a mound of blankets. She was tired. I now want to say she was sick, because that was true, but it's more true to say she was dying. In her mind then, though, things were as they'd always been when she was at the apartment with Papa (whose first name I don't remember). I found that out when I asked for the garbage can. "Right over there, Johnny," she said, looking at my father as if he'd asked. "By the fridge."

My father had a small fridge in his room. Filled with that yogurt and Pepsi. On those summer visits I'd hear him in the middle of the night. Through the dusty glowing air he'd walk slowly to the fridge, cigarette hanging from his mouth, oxygen tube in his hand like a vacuum cord. When he'd get what he wanted, sometimes a yogurt, sometimes a Pepsi, sometimes both, he'd turn around and head back to that chair. The way he plopped down and cried in agony, I can still hear it: a deep, pained groan with him slapping an arm of the chair in his frantic attempt to find his dropped cigarette. Because of the sores on his legs, which looked like burned flesh, he had to keep his legs up so the blood would flow better under the wrappings, flow right under all the weight he carried (he was obese in those years, and he never got skinny and took to wearing only sweatpants). But that chair, his mother's, was broken and couldn't allow him back either, so he'd cross his legs sometimes and say to me, "Hey, help your father," and I'd go to him and help him lift the heavy leg and set it atop the other, as if that were the only way we could find him comfort.

My father always complained, but never about his health, at least not in front of me. To him, his illness was just something he had to carry, though sometimes he'd hint about knowing what bad shape his body was in, like when he saw the ocean at St. Mary's beach and said he wished the wraps could get wet. "I'd just go up to my knees," he said, and then he didn't mention it again, as if he realized the smallest of waves could push him over. For the most part, he complained regularly about three things: first, how he didn't want to sell his mother's Hummels, second, how he wanted to see more of me. The latter he'd usually tell me as I slept late at night. He'd lean from his recliner and reach for my foot sticking out from under the blanket. "Stay until October," he'd say, tickling me and squeezing my toes.

I'd always get annoyed when he did that, and the annoyance, I remember, always came with a feeling of breathlessness. I'd kick, and with whatever air I could muster I'd yell, "*Stop* it! Sleep like a normal person and maybe I'll think about it!"

I now wonder if I was meaner than I should have been, but sometimes I now think I wasn't firm enough. I was only a boy, and he was my father. I never would stay until October like he wanted, but once I was there during that month.

My wife, who wasn't yet my wife at the time, was with me for that visit. We were going on vacation to California—

which ended sooner than it was supposed to—and we were flying out of New York. I had told my father our plans, had given him our itinerary over the phone (as he wrote it down in his black appointment book, or so he told me later), and he asked me to visit, asked me to stop off and see him before our flight, saying he wanted to meet her. I was twenty-three at the time, and I'd been free of that room for five years and dreaded returning, but my wife pushed me, said she wanted to meet him. No, she *told* me she would meet him. All she'd known of him was that he liked to call me on Sundays and talk to me as he got tired and began to forget my name, calling me Rick or Dan or Ed or Mick or any of the other names that the tenants who lived in the same house as him went by, until he'd finally fall asleep with the phone to his ear, and I'd hang up.

The house my father lived in, the one I stayed in whenever I did visit, had a lot of tenants. Nine plus him. Like him they each rented a room, except for Bill, who my father called Bilbo the Dildo, and who rented the entire basement that stunk of mold and wet. To my father, the tenants were crazy—this, by the way, was the third thing he complained about when we'd talk. They were constantly stealing his money, he said, always stealing his yogurt and his Pepsi, and when he couldn't find his cane or his top dentures (which, as he slept, always fell from his mouth and into his top shirt pocket), he'd blame them. "You took it, didn't you, Dildo?" he'd say at Sunday brunch while Marlana, also a tenant, breaded eggplant. My father wasn't crazy, only on occasion, like when my wife and I showed up that October.

We arrived late for that visit. He was waiting for us outside on the red chipped-paint porch. Moths clung to and patted at the bright bulb overhead, and he swatted at them with a cigarette in his hand. He tried so hard to help my wife carry a small bag, and while trying he turned around to go back inside with the bag and lost his balance but caught himself. I couldn't let him carry the bag then, and for that I caught hell, but I carried it.

We were there for two days, and both days it rained, rained, rained. His dark room was even darker during such weather, when the rain outside fell and tapped on the air conditioner, which my wife and father took turns turning on and off. Like my father, my wife liked it cold. She was always getting hot, still does, which is why she likes to read down back in that shaded wood, hidden from the sun, but I think on that day in October, when she and he first met, she kept the AC on to push around the stale smoke my father had blown into the room before we arrived.

That first night and day we spent there, I witnessed a different man. He didn't smoke in our presence, didn't get up all night for his yogurt and Pepsi, didn't wake us with any pained noises. On that first morning I woke to find him gone, and when he came back I found he'd been to McDonald's and brought back eleven fruit parfaits which he'd spread out on the kitchen table for everyone, even Bill, to eat. As rain fell in the afternoon, he borrowed a kerosene lamp from the dumpster diver downstairs, Dan, and it ran out of kerosene quickly, and my father said he wouldn't pay his rent until the light in his room was fixed, then, with the remote control, turned the TV to a brighter channel, then showed my wife his mother's Hummels, taking each off the shelf to do so. As she looked at them, turning them over in her small hands, he asked her about her, about her parents, where she and they grew up. "Oh, you have a brother?" I remember him asking. "What's his name?" And after he'd asked what she studied in college: "Botany? I used to keep a real nice flower garden. He'll tell you." And he pointed at me, then rattled off a list of flowers he'd once had. (I don't remember the flowers, but I don't see how you can know so many flowers without ever having had any.) He also asked what her father did for work. "Fells trees? What about your mother?" he asked, and he also asked what her favorite TV show was, then checked every channel to see if it was on, then asked which show was her least favorite only to learn it was one of his favorites, but he agreed with her that it was terrible. He asked her how many cats she had, what their names were, how old they were. He asked question after question, each one so simple, which showed he'd thought about them carefully, had wondered at them, had true interest. I'll never forget how, right as the questions ran out, he and I locked eyes. We didn't say anything right then, because we didn't have to. We both knew it was a moment that should have brought us closer—the extending of a family circle—but all that moment did was tell us how far apart we were.

My father was not good that night, or perhaps the night was not good to him. It was like I was a boy again. He didn't sleep at all, and as I had so many times before, I woke on his bed to him tugging on that suitcase between the mattress and box spring, and I had to get up so he could pull it out, and when he did my wife began rolling off the mattress, and I had to catch her. I was annoyed, and I asked why he needed to pull the suitcase out *then*, asked why he couldn't wait.

"Because waiting never ends for me," he said, not kindly.

He went to his dresser drawer and pulled out a stack of

old black appointment books, and instead of the suitcase he used them to keep the mattress level. He went downstairs with the suitcase, and for the rest of the night I sat on his recliner and watched the TV on mute, occasionally taking his oxygen tube and slipping the nasal cannula around my head and plugging my nose, reaching out in the dim light for the tank's knob. I was wearing it, my nose plugged, breathing in and out and in and out, when I heard him come up the stairs. I took the cannula off my face, set it on the arm of the chair, met him halfway on the stairs, asked in a low but annoyed voice what he wanted. He said in a voice as annoyed as mine that he needed his cigarettes and a book of matches, and I told him I'd get them, but he said he could get them, and I said I don't want you to wake her, and he looked sorry and said yeah, don't wake her, and he let me get the smokes. Later, and with no argument, because we both didn't want to disturb her sleep (yet I think in reality we both wanted to let any annoyance we'd felt rest, too), he let me get for him a yogurt and a Pepsi, then another yogurt and another Pepsi until he stopped asking for things because he'd passed out downstairs on the back porch futon.

"Is he sick?" my wife asked me after she'd woken at dawn, as we stood in the hallway. There were no parfaits, no tenants floating around, just us in the hall and my father around the corner and on the back porch, sitting up on the futon and nodding off with the unzipped suitcase at his feet. "Should he go to the hospital?" she said. "I just looked at him, and he doesn't look right."

I told her we should just let him sleep, that he'd wake rested in time to see us off before our flight—we'd arranged a shuttle to pick us up so we could leave our car, which my father had sworn he wouldn't drive, at my father's place. But he woke soon anyway, and we heard him rummaging in his suitcase as we sat in the kitchen drinking coffee, and she said, "What's he doing?" I couldn't bring myself to tell her what he kept in that suitcase, or that his men brought them to him in bottles with the labels peeled off. I couldn't ruin who she'd met, who I had wanted him to be, and who I'll always tell myself he wanted to be.

Then it was past noon, an hour after she'd asked what she'd asked, and I hadn't really answered, and the shuttle was supposed to arrive at three. My father hadn't stirred one bit during that hour, and then all at once he started to groan—this deep, pained groan I can still hear when I listen hard enough. I don't think it was the noise he made that angered me but rather how the noise struck my wife. Her eyes got wide, and she put a hand over her chest, and I got up and went out to where he lay on that back porch.

"What the hell is the matter with you?" I said.

"Get me some scissors," he said, one eye closed, the other partially open.

And then I saw. In his sleep, or perhaps in some waking moments, he'd undone the wraps around his legs, had picked at the sores there, had peeled back a piece of skin that was now still attached. My wife never saw because I told her to stay off the porch because the mess was his mess, my mess, our mess. I would tell her years later, though, about how circular that pool of blood was, how it grew wider and wider.

I wouldn't get him scissors, but I pretended to look for them. I found them in the top drawer next to the kitchen sink, and I took them and slid them under the stove. When I returned to him, saying there weren't any, he blamed the tenants, said they never put anything back, and the flap of skin was like a torn cuticle beside a fingernail or a moist brown root buried under the earth, and he yanked at it and screamed and the red flowed down and over his darkened socks and pooled wider and wider on the floor until finally—when I knew the skin wouldn't come off and he would soon unravel himself down to the bone—I went to him, wrestled his slippery hand from his leg, and bent his hand toward his wrist until he sat back and quit.

"Why?" I asked. I know it makes sense to think that question was directed at his behavior, as in why did he peel back his flesh, but since that day I've had a lot of time to think about what I meant by why, and what I meant was why everything, why all of it, from the dirt below our feet up to the sky above our heads and all the space and the things taking up space in between. My father looked at me then, and I at him, and he said, "Because, you have to go—you always have to go and leave me be. That's how it works. You're not me."

But I didn't go. Or I couldn't yet, because the blood pooling between us was his blood, our blood, my blood. I cleaned up our mess and rewrapped his leg with gauze and medical tape (he kept a pink foot basin filled with first aid supplies upstairs between his recliner and oxygen tanks), then told him to make another appointment to get his leg wrapped properly. And before my wife and I left, before the shuttle honked for us outside, we helped my father upstairs. With blood all over my hands and shirt, I stood beside him, holding him by the elbow. My wife followed behind us, saying, "You'll be all right, Dad, you'll be okay," while looking at me and rubbing his wide, wide back as if she were addressing or comforting the both of us.

When we got him to the room—or perhaps she got us both there—my father plopped down in his chair.

"We can stay until you're better," she said. "We don't have to go."

The shuttle honked.

"I'll be fine," was all my father said, and as he rested in his recliner, he gave a tired goodbye to her, gave her a hug, a kiss. Then, when she went out the door with her bag, he said, "Hey," and he rubbed his fingers together, trying to remember my name. "Oh, you know it," he said, and he told me to get his oxygen tubes and his cigarettes, which were downstairs. "And turn on the AC," he said.

After I did all he asked, he said nothing to me. I watched him, waiting for just a word, but none came. He sat in his recliner, oxygen tube curled around his ears and into his nose, a lit smoke in his hand, his eyes shut and three fingers on his forehead, thinking. But I couldn't wait any longer. I grabbed my bag, and as I closed his door behind me and walked down the creaking stairs, he called to me urgently, knowing, I think, how grave of a place he'd had us in, and he kept saying, "Wait, wait! Come here, please, son! Wait! Honey! Come up here!" We all knew he was too weak to follow me, let alone chase me, and I opened the front door, passed through it after my wife did, and closed it behind us.

But our vacation, the one we'd been taking to California, never really happened. We were out there only for one night, then were getting ready early in the morning to go have breakfast and then go to the beach, when Bill called and told me. I don't remember much of the flight home. Mostly I remember waiting to board the plane and playing over and over again the voice mails my father had left me, the ones I'd ignored and refused to listen to until it was too late. He sounded normal in those voice mails, the opposite of how he'd been: "Call me, please? I have to tell you something." And "Please, just call me. It'll take just a second." And "Goddammit, Dan—I mean Rick, I mean Bill, I mean Ed, I mean Junior—would you please just call me back? *Please*. Okay. Goodbye."

It's been years since that cell phone broke—two daughters ago, at least—so I can't say I remember precisely what he said in those voice mails, much as I'm sure he sounded normal in them. I do remember that, when my wife and I returned to the town where he rented that room, my wife didn't let the shuttle take us down the road to the boarding house (she insisted I stay in the shuttle while she walked down the road to get our car), so I didn't see the house in person, but I had that newspaper, the one with the article before I clipped the article out and hid it and it yellowed and I began kneeling secretly while reading it, my only prayer. I've been reading it secretly even though I know exactly what it looks like, "Fire Leaves 9 Homeless, 1 Dead" over a photo of the red house blackened and mangled, twisted like the tube that once ran across my father's floor. It will always be clear in the photo, and in my mind, that my father's room no longer had walls and was blasted open, and that I'd never be able to make anything else out—in the photo, there would always be dense black ink where the printer printed black. But I never need a clear image to know what was buried under the gray ash and all that debris: a made bed, burned and soot-covered, but a made bed nonetheless, numerous shattered Hummels and a single surviving one, a broken recliner, an old TV, empty charred yogurt containers and aluminum Pepsi cans, a dumpy air conditioner, crisp and completely black appointment books.

Sometimes, after I look at the yellowed article, I wonder if I can help my wife garden in some way she'll appreciate. And I sit up on our bed and rub my joints, extend my leg out, then in, stretching it. I do that with my other leg, too. When I'm done, I stand up and go to the closet, where I hide the clipped article without caring much about whether it'll go lost. What's it worth, anyway? I know the story so well.

Or maybe I don't. Maybe I don't remember how poorly I handled those visits, how rough I was with my father despite trying to be otherwise. When I question my memory like this, I sometimes sit back down on our bed for a minute, and then I decide to go out there, to be with my wife, even though I know she doesn't need my help. I go to knock on the window to say I'll be right out, but often when I do this, she's gone. And I again see that, way down behind the house and above the oaks and maples and birch trees, a thin line of smoke rises. How long she's had a fire going is something I never know, and I don't know how long it will keep burning. But I do know I'll bring along some more wood, an armful, enough to keep it going a while longer.

THE ONLY WAY

T. E. WILDERSON

I didn't decide to give up my baby 'cause he's half black. Really, I didn't. I just know I already have four mouths under the age of five to feed with the pay from my Mickey D's assistant manager jobby-job, and I'm the only one who's been paying for their food. Not that I'm saying I'm raising them all by myself. Mrs. Ouellette, the last in my run of foster moms, watches all four when I work. She's retired from foster care now, which is why she can babysit. And she does it for pennies for me, really. Maybe it's her way of doing her old kid a solid? She was one tough biddy when she was my moms, but we was tight and stayed in touch after I moved out and into my first halfway house. You know, where it was all girls like me, where we knew other people called it Ronald McKnocked-Up House.

Some days, usually when she's had trouble getting my littles down for the night, Mrs. Ouellette has a tight jaw when I get home. Which is not what I need after a double shift, especially if I had a no-show or two. Can't say I blame her, though. Them kids are a handful. The very last thing I need is for her sciatica to get too bad and she can't help me, or, worse, that she up and dies. That could mean the foster system for my kids, and like I say, I been there, so I'd rather we all live in my Honda Accord, which I done, too—I mean, in my moms's car.

Don't get me wrong. I'm not looking for a pat on the back for working on my feet till they squeal and then coming home to be a good moms to Ty, Daisy, Kaitlin, and Zach. I'm just trying to remind myself of how come I'm waiting for two virtual strangers to make it here to the hospital so they can take my newborn.

Two strangers who, when I met them, both looked like they never so much as got a speeding ticket, and like they might crack to pieces if I talked too loud. Who also looked just as nervous the four other times I seen 'em. I think they was afraid I'd decide not to go through with the adoption—you know, they wasn't counting their chickens or whatever.

Gretchen and Ben—that's these people's names—they've been staying at the Marriott out by the airport for seven days now. They got here on my due date, September nineteenth. They was supposed to come when our adoption lawyer, Larry Loeffler, called them to say I'd gone into labor, not any sooner. So I kinda freaked out at first when they came to town early. I was afraid they wanted to be there for the birth even though I'd already said no way to that.

Turns out they understood that part. They just wanted to see the baby as soon as they possibly could. But the thing is, I didn't want them to see him before I was *ready* for them to see him. But I hadn't thought to have that put in writing with Larry, who promised me they was just eager, not to worry, that the clock for the seventy-two hour "grace period" would start ticking right when I gave birth, so I could decide if I truly agreed to terminate my parental rights.

Meaning I'd be formally and legally and finally consenting for the adoption to go ahead, meaning everything would be final-final and they could take my baby boy.

Larry said that since my baby's daddy, Darius, already signed away his parental rights months ago, things from now on should go real smoothly. Gotta say, though, the day I told Darius I wanted to give our baby up was more painful than any childbirth. Because Darius didn't say a word. Not. One. All that happened was his jaw muscles kept bulging like he wanted to yell or whisper something but couldn't 'cause his mouth was wired shut. He blazed holes straight through me with his eyes, and there weren't no words that coulda hurt more than that silence. Then he just turned and walked out of my apartment. I jumped when he slammed the door behind him. I'm telling you, even the room shook. I'd thought he was gonna understand it was our only real option 'cause we basically already had seven kids between us. Where would we fit one more?

And really, if anyone's to blame for my situation, it's my cousin Jason and his crackhead girlfriend, April. Jason got out of being locked up for some bullshit I know he couldn't of done 'cause they mandated rehab instead. I mean, he's stupid, but he ain't stupid enough to rob a bank wearing a dress, sunglasses, and a blonde curly wig. That's too whack, even for him. He's more of a Halloween-mask-type robbing fool. I mostly blame April 'cause if he and April'd stayed clean after the hundredth time they *said* they would, I wouldn't of had to step up to keep their two kids out of the system. Like I said, I myself spent time in foster care, so I know that's the kinda shit you can't scrub off any easier than tar on white bumper-toed tennis shoes. So, no way was I gonna let those two kids have to deal with that, so, hey, I did what I did.

And I don't think I was wrong to report Jason and April as unfit parents. When they left them kids for me to babysit and didn't come back for five days, I was just doing what anyone with a spine would. And all April said after they finally showed up and I told them I'd called Child Services was that she and Jason had to go 'cause Cool Boy, their dealer, was waiting. See what I'm saying?

Jason hasn't been right since his moms OD'd. And this is my *cousin* Jason, so, yeah, his moms was my aunt, my aunt Chrissy. And not long after she, Chrissy, OD'd, Jason, who wasn't exactly Mr. Just Say No anyway, fell in with April. I thought it was kinda wrong how April put this spell on him when he was obviously in a bad way. Point is, April's entrance into Jason's life is when shit for him started going *really* downhill. I turned out luckier than him, if you count getting pregnant at fifteen-and-a-half lucky. And nobody could convince me to give up Ty, my first baby, so Mrs. Ouellette—this was when she was still my foster moms—got me into the Ronald McKnocked-Up House. Then I almost finished high school. Then I slipped and got pregnant with Daisy, so now I couldn't keep up with everything, which left me a semester short of graduating. But then the state moved me to a new house, one that had childcare, so all I had to do was take some job skills classes. That and work on getting my GED, which I aced. I was doin' alright then. That's when I started working at McDonald's. Only six months at the register before I got my first promotion.

My pops, if it matters any, left years before any of this.

Poof, he just vanished, and then my moms couldn't find work. Even with government assistance, she wasn't able to keep a roof over our heads, so that's how we ended up living on the street, in her station wagon.

One night we was parked in a place that, looking back on it, was super sketchy. I'm not sure how long my moms was gone 'cause I'd fell asleep. I just remember being woke up by this bright light shining on me in the way-way back. Then I heard my moms, who another cop had by the shoulder. She was across the street but close enough I could see she was red in the face and crying, yelling out at me that I shouldn't be afraid, that she'd come and get me soon. At the time I didn't understand why I couldn't go with her. I mean, it would be a long while before I found out she got caught up in a prostitution sweep. Anyway it was dark but the snot running from her nose into her mouth was shiny enough for me to see. I wanted to yell *Wipe your face with your sleeve* but then realized her hands was cuffed behind her back, with her jerking now and then like she was trying to shake loose. I was so focused on her that the cop shining his light on me got huffy. *Come on out, you're not making things any better*, he said. So I climbed over all our stuff packed in the middle seat up to the driver's side and got out, just in time to see the other cop butt my moms's head on the doorframe as he pushed her inside a squad car.

I wanted to run, scream, and cry all at the same time right then. What I did was stand there with this bald cop under a dim yellowish streetlamp watching my moms crying and hanging her head while she was caged in a patrol car. I'd just turned twelve the week before, and she and me celebrated with cupcakes in our old neighborhood park. Ate them sitting on the swings, no presents for me, but I was happy that day.

• • •

My moms never did get back with me. After they put me in the system, she'd send me letters, which I thought was super weird 'cause she liked talking on the phone so much. Plus there was never a return address on those letters, and one day one arrived that I guessed my Aunt Mallory had written. I mean, she *tried* to write like my moms, but you could tell the slant of some words was wrong. I guess they had this worked out so I wouldn't know my moms was in jail. Or prison. Or nowhere. My Aunt Mallory lives in a trailer park in San Diego and has never had any space for me. But she and my moms was in touch back in the day. The last real letter I got from my moms was so full of meanness I tore it to pieces then lit the pieces on fire in the kitchen sink. Watching them torn-up pages burn helped, but the words was already stuck in my head—see, she'd found out about me getting pregnant, I guess 'cause my aunt Mallory had been in touch with Mrs. Ouellette. Mama wrote, *You keep spreading your legs like that your life is gonna be one long tragic fairy tale.* Hmm. I'd always thought my fairy tale life had become tragic the night she was arrested on Decker Avenue. I mean, *sure* it hurt when my pops left, but then it was the two of us, a mother and daughter alone together and all tight like that, thicker thieves than we ever was.

Those words—*tragic fairy tale*—ran through my mind when I knew I was pregnant for the second time. I didn't tell no one about that right away. Not Mrs. Ouellette, not anyone at the McDonald's where I work, and of course not my moms. I mean, how could I?

• • •

It's raining. Not hard, though. Just enough for there to be like little water freckles on the window. I'm feeling a little queasy. In about two and a half hours, Larry, Gretchen, and Ben are coming to take my new baby. That's when the shit's gonna get really real. That's when I sign the papers saying *it's okay* for Gretchen and Ben to take him. Larry told me that they've seen him, held him, fed him. More for the Things Veronica Don't Need to Know file. I thought I'd been clear with Larry that I didn't want any baby updates, thought he understood this from jump. I'd arranged for a "semi-open" adoption. I'd had Larry write it out so it would be that me, Gretchen, and Ben could know a little about each other, and we could be in touch while I was pregnant—but that then, that was *it*. I don't want pictures of this baby boy taking his first steps, smearing his first birthday cake all over his face, going to his first day of kindergarten. No. Just no. I haven't seen him since moments after he was born and they'd cleaned him up. I held him, even squeezed him a little, but I could barely look at him. I didn't wanna see any of Darius in him. Or me in him, either.

I had called Darius when I was going into labor, to tell him the name of this hospital. I didn't want to mess things up for him by saying why on his answering machine, just that he needed to call me or Mrs. Ouellette immediately. He hadn't answered any of my calls since after the night I told him I was pregnant. I'm sure that, if he didn't have to take care of his three brothers, he woulda taken our baby. But his moms has MS, so he has to take care of her, too. He had to quit McDonald's and is paid by the state so he can be her caretaker all legally and stuff. The last time I heard his voice was when I was leaving a message (for the nine millionth time) to call me after I'd sent him a long letter 'bout how I found Larry. On the machine I was telling Darius that we needed to meet up so he could sign the papers, and suddenly he picked up. But all he said was "Just mail them, Veronica," and he hung up.

I'd be lying if I said I didn't cry for the next three days. What was worse was he didn't sound sad or mad. He was just calm, almost like he was telling someone they'd called the wrong number. It had already been a moody day. I'd been in court that morning for the hearing to make me legal guardian of Jason and April's two kids. That's right. Two. Kaitlin and Zach. So I felt clammy and dizzy the whole time in that courtroom. But there was no one else to take care of those kids—Jason and April didn't ever show at this hearing. April's whole family lives in the bottom of a Wild Turkey bottle. Except for her older brother. He's on the pipe.

When Darius and I was dating, I used to call Darius's moms just to see how she was doing. She was always real nice. Even told me she didn't mind none that I had four kids. Or that I was white. One time, when I was over at her house, she leaned in close and whispered, *You not like them other snow babes Darius bring around. Your heart is large. I can feel it.* I guess I probly shoulda been mad she said this. I mean no one had ever called me a snow babe to my face. Darius was the only black guy I'd ever dated. Instead, I took the compliment and ran.

Anyway I liked the way she talked all southern. It always

sounded like she was about to have you sit on her lap so she could rock you and hum in your ear. But after I told Darius The News, nobody ever picked up the phone in that house. Always the answering machine from then on out—except for the one time I just mentioned.

It wears him down, caring for his whole family like he does. Point is, he's *got* a family, and they're all the same blood, unlike my crew. My kids with their different in-the-wind daddies and Jason's two. I still say I'm lucky, though, since Mrs. Ouellette has my four little ones while I'm in the hospital. Sometimes I think Mrs. Ouellette is the one person who isn't looking down at me. Not that she's the cuddly type. But for a woman who kept locks on the fridge and the kitchen cabinets, my sense was that she always did care. When I got my GED, it's her who I called. By that time, Jason was already pretty far away into his own little world-'o-crack, and like I might have said, I usually didn't even know where he was, so Mrs. Ouellette had a "graduation" party for me. Chocolate sheet cake with white frosting and "Congratulations" written in red icing. She squeezed her arm around my shoulders when I cut into that cake and smiled in a new way that warmed me like the sun. That was the most proud moment I ever had. Is it horrible that I didn't feel any pride the times I gave birth? Satisfied, happy, fluttery, and full of love of course—but not *proud*. When I broke it to Mrs. Ouellette I might be having baby number three, she looked more shocked than she did the next day when we found out for sure. Then I told her my plan to give the baby up, and she nodded like she was relieved.

I maybe haven't reached the relieved phase yet. Partly I doubt I ever will. It was Mrs. Ouellette who spoke on my behalf at the hearing to gain legal custody of Jason's kids and support my officially adopting them. It was raining that day, too.

• • •

I check the clock. Damned if only half an hour's passed since I last looked. So that's less than two hours to get right. With myself and this decision. I'd say with God, but it's been a long while since I've been a believer. It's the only way, though. I mean, giving up this baby is. The *only* way—I can say that out loud to Larry, to Mrs. Ouellette, to Darius, to Gretchen and Ben. Then to social worker after social worker after social worker, each appointed by somebody with power I don't have. And I've said it was the only way—silently—when my baby boy was still inside me. Said it to a piece of me I'm gonna let two near-strangers take in 117 minutes.

That is, if they're on time. Part of me's mad since they *will* be on time 'cause they're prompt sort of people. Punctual. Gretchen will probly be wearing a Laura Ashley dress, one that would take me three full shifts to pay for. And Ben will have on an Izod polo shirt. Just wait. Dude irons creases into his jeans, which I never seen anybody else do. *It's the only way*, and everyone I talk to seems to agree. Even that psychic I called on one of my more sleepless nights said, *You're going to make a huge decision in your life, but it will be the right one.* Darius, mad as he might be, must know this gotta be true, too—otherwise why would he have been so calm when he did finally pick up the phone? And if I was still in touch with my moms, wherever she might be if she's still alive, I'm sure she'd agree. If not, that's another for Things Veronica Don't Need to Know.

The last time I saw her, I was going to work on the 94B Express bus. I like to sit all the way in the back. This particular 94B Express stopped, and my moms got on wearing this shag-nasty rabbit fur jacket, a miniskirt, and silver strappy heels. Never mind the six inches of snow on the ground. I couldn't hear what her and the driver was saying, but they was clearly arguing. The bus driver shooed at her to get off and opened the door. This clown sitting next to me said, *Get off the fucking bus already, damn*, and my moms turned and took a step down. But then she stepped back up and yelled, *Fuck you, fuckers! I hate you all, y'all nothing but a busload of bitches!* Then she got off for good. When the bus pulled away from the curb, she flipped us the bird. She never saw me. Which was fine 'cause I was six months into my second pregnancy. I mean, the last thing I wanted was for her to see me in that condition. Not after that hurtful letter she sent, which I guess could be the last letter ever between us.

• • •

Except for Larry, no one's visited me here. Every time someone's come around that curtain, though, I've secretly hoped it's Darius. Which is stupid. He has no idea I'm here, for one. For two, he apparently used up all his feelings for me when he picked up the phone to say, *Just mail them, Veronica.*

Gretchen and Ben are naming my baby "Matthew." Larry let this slip, and he looked super sorry after that because obviously it was also on the list of Things Veronica Don't Need to Know. Now, any time I might see a little mixed boy named Matthew about my baby's age, I'll wonder if that's *my* Matthew.

It helps that Gretchen and Ben live a thousand miles away. Larry said I was lucky to have found them on account of my baby being half black, since blond-haired, blue-eyed boys was what adopting parents want most. My hair's dishwater blonde and I got brown eyes, by the way, and in the split second I fully looked at this baby before the nurse walked off with him, all I could see was a head of slick, bone-straight dark hair and skin just a bit tanner than mine.

Gretchen and Ben told Larry to tell me that they could raise the boy Baptist, if I wanted, and I figure they said that because they think black people are all Baptists. The joke's on them because Darius is Catholic. Like, he and his moms watch Mass on television every Sunday. Maybe what Gretchen and Ben was trying to say was that they'd raise this baby to know other black people? When I was picking possible parents, that kinda stuff never crossed my mind.

Ben is an actuary, whatever that is. Gretchen's gonna be a stay-at-home moms, something I'll never get to do. Not that I can see in any version of the future. Though I am trying to move up to full-on manager at my McDonald's. That's about as far as my dream goes. Scratch that. I dream of seeing my kids walk across a stage getting their high school diplomas. Then I'd truly feel proud.

I get this horrible cramp, and it hits me. What if Darius never told his moms why he stopped seeing me? What if she has no idea she's a grandma? Like I said, with all the messages I left on their machine, I was careful not to hint at my condition. Because of his younger brothers, mostly. But now I hate the thought that his moms might not have a clue. Not gonna lie, I thought about going to his house after being ignored this last month. His moms always sits in a chair in the living room by the window facing the street. Always unless it's time for *General Hospital*, and she has to be helped to her TV-watching recliner then. So I always knew that, if I didn't time a visit right, she would've seen me coming, big as a house, up the walk. What if I'd grown a spine and gone there to talk to Darius? I can't imagine what her thoughts on the matter might be, snow babe or not.

I also wouldn't lie by denying I've often thought back to those times when I'd spend the evening at Darius's watching television. Once his moms's favorite show *Amen* ended, he'd carry her over to her bed. It always amazed me how somebody lanky as him could carry his moms like she was a toddler. Then, he'd get her a glass of water.

After that we'd watch reruns of *Hunter*. Darius loved cop shows then, and I'm guessing he still does. We got to do this about once a month when Mrs. Ouellette would insist on babysitting so I could go out.

But mostly, Darius and me stole time. He'd slip over to my place when everyone in his and my houses was asleep. Never stayed more than a couple of hours, since he was afraid his moms would wake up and call for him and he wouldn't be there. But, clearly, we found time to get busy. When I think about how good a pops Darius would be, having seen him with his brothers, I always get all twisted, and right now is no exception. I mean, he's got responsibilities, just like I do. But ever since I taught him the right way to make a Big

Mac his first day at work, all I wanted was to wake up to his dimpled smile and long eyelashes every day for the rest of my life.

But, even if I'd never gotten pregnant, we coulda gone on only so long the way we were seeing each other. We only ever been on one "real" date, and we worked on Valentine's Day, but that didn't suck 'cause at least we was together. We celebrated a couple weeks later at Murray's Steakhouse downtown, the kinda place with white tablecloths and two people waiting on you. We shared the filet mignon. It came with two onion rings on top so good I can never go back to fast-food ones. Darius let me pick the movie we went to after we ate, and I chose this romantic comedy I can't remember the name of now. He's the type to go along and enjoy whatever. When he picked me up that night, he gave me a red rose, but the smell of his cologne's what made my knees weak.

I saved the rose petals, though. Pressed them in my favorite Judith Krantz book, *Princess Daisy*. I love me my romance novels. Reading them is like reading daydreams. Darius was my Prince Charming, for sure. My other two kids' fathers was both chuckleheads. Looking back, I'm not sure how I let myself mess with either one. Let's just say neither have their high school diploma or GED. My boy Ty's daddy had a Camaro like my pops—I guess that's why I liked him. His car was white, though. He got locked up for selling a stolen car the day I found out he'd gotten me pregnant. He was sentenced ten years in Stillwater. If he's gotten out early, I couldn't say. I can tell you he ain't never seen his son, not up close, close enough to hold. I dunno what Daisy's last name should be. It was like that.

You know who else ain't never seen my kids? Any of their grandparents. Which bums me out when I think of it. So, I try not to think about it. One of the things I liked about Gretchen and Ben was both their parents are still alive. And together. So, okay, this new boy of mine might not have Darius's moms as his grandma, but he'll have *four* other grandparents. I only ever had my pops's moms, Nana June, though she died like a year after my pops left. Last time we saw her in the old folks home, she didn't remember us. She called my moms Helen. Whoops. That was my pops's high school sweetheart. My moms's first name is Margie.

The desire to go see my baby boy in the nursery hits me. Hard. Realer than the pain in my boobs, which are full of milk. They gave me some medicine—Parlosomething—so I'll stop "lactating," but it hasn't taken full effect yet. So instead I just been oozing milk all day, and my boobs feel hard as bricks. They told me I could use a breast pump if the pain was too much, but if you ask me, that seems wrong. I'd feel like I'd be sending my body mixed signals.

I can't feed another mouth, though. This really is the only way. Five is a lot of kids for a single moms. So, it's not about whether or not I love my new baby. Because I do. That's the only clear thing. And as Larry says, giving him up is the greatest act of love.

Maybe. But maybe I'm also selfish for wanting my baby now? All to myself? And it don't matter none that I'd have one mixed baby out of five. I'm afraid that if I tell the truth, it would be this: I love this baby the most 'cause I love Darius more than I've ever loved anybody else. Ever.

• • •

I use the milk pump, but only a little, and only to ease the pain. I'm fixing my stupid hospital gown when in busts the last person I expected, Jason—you know, my cousin Jason. I don't wanna start off fighting, but he's supposed to be in rehab. The fact that he's here means he's not only fallen off the wagon, the wagon's probly rolled over him. Kinda the way he rolled his Bronco over April that night they had a huge fight in the Liquor Lyle's parking lot. And, I mean rolled literally, cracked her pelvis and broke her right leg. Now, if you watch her, she walks with a slight limp.

"Hey, girl," he says to me now. "Look at ya." His eyes are all red, he's pale, and the corners of his mouth are white and crusty.

"Hey, stranger." I couldn't help myself.

He kisses my forehead with cold lips.

"So, where's the bambino?" he asks.

I wanna break his teeth and watch him swallow them. Instead, I say, "The nurses have him."

"Oh," he says, and I realize I may have sliced open his face with my eyes.

"Yeah. You remember I'm giving him up, right?"

He just looks at me, kinda bug-eyed. Like maybe he's wandered into the wrong room and thinks he's talking to a complete stranger. He flops down in the visitor's chair. Then I see it, tucked into the front of his jeans' waistband. A damned handgun.

"What. The. Fuck," I say. Like really, dude, I wanna say, 'cause I'm wondering if he's thinking of hitting another bank. I stare him down.

"Oh," he says. "Yeah." He half-smiles and gives me this wave as if to say the gun's nothing.

Nothing? My cousin has a gun up here *in Abbott-Northwestern Hospital* for all the world to see? It's not like we come from gun-toting families. "Why the hell you need a gun for? Do you even have a permit for that thing?"

He laughs, kinda nervous-like. "I . . . Some shit happened. So I gotta watch my back." His eyes are darting around like somehow there might be somebody hiding in this tiny room. "You still taking care of my kids?"

Now my cheeks are real hot. "*Really*, Jason?" I say, and he stands and hikes up his jeans and starts to leave, and we notice that Larry, Gretchen, and Ben are hanging out by the door.

Jason does this cartoony double-take and asks me, "That them?"

I nod, and he looks at me like I'm a stranger again, like I'm homeless and on a sidewalk with a sign that says ANYTHING HELPS. Like *I'm* the fuckup. I have to wave at Larry and Gretchen and Ben for them to come in. Maybe they saw the gun, and that's why they're hesitating.

"Sorry to interrupt," Larry says. He's got his briefcase in one hand and a brown folder in the other, and I introduce Jason to him and Gretchen and Ben. Jason crosses his arms in front of himself to hide the gun, but we can all still see it. He's all smirky like he's got a purpose to be here. The irony of the situation is clearly lost on him. I mean, if I wasn't taking care of his kids, there'd be no need right now to be giving up this one of mine.

Gretchen is clutching her bag like she's afraid Jason's gonna mug her. It's the preppy kind that's got a circle wood handle and a monogram. Probly more of her Laura Ashley collection. My stomach hurts like I swallowed rocks. I check the clock. They're ten minutes early, and now I'm mad, really mad, like something's been stolen from me. I had planned to spend the next few minutes figuring out what to say to them as they left. *Good luck? Thanks? Have a nice life?* But right now, with Jason looking at me in addition to them, I'm completely blank.

Worse, nobody else is talking. And now Jason's eyes start to glaze over. Ben has a Dayton's shopping bag, which seems odd because if it's for me, he ain't offering it over. I'm feeling more than a little light-headed.

Finally, Larry speaks up:

"You okay to do this?"

Gretchen shoots him a fierce look that I never woulda guessed she was capable of, and Ben puts his hand on her arm. For a split-second, I hate Gretchen. With her goldilocks blonde bob and her toothpaste-commercial-perfect teeth. But . . . she and Ben have been real good to me. They've paid my rent for the last five months, given me an allowance, and covered all of my doctor bills, and they're gonna pay the whole bill Larry's gonna charge for this deal, plus give me five *thousand* under the table when all of the paperwork is final-final.

And Larry told me if I pulled out of the deal, I'd get zilch. I'm not sure why I'm thinking any of this 'cause my mind's been made up. Now's not the time, but I have one of my fly-by daydreams: I show up at Darius's house with this baby, the baby starts crying, Darius starts crying, Darius gets on one knee to ask me to marry him.

Ha ha ha. *Snap out of it, Veronica.*

Then Gretchen blurts, "We have an infant seat in the car. We're ready to bring Matthew home. That is, if you . . . you know. *Sign.*"

"Yo, she ain't gotta sign nothing," Jason says.

"I'm sorry," Gretchen says to him. "This concerns you *how*?"

"If she don't wanna—"

"Okay, okay everyone," says Larry. "Let's not get riled up. Veronica, are we good?"

My anger at pretty much everyone is causing me to be tongue-tied. I don't know who I want to look at least.

"She agreed," Gretchen says. "Ben, *do something*—Larry, can you remind her what she promised us she'd do?"

Then Larry, Gretchen, and Ben are talking loud at me all at once, and I can't make out anything anyone is saying. Larry wipes his forehead with the back of his hand, and I can't take all their noise or even the sight of them, so I cover my ears and close my eyes. I wish Jason would pull out his gun, wave it around, and tell them all to *back the hell up*.

But he's not. I open my eyes and see him staring at me. Yes, his eyes are red, and no, he'll never amount to much. But he's *family*, and I don't care if Gretchen and Ben play only gospel music for this new baby boy's entire life, or travel to Africa so he can find his roots, or bring him to see the Harlem Globetrotters, or even *move* to Harlem.

I'm his moms. I'm gonna make it work. I'm gonna have my fairy tale.

And if it's tragic to you, so what.

VIEWS

PATRICIA GARCÍA LUJÁN

Before it happened, Alex asked her third-grade music class to look for objects in their kitchens that could be used as instruments. She gave them twenty minutes for this assignment, even though she knew it would take them less than that. She wanted to give them a chance to stretch their legs and get away from the screen. They always looked so pale inside their little squares, blue light reflecting off their white, glazed foreheads.

During the break, Alex paced her small apartment, then hung her head as far as she could toward her toes, forcing a rush of blood across her body. She got up, light-headed, and looked out the window. Anorexic palm trees dotted the landscape. When she'd first moved here from Venezuela, she feared the trees would snap in half. They seemed so fragile, so unnaturally tall and thin, like most people in L.A. But the weather here made it easy for them to endure, the rain nonexistent, the sunshine relentless.

When time was up, the tiny squares slowly repopulated with faces. All the mute buttons burned red. Alex asked her students to present their findings, and the first kids—the ones with easy smiles and tidy beds in the background—shared their makeshift instruments energetically. One shook a pepper mill; another ran a wooden spoon down a metallic cheese grater. Then Alex called on one of the quieter boys. This one rarely spoke. His eyes were always focused elsewhere, his square sometimes black.

Alex unmuted him and caught him by surprise. Moaning and grunts took over the audio, as well as the sound of skin slapping against skin. A woman begged for more. The boys started to giggle, while the girls sat in silence, their eyes betraying their confusion. Alex scrambled to hit the mute button, but by the time she reached it, the quiet boy had already left the room. She looked at the clock in the corner. It was ten thirty in the morning.

• • •

Three freeway exits away, Adrian stared at rows of blue-and-yellow pasta boxes, searching for the bucatini. On the shelf was linguini, spaghetti, rigatoni, penne, fusilli, pappardelle, but no bucatini in sight. He moved the boxes around and peered at a dusty black void behind the products. Nothing. He grabbed a box of fettuccini, close enough, and sent a text:

Would you like this substitution? Please reply with yes or no.

He waited, received this response:

is there no bucatini?

He tapped the x on the screen and put the fettuccini back on the shelf. He pushed the cart along and continued to make his way down the list: eggs, yogurt, collagen powder, salmon filets, mayonnaise, capers.

While he dispensed almond butter into a plastic container, his phone vibrated in his pocket. Another order. He pushed the items in the cart to one side and again paced the aisles, searching for brioche bread, grated Parmesan cheese, canned tomatoes, oat milk, kombucha.

At the checkout line, he saw two others wearing the same blue vest that hung over his shoulders. He placed the items on the conveyor belt and checked his watch: six minutes to spare. As the cashier rang up his orders, Adrian played a game with himself in which he tried to guess the final amount for each customer. This time he was under, again; the totals always exceeded his estimations.

He folded the paper bags and sealed them with a sticker. Placed the produce in thickly insulated silver bags. Inside one, raspberries were already releasing a sugary red sweat. He placed the bags in the trunk of his car and typed a couple of addresses into the map. A swirl of red lines materialized on his screen.

The ETA let him know he wasn't going to make the deadline.

• • •

"Okay, who wants to go next?" Alex asked her class, pretending the interruption had never happened.

"Miss Alex, what was that noise?" said one of the girls, a precocious one. Alex could see her trying to stifle a smile.

"That was, um," Alex bit her tongue. Last year, a fifth grade P.E. teacher had said boys shouldn't be allowed to compete in girls' sports, and a flood of angry emails had swarmed the principal's in-box the next day. Alex had sat through a combative parent-teacher meeting, where half the adults yelled at the P.E. teacher while the other half of the room defended him. Coach did survive the fallout that time, but the following year he was quietly replaced.

More kids began to raise their hands.

"Why did Ben leave?"

"Is he coming back?"

"Miss Alex, can I go to the bathroom?"

She let them talk over one another to buy herself time. There were only three more minutes until class was over.

"I know what it was, my brother showed me that once."

"Is Ben in trouble, Miss Alex?"

"Why was the woman yelling 'harder'?"

"Was someone getting hurt?"

Once class was over, Alex sent an email to the principal explaining the situation. She said the boy had watched something inappropriate during class and that she wanted to discuss with her how to handle this going forward.

Need more detail, the principal replied. Her emails were always curt; she rarely got on the phone.

It was explicit, Alex wrote. *Sexual.*

What exactly did you see? the principal replied in less than a minute, and Alex admitted she didn't see anything, only heard, as did all the other third graders in the class.

Are you sure? the principal asked. *Could it have been something else? We need to be sure.*

Alex rolled her eyes. She'd never respected the principal; no one did. The woman ran the elementary school like a store and treated parents as customers who were always right. Alex found her blind deference embarrassing. She had attended a school run by nuns, who'd disciplined with wooden rulers and threats of eternal damnation. She'd hated every minute of it, but at least those sisters had understood authority.

Positive, Alex replied, before adding: *Unless you think a woman yelling HARDER could be something else?*

She deleted the second part before hitting send.

• • •

Adrian dropped off eight bags on the doorstep and snapped a photo of them. He tapped on a check mark and strode back to his car. One delivery down, another four to go.

The next destination was a small home in Silver Lake painted robin's-egg blue. Near the door, a hammered-down sign greeted Adrian: IN THIS HOUSE WE BELIEVE, above a long list of declarations in a rainbow of colors. The sign stood erectly in the lawns of the homes on the right and the left, too. Adrian smiled at their uniformity, how the whole block agreed to blast out the exact same banal points of view: *Science is real. Love is love. No human is illegal.* As if saying any of these things was brave, as if it changed anything.

Adrian wasn't sure what he was, but he knew he wasn't legal just yet. He'd been stuck in immigration limbo for more than four years now, even though his lawyer had said his status would be taken care of in one. "Asylum is your best chance," the lawyer had told him when they'd first met in his office, with dozens of people speaking in Spanish crowded outside of his door. "You'll need to claim that you feared for your life, and that that's why you're here."

"But I did fear for my life," Adrian had said. "Every day."

The lawyer had then explained how, after they submitted the paperwork, Adrian wouldn't be able to go back home again.

"Never?" Adrian had asked with a pen in his hand.

"Not until you get your blue passport. Which could be, give or take, another six years."

Still, Adrian had signed the paperwork in black ink.

Now, after setting a bag filled with toilet paper and a stack of plastic water bottles on the front porch, Adrian took the photo, clicked on the green check mark, and rushed back to his car. He turned on the ignition.

Ding.

A tip had come in. Two dollars from the toilet paper lady.

. . .

Later that afternoon, Alex sat in static traffic on Santa Monica Boulevard on her way to Bel Air, where she was about to listen to a seventh-grader play "Clair de lune" for an hour. While the school remained closed, Alex thankfully still found work as a private music tutor. Between rent and the car lease and the soaring price of gasoline, her teaching salary wasn't cutting it.

Her class started in fifteen minutes, but the jam showed no signs of untangling. She typed the address into her phone and felt relieved when the ETA said she'd arrive just in time. She then pasted the same address on Zillow.

Peeking into the homes of her students was a secret hobby. She liked to ogle their sprawling kitchens, free-standing bathtubs, theater rooms, and infinity pools. All of them had an unreasonable number of bathrooms. All of their selling prices featured zero after zero after zero.

In Caracas, such ostentatiousness was unimaginable. Showing off money there only attracted trouble—not that her family owned much. But in L.A., everyone exposed themselves with abandon. They parked convertible cars on the street with the roofs down, shopped for groceries with gold watches on their wrists, and lived in glass houses with large spotless windows that allowed anyone to see all the way inside. Lives constantly on display.

Ding.

A voice note from her mother.

Lately, they communicated through these rambling missives, each one getting back to the other whenever they could. The California time difference partly to blame.

Her mother had heard on the news something about fires in Santa Cruz. *Is that near you?* she asked on the voice note. *Also, could you check on the deposit? You know we can only pay for your father's medication in dollars.*

Alex picked up the phone and hit the blue mic icon on the screen: "Hola mami," she started, but her message paused when another notification buzzed in.

NEW MESSAGE FROM ADRIAN, her dashboard read. She held her phone higher to read texts as they came in:

Not sure I can make dinner tonight

way behind on my route

trafico de mierda

i'll let you know

te amo

The choke hold of traffic eased, and Alex dropped her phone in the drink compartment. She'd get back to them later. Her foot pressed on the accelerator, the sky now toned down to a pale yellow.

She lowered the window hoping to catch a bit of breeze, but the air smelled of exhaust, or maybe it was smoke. She'd stopped being able to tell the difference.

• • •

That night, Alex and Adrian were invited to dinner at her friend Luisa's house. Alex had met Luisa when they'd both worked on a music video together a few years ago—Luisa as a listed production assistant, Alex as an unacknowledged gofer. The two had become quick friends after they'd picked up on each other's accent, that breathy coastal lilt more commonly found in Miami, rare all the way out in California. They'd stuck to each other like new lovers.

This was back when Alex was still trying to sneak her way into the music business. Her plan back then was to take any odd job where she might bump elbows with someone important who could pluck her from obscurity and into a studio. She built sets, fetched matcha lattes, nannied famous spawn. The only break she got was someone connected her to a job teaching music at a private school. She took it, telling herself it was a temporary solution to the pile of bills sprouting on her kitchen counter. Three years went by and she'd lowered the stack, as well as the lofty aspirations she once had for her life. Her dreams now towered over her, well out of reach.

Alex arrived just as Luisa was setting the table outside in the backyard. Luisa lived with her husband, Joaquin, in a small bungalow-like house with a garden and a golden doodle. Alex arranged the place mats and slipped linen napkins into wicker rings while Luisa poured a bottle of wine into a glass decanter.

"All of this for me?" Alex said, her sarcasm masking the pang of insufficiency she felt while she admired Luisa's steak knives and the fresh tulips dangling from the vase. Alex thought of the chipped plates and mismatched mugs stacked in her cupboard. The many times she and Adrian used paper towels as napkins. How he'd tear a sheet in half because he thought Bounty was too expensive.

"Where's Adrian?" Luisa asked, and she drizzled olive oil over the flaky salt on a bowl of salad. "I'm making lamb chops. Trying to impress the chef."

"Former chef," Alex corrected.

"Just because all the restaurants are closed doesn't mean he's not a chef anymore."

Alex shrugged. "He would argue the opposite. Anyway, I don't think he's going to make it. He texted saying he's behind on his route again."

"Is he still doing deliveries? I thought he wanted to quit?"

Alex scoffed. "Don't we all?"

"Well, if you're looking for work, I need a model for next week," Luisa said. "You'd be perfect. Everyone wants your ethnically ambiguous look these days." With her own sarcasm, she drew air quotes with her fingers.

Luisa made a living shooting social media ads on her phone for juice stores, makeup lines, and other companies with identical sans serif branding. Everyone hired her off Instagram. Her popular account featured a mélange of sparse interiors, contemporary art, and French New Wave movie stills. Alex found it fascinating how Luisa managed to build a career from simply posting other people's pictures on her feed.

"Sure, count me in," Alex said. She'd modeled for Luisa a few times before. The work didn't pay much, but Alex believed in saying yes to any opportunity, especially one that could help her get discovered. She fiercely believed in the law of attraction. Chose to believe the universe was conspiring in her favor. Her big moment would come, eventually. All she had to do was stay open to all possibilities.

"Perfect," Luisa said, and she massaged the spinach leaves with wooden tongs. Then she asked Alex about her day.

"Well," Alex said, "one of my eight-year-old students was watching porn in the middle of class."

Luisa perked up. "Eight?" she said. "Dios. Has this ever happened before?"

"Never," Alex said. "Phones aren't allowed in school. But now that they're alone in their rooms all day? Who knows what they're up to."

"Where are the parents?" Luisa asked. "Aren't they around?"

"Please, the only time I ever see parents is when they pop in and ask the kids to keep it down, then shut the door."

"Can't be easy for them," Luisa added, and she took a seat on a wicker bench, crossing her legs. "Joaco and I work at opposite ends of the house, and some days we want to kill each other." Luisa mimed a strangling motion with her hands and shook the invisible neck between her fingers.

"At least you get to see each other. Adrian's shifts are insane. We're never on the same schedule anymore."

The sound of a creaky hinge interrupted them, and out walked Joaquin in sweatpants, Adidas slides, and misty eyes. He greeted Alex with a kiss on the cheek.

"What's the word?" he asked, and he took his seat next to Luisa. Their bodies immediately gravitated toward each other, his hand on her leg, her head on his shoulder.

"One of Alex's students was watching porn during her class."

Joaquin let out a laugh. "So what?" he said. "Every guy watches porn."

"He's eight," Alex replied.

"Oh." Joaquin sucked in air through clenched teeth. He pulled out a metallic box stamped with a sticker of a lime-green medical cross. He opened it and a pungent, sour smell graced the air.

"He's not wrong, you know," Luisa said as she started to place cherry tomatoes onto small green plates shaped like leaves. "Men are pigs. You should see Joaco's WhatsApp—it's disgusting."

"Luisa, what goes on in my chats is confidential."

"It's gross," Luisa said, and she shifted away from him on the bench. "Show her."

"No way," he said. Then he crumbled a bud of weed with one hand while his other palm held a fragile sheet of rolling paper. Luisa snatched the phone from his pocket. "Hey," he yelled, but he kept his hands occupied with the joint.

Luisa punched in the passcode and, within seconds, pulled up a screen full of texts, photos, and videos.

"Look." She waved the phone out in a semicircle as if she were presenting evidence in a court of law. "This is what they text each other twenty-four hours a day."

Alex narrowed her eyes and focused on the chat screen: Open mouths. Pinched nipples. A famous movie star's legs spread wide, no underwear. Fingers circling a hairless vagina, pink and smooth like clay.

Luisa kept scrolling. Her index finger tapping, tapping, tapping until the images all became a blur of flesh.

"What's going on here?" Adrian said, surprising them from behind. He'd let himself through the gate to their backyard.

"Taking advantage of the distraction," Joaquin said, and he yanked the phone out of Luisa's hand. "Just these two watching dirty things on my phone."

Adrian laughed. "Dinner took an interesting turn. What did I miss?"

Alex got up from the table and greeted him with a kiss. "Long story," she said. "We'll catch you up."

Luisa poured a glass of wine and handed it to Adrian. "We were talking about how all men are sexually depraved."

"Depraved is a bit dramatic," Alex said, and for the first time she wondered about Luisa and Joaquin. Whether they had quiet sex in the dark.

"I agree with Alex," Joaquin interjected. "There's nothing depraved about these videos. This is simple supply and demand. There's an engaged consumer base and these products are geared toward their satisfaction."

"You've been working in marketing too long," Adrian said. He pointed at the lit joint in Joaquin's hand. Joaquin handed it over and Adrian took a hit. "Before you know it, you'll be talking like those robots at work. Everything is a KPI or a POD or a who-the-fuck-knows. When did we stop using words?"

Alex laughed, even though she could sense the simmering anger beneath Adrian's humor. He hated that job. She rubbed his lower back.

"Ay si," he said, and he closed his eyes. "That's nice."

"Sorry if I find it depressing that everything is for sale these days," Luisa continued as she refilled everyone's glasses. "Like, oh my God Joaco, show them that video of the couple."

"You're obsessed," Joaquin said. Still, he swiped open his phone.

"This guy Joaco knows from Caracas," Luisa explained while Joaquin scrolled. "Him and his wife make videos of themselves."

"What kind of videos?" Adrian asked.

"Aha," Joaquin said, and he held out his phone. "Here we go."

He hit play and a petite, young woman in black, lacy lingerie appeared on the screen. She slowly got down on all fours. "Very good," an off-screen voice said, and then a hand pulled down her underwear.

"You know these people?" Alex asked.

Joaquin nodded. "I went to school with his older brother. Apparently, they're making a killing with these. They have thousands of subscribers."

"Please," the woman on the floor whispered. "Please, I want it." The lower half of a man's body appeared. She opened her mouth and let him in. Her hand held on to his hairy, muscular thigh. A diamond ring sparkled with every push.

"Why don't you see his face?" Alex said. "Why only hers?"

"I guess they want other people to imagine they're the

ones fucking her mouth?" Joaquin said, and everyone laughed.

Once the man was finished, the woman on the screen closed her lips and swallowed. The muscles in her throat clenched, then released. She looked straight at the camera and smiled. Joaquin swiped off the phone.

"Isn't it crazy?" Luisa said, her cheeks flushed. "These people are married."

"People have done crazier things for money," Joaquin said.

"Tough economy," Adrian added, and everyone laughed.

• • •

The four of them polished off five bottles of wine, Alex drinking a few more glasses than the rest. She said she was fine to drive, but Adrian insisted she leave her car at Luisa's, and Alex said fine, she'd pick it up tomorrow.

They got home late. Once inside their little apartment, they automatically completed their evening routines side by side. He flossed. She removed her mascara. Her face was left dewy, covered in a soft sheen of oil.

In bed, she found sleep impossible. Her mind raced with possibilities. What-ifs materializing one after another. She reached out to him, but he was already more asleep than awake. She started to kiss his neck and his eyes opened. He grabbed her by the waist and pulled her to him.

They started having sex. She on top, her shoulders pulled back, her eyes on his. Unlike most of the women Adrian had slept with before her, she liked her body and enjoyed showing it off. When they fucked, she told him exactly what she wanted, where, and how. She whispered things in his ear that would make him come immediately. Inspired him to say things he never imagined leaving his mouth. He loved her lack of inhibition, her freedom.

She was getting close. She climbed off him, turned around and got on her hands and knees, her face toward the wall, away from his. She arched her back. He got up and grabbed her by the hips. She turned and said something he didn't understand. He asked her to say it again.

"Grab your phone."

"Why?"

"I want you to film me."

He laughed. "You're drunk."

"Film me."

• • •

Adrian usually went along with whatever Alex wanted. He didn't like to say no to her; it was a pointless exercise. She always exhausted him into a yes. That's how they'd ended up in L.A. She was the one who'd pushed them to leave. He'd never really thought about it before he was with her. Even though so many people were leaving, to him, starting from scratch elsewhere, away from family and friends, seemed difficult and unappealing.

Not that life in Caracas had been easy. But Adrian had been one of those people who adapted rather than complained. He'd taken every small indignity from the government in stride. If there was no meat on the shelves, he'd eat fish. During water outages, he would go to the beach, and he'd never mind the salt on his skin. But Alex had refused to live that way. She hadn't been able to stand the supermarket lines and the power outages and the constant fear she said pricked the soles of her feet like barbed wire.

"We're like little crabs in a boiling pot," she'd told him one night. "You don't realize it, but we're slowly being cooked alive."

She'd said they could be earning in dollars. She'd said they could save, help out their families. Maybe he could even open up his own restaurant.

She'd presented endless possibilities for their lives. Didn't he see that there were dozens of opportunities? He only had to be brave enough to take them.

"Things can only get better for us," she'd said. "Things will be better."

And he, as always, believed her.

. . .

When they finished, the phone was still in Adrian's hand, his fingers clenched around the glass screen. His chest rose and fell quickly. He was still trying to catch his breath.

Alex reached over and took his phone. He raised his head off the mattress. "Hey, what are you doing with that?"

"I want to see," she said, smiling at him.

He got up on his elbows. "Oh, is this a performance review?"

She laughed. "I have no complaints. I'm just curious."

Alex looked at the clip. She thought she looked good, even though the camera had been at a strange angle.

"What if we did it?" she asked. Through the small speaker, she heard herself moaning.

"Did what?"

"You know, put this up," she said, and she turned the screen to him. "Make people pay to watch us."

He scoffed. "Now I *know* you're drunk." He lay back down and closed his eyes.

He fell asleep easily, as he usually did once they were done. His body relaxed, his chest movements becoming steady and evenly paced.

Alex stayed up for another while, blue light flushed across her face. She ran her index finger across the screen, and the video raced forward, then back, forward, then back.

• • •

Traffic, as usual, was uncooperative. Alex pulled up her phone and swiped open the latest news alert. A chart showed lines going up, up, up. On a map, the shape of California beamed a crimson red.

Frustrated, she put the phone down. Ahead, the Hollywood sign winked at her from the mountain.

She'd always known she'd end up here. The City of Angels had always seemed like the final destination for her. Her crush had begun early, when, as a girl, she'd spent hours in the afternoons watching dubbed reruns of rich Beverly Hills teenagers who wore sunglasses to school and handsome lifeguards who saved people from riptides and sharks. Whenever she'd visited the beach with her family, she'd looked for their red swimsuits. But there never had been anyone keeping an eye on the water. Whenever she'd gotten caught in a current, she'd understood that it was up to her to swim out of it herself.

Half an hour later, she arrived at a large house decorated

with hedges trimmed in the shapes of animals. Because she was running a few minutes late, she sprinted to the entrance, then rang the bell. While she steadied her breath, a woman in uniform opened the door.

"Goo afternun," the woman said. "Mask?"

Alex replied to her in Spanish, but the woman didn't respond. Alex searched her bag and fished out a wrinkled blue mask. Once she pulled the elastic behind her ears, the woman let her in and pointed at a tray in the entrance.

"Estep there, please."

Alex stood in a tray with shallow water and a foul smell.

"Bleach," the woman said. "La señora is very careful."

She led Alex past the winding staircase and into an airy terrace, where a young boy sat in front of a piano, his shoulders slumped.

Alex heard the clack of heels on the terrace's marble floor. She recognized the boy's mother walking toward her. The boy didn't turn around. His gaze remained fixed on the white and black keys.

"Oh great, you're here," the woman said, careful not to get near Alex. "Before you start, you should know we're trying out a new medication on Jake, so he might seem a little drowsier than usual."

"Okay, good to know," Alex said, and she patted the top of the boy's head softly. "I'm sure we'll be fine."

"Ah-ah," the woman said, wagging her finger. "No touching, remember?"

"Right." Alex stuck her hand in her jacket pocket.

"I'll be back in an hour. If you need anything, Dolores is here."

Alex stood beside the far end of the bench. The boy

turned around and said hello, as if he'd noticed her presence only then. His eyes were small and glistening.

"Should we try that Beatles song today?" Alex asked.

He gave her a weak smile. It stayed on his face as her fingers started playing the first chords of "Let It Be."

"Now your turn," she said.

The boy looked at the keys as if unsure of how to proceed. He rubbed his eyes.

"Miss Alex, I don't feel well."

She wanted to reach out and comfort him, but she suspected there might be cameras looking at them. She'd spotted cameras in some of the other homes she'd visited. She imagined the boy's mother combing through the footage, looking for any excuse to fire her.

"Maybe we can try something easier?" she asked.

The boy closed his eyes and shook his head. He started to breathe quickly.

"Are you okay?" she asked.

He turned in her direction and threw up, rivulets of vomit now dripping from between the keys.

• • •

Adrian stood in line in the supermarket for the third time that day. He pushed his way through crowded aisles and picked over produce shelves. He hated going to the supermarket after five. By that time, so many items were out of stock, his orders full of declined substitutions.

Before this job, Adrian loved to be surrounded by food. He'd get up early on Sundays and walk down the open-air market in Chacao that smelled like ripe papayas and burnt butter. Plastic crates had towered with rainbow-hued peppers, feathery cilantro, and hairy yuccas. Corn cachapa mix had sizzled on a greasy skillet. He would order a tart passion fruit juice and would never leave without also buying a bag of crispy, fat-lined chicharron skin.

Back home, the food had felt alive. Here, everything lay suffocated under layers of plastic.

He loaded the orders into the back of his car and set off. The map directed him toward the highway, but he decided to take a back route instead and spiraled through narrow streets.

His dashboard blinked orange. The car was running low on gas. He checked the clock and calculated that he had some extra minutes to load up the tank and still hit his delivery windows. He searched for the nearest gas station and pulled up to one as the last rays of sunlight beamed over the city.

He slid the nozzle into his car and watched as the total shuffled up, up, up on the screen. He used to joke that his complete distaste for numbers was the reason he became a chef. While his friends had headed off to study engineering and business, he instead had gotten certified in specialties like sous viding and open-fire cooking and pastry decoration. For a while, he'd chopped and plated meals inside sizzling kitchens of trendy Peruvian, Japanese, and Italian restaurants that were popping up all over Caracas. His friends would show up and ask the waiter for the chef, and Adrian would oblige and play his part. He would step out in his white uniform and introduce every elaborate dish on their table. Their mouths would water, and they'd look up at him with admiration.

Now his whole day consisted of nothing but numbers. The number of orders, the amount of packages, the estimated times of arrivals, the measly tips, the performance reviews, the overdraft fees. None of them ever amounting to anything, he himself always falling behind, always racing to a finish line that kept dragging further and further away.

Next to the gas station, a row of tents huddled under a bridge. An American flag draped over one of the nylon roofs. Adrian wondered how someone could still pledge loyalty to a country that left them without a home. But that was the thing about Americans—they somehow still believed they were better than everyone else, even when they slept on the street.

While he waited for his tank to fill, he noticed that a man in a soiled shirt with a plastic lanyard hanging from his neck was staring at him. Loose tracksuit pants hung from the man's protruding hip bones.

"Hey," the man yelled, and he headed in Adrian's direction. The numbers on the screen continued to climb. Adrian willed them to hurry up.

Before the man was close, Adrian could feel his stench, a sharp tang that would've been worse if not for the gasoline's overpowering aroma. Thick dark circles obscured the man's eyes. Small red sores were sprinkled over his face, his mouth a downturned line.

"Hey man, help me buy some food?" he asked, and Adrian could see he still had a few teeth left, most of them as gray as his skin.

Adrian never carried cash, but he performed a search through his pockets anyway. He patted the back of his jeans, stuck his hands in his jacket.

The man jittered while he waited. Up close, he seemed younger, maybe only a few years older than Adrian, who tried to imagine the man with clean hair and a good pair of sneakers. He wanted to ask him how he'd ended up under a bridge. It probably happened suddenly, Adrian thought. Over before he even realized it. Adrian had felt something similar lately. One morning, he'd woken up and couldn't recognize himself anymore. It was as if he'd slipped into another person's body, someone who spoke another language and lived somewhere else—and now he was stuck inside with no way out.

His phone pinged, another new order.

"I got nothing," Adrian said, raising his hands in an apologetic manner. "You want a sandwich from inside?"

The man looked him in the eye, then spat at his shoes.

"Fuck am I gonna do with a sandwich?" he said, and he walked away.

• • •

Alex was already in bed by the time Adrian made it home that night. She heard the door open and close as she lay in her underwear under the sheets. In the living room, her dirty clothes swirled inside the washing machine.

She'd been on her phone for a while. A couple of hours, perhaps, taking mental notes as she scrolled through endless profiles of naked women with smooth, perfect hips, barely parted pouts, every inch of their bodies soft and bare.

She heard the beep of the microwave and assumed Adrian was heating up some old takeout. He never cooked anymore; he was always home too late or too tired. He deserved some rest, she thought. She would do this for him. She only had to get him to see that, which wouldn't be easy.

But she'd put thoughts into his head before. Dangled ideas in front of him and then watched him arrive at a conclusion, as if he'd came up with it on his own.

Sometimes, she was amazed at how effortless it could be.

• • •

"I thought you were messing around the other day," Adrian said. "I can't believe you're serious."

She'd pounced on him as soon as he'd walked into their room. Hadn't stopped talking about her big idea. Hadn't even given him a chance to take off his shoes.

"I went ahead and set up a profile," she said now, and she handed him her phone, which felt hot in his hand.

On the screen, her glossed lips sucked on an index finger.

"I don't even have to show my face," she continued. She took back the phone to point out how the photo cut off just above the tip of her nose.

"A lot of girls post like this," she added. "I could be any of them. No one would ever know it's me."

"I'd know," he said to her.

"I read all about this one platform," she said, pulling up a *New York Times* article, her voice quick. "The numbers are amazing."

More numbers, Adrian thought. He could never escape the numbers.

"Could we at least try it once?" she asked. "See how it goes?"

He stared at her and wondered if she was stuck inside someone else, too. He wanted to search her eyes for a sign that she was still in there, but she wasn't looking at him, her gaze on the screen as she tapped it once, then again. Its light was reflecting off her face. She looked beautiful and hideous at the same time.

"It could be fun," she said. She handed back the phone and took off her bra. "Let's just have some fun."

Adrian's hand was squeezing the phone. The red record button stared up at him, daring him to touch it. The only numbers on the screen were pairs of double zeroes. He let his finger press down.

LUCY LUCY LUCY

NIKKI DOLSON

When Angela cornered Lucy in the girls' locker room and said, "White girl!" there was a moment when Lucy wanted to tell her how she wasn't white or black, only the perfect mix of both, which is what her father liked to say. Instead, she turned away as her mother had taught her to. Her mother would say, "Don't fight. Be better than those petty girls, baby."

One of the LaLas, either LaDonnia or LaTasha, freshman girls who'd once been friends with Lucy, yelled, "Cut her hair!" and laughed.

Lucy grabbed the long thick braids that trailed down her back and tried to think of a comeback—something, anything—but before she could, Angela spun her around and pushed her hard. Lucy fell back against the metal lockers, her head colliding with a lock, the pain making brilliant spots of color in front of her eyes, and with that, Lucille Jones was done turning the other cheek. She swung first and kept swinging, her fists connecting with the body beneath her until Coach Daniels blew her whistle. She stopped midswing, breathing hard. Stood and wiped her hand across her face. There was a long streak of vibrant red across the pale skin of her palm. She was bleeding but felt nothing other than the ecstatic beating of her heart.

On the floor, in the middle of a mess of backpacks and clothes and books, Angela, furious, was still trying to kick Lucy as Coach pulled her away. Behind them, the LaLas stood, disbelief twitching off one girl's face and onto the other.

In the principal's office, each girl had a chance to explain what happened. Angela said Lucy started it, and that was all she had to say. Lucy explained the situation as calmly as she could, described the previous altercations, the constant teasing, and the threats to cut her hair, finishing with, "Then she pushed me into the lockers, Mr. Allegretti."

Mr. Allegretti opened his mouth then closed it. He sent both girls out of the office where they sat in white plastic chairs across from each other. Angela glared at Lucy, who wasn't worried until their mothers showed up.

The Lucy Lucy's mother wanted her to be had "good girl" friends. Friends who did their homework and didn't sass or roll their eyes. This Lucy told her parents about her good day at school even though most days weren't good at all. At school she kept her head down and tried to disappear. At school there was nowhere for her to hide. She didn't fit anywhere. Pale as she was. Mixed like she was. Different as she was. The various versions of Lucy were always on her mind.

Angela and her mother went into the principal's office first. While Lucy and her mother waited side by side in the chairs, Lucy watched her mother carefully. She sat stiff and unmoving like the collar of her uniform shirt. She had mentioned more than once to Lucy how much she hated the green polyester pants that hugged her hips and the jungle-patterned shirt she had to wear for her job as a blackjack dealer at the Tropicana Casino. She didn't look at Lucy. She seemed to be studying a banner in the hallway that read "Tiffany Carter 4 Prom Queen—CLASS of 1988 RULEZ!" in alternating primary colors.

"Nice girls don't fight," Lucy's mother finally said.

"She called me 'white girl,'" Lucy said too quickly. Her mother's mouth tightened, but she didn't look at Lucy. "*And* she threatened to cut off my hair."

Her mother loved her hair and frequently mentioned how lucky Lucy was because she wouldn't have to endure relaxers and hot combs as her mother had when she was little. Honestly, Lucy didn't care much about her hair, which was long and, when not properly restrained in braids, expanded into wild curls. Most days she struggled to put it in manageable braids and, occasionally, a fat barrette.

Now her mother turned to her, smoothed her hand over Lucy's face, covering her eyes until Lucy relaxed and leaned into her palm. Her mother lifted her hand and said, "Well, if she started it, then I can't blame you."

Lucy's mother argued down a two-week suspension to three days of detention, citing her daughter's excellent grades and good behavior in the face of such obvious bullying, finishing with: "That girl provoked an altercation with my daughter. Now we need to think about what lesson needs to be learned here. The lesson is sometimes you have to fight back."

• • •

On the first afternoon of detention, there were five detainees including Lucy. A redheaded boy she didn't know made endless paper airplanes in different shapes and sizes. Lucy watched the planes fly for fractions of a second then plummet to the floor. The others were the LaLas and a girl named Therese.

Therese was seventeen and still a sophomore. The story was she'd failed eighth grade, then managed to fail so many classes her sophomore year they couldn't let her become a junior. The better story was Therese's parents had split up the summer before, after a very public argument in the Lucky's grocery store parking lot, which ended with her mother being taken away in handcuffs for assault with a deadly weapon, namely, her 1974 two-door, butter-yellow Subaru. Therese's father then left town for a job in Ohio, and now her mother, on serious probation, worked nights and drank during the day. Therese was always in detention for one thing or another. She didn't seem to care what anyone thought of her, and now she had a magazine spread out across her desk, the LaLas clustered around her like mosquitos, their voices buzzing. Lucy could see the slick pages with models on them. Therese caught Lucy looking her way.

"Hey you!" Therese said. The LaLas turned to look at Lucy, matching unhappy expressions on their faces.

Lucy gave a quick little smile to Therese, then looked out the window at the school band practicing on the field. There was a squeal of metal against linoleum, and Lucy turned back to see Therese weaving slowly between the desks. Her hair, done up in small braids with pink beads twisted in, brushed her shoulders. She wore jeans and a neon-pink T-shirt, pink lip gloss shimmering on her lips. Lucy felt a little plain in the yellow, short-sleeve button-down her mother had bought her.

Therese sat on the desk in front of Lucy, her butt on the desktop, her feet on the seat. She tapped her fingers on the glossy magazine on her lap and stared at Lucy for a long moment. For her part, Lucy just blinked at her, unsure of what to say. Therese had six inches on Lucy to go along with their three-year age difference, so Lucy wasn't so sure a fight with her would be worth the risk.

Therese opened her mouth to speak, but then they all heard footsteps coming down the hall. The redheaded boy put his head down on his desk with the wreckage of failed flights all around him. The LaLas slipped back into their seats. Lucy straightened in her chair, but Therese didn't move. She kept her head down like she was completely absorbed in the magazine, the tips of her braids dusting the pages as she turned them.

"Therese, take a seat."

It was Miss Winthrop, the substitute teacher who taught freshman and sophomore English. She didn't look much older than the seniors who walked the halls. Every day she wore her dark blonde hair in fat curls that covered the front of her shoulders and a watch set in a big silver bangle bracelet that slid up and down her arm.

"Therese," Miss Winthrop said.

Therese didn't acknowledge her.

Lucy whispered, "Therese?"

Therese glanced up from the page and winked at Lucy. Slowly, she stretched one denim-clad leg out, then placed her booted foot on the floor. She slid herself down to sit at the desk the correct way and went back to her magazine. The

LaLas giggled. They reminded Lucy of the Siamese cats in *Lady and the Tramp*, so terribly happy when others suffered.

"Thank you," Miss Winthrop said, her voice hard. "Now we all know why each of you is here. I hope you've been behaving yourselves. We have"—she looked at her watch—"another forty minutes together, and then you're free to go."

Therese pulled gum from her pocket, unfolded it from its silver wrapper, put it in her mouth, and proceeded to pop it loudly.

Lucy saw Miss Winthrop narrow her eyes. "Therese, is your homework finished?"

Therese flipped another page. "Sure."

"So your book report is finished for my class?"

"Yep, it's all up here, Elaine," Therese said, tapping her temple. She'd said Miss Winthrop's name as if she had a right to. Like they were friends.

"Therese, come with me," Miss Winthrop said, her hands clenched into tight fists at her sides.

Therese hopped up from her seat with a smile forming on her lips. She tossed the magazine onto Lucy's desk, winked again, strutted past Miss Winthrop and out into the hall. Miss Winthrop followed her out, shutting the door behind them.

After five minutes, LaTasha got up, peeked through the window in the classroom's door, and shook her head.

LaDonnia turned to Lucy, said, "Let me have that *Vogue*."

"It's Therese's," Lucy said.

"Come off it, white girl," said LaTasha.

Lucy glared at her. She stood, and, with the *Vogue* in one hand, tried to walk like Therese, with her head up and shoulders back. As Lucy got closer to the door, LaTasha backed away from it. She was taller than Lucy, most everyone was, but Lucy saw a flicker of fear and let her own smile form. She paused beside LaTasha, then flung open the door and walked out of the room. She heard LaTasha whisper *Bitch!* as the door closed behind her.

Lucy headed down the empty hallway to the bathroom, her sneakers near silent on the scuffed floor. As she approached the last classroom, she heard someone's hiccuping sobs. She edged close to that classroom's slightly open door. She saw Therese with her back against the wall next to the blackboard, tears streaming down her face. Miss Winthrop stood close to her, one leg between Therese's parted legs, one hand on the wall and the other holding Therese's face, her thumb stroking her cheek.

Lucy didn't breathe.

"You can't do this," Therese said. Her long black braids mingled with Miss Winthrop's blonde curls as she put her head down onto Miss Winthrop's shoulder.

"Therese," Miss Winthrop said, "I told you. I can't stay. They didn't extend my contract, but we have until the end of the school year. We have weeks before I go."

"Stay—you can work at another school," Therese said, her voice muffled.

"The school districts aren't hiring here. It's bad all over, Honey. We've talked about this. You have to stop this behavior. You're so smart. You're so beautiful."

Lucy watched Therese lean in and kiss Miss Winthrop on the lips. Miss Winthrop's pale hands cradled Therese's face. Therese clutched at Miss Winthrop's waist, their bodies pressing together, and one of them, Lucy couldn't tell which, let out a low moan. Lucy gasped and ducked away, nearly tripping over her own feet as she ran around the corner and into the safety of the bathroom.

She gripped one of the white porcelain sinks in front of the wall-mounted mirror and tried to breathe slowly. Blood pounded in her ears. She touched her own lips and wondered what it'd be like to kiss another girl. Her kissing experience was minimal. Leroy was the boy she had liked all during eighth grade, but he'd been going with another girl. But that had ended with the school year, and come summer, at a fair, Lucy found herself standing in line with Leroy for the Ferris wheel. They'd shared a carriage, and when they lurched to a stop near the top, Leroy had leaned over and kissed her. She remembered grabbing his arms and gripping tightly as if she was going to push him away, when all she wanted was to pull him closer. She remembered touching her tongue to his lips and how rough they'd felt. She remembered the firm curve of his biceps under her sweating palms. They'd parted when the ride jerked to a start again, each of them looking away, trying to act as if the kiss could never possibly be the highlight of their summer. Now he was a freshman at another school, and she was hiding in a girls' bathroom.

The door to the bathroom burst open, and Therese was there, frowning at Lucy. Lucy turned on the faucet and began washing her hands. Therese let the door close behind her. She walked up to the sink next to Lucy, dropped her tote bag on the floor, and leaned back against the sink with her arms folded across her chest.

"I know you saw," she said. She didn't sound angry.

"I won't say anything," Lucy said.

"I know you won't," Therese said. Lucy heard the threat

and envisioned her end, laid out cold on the floor of the bathroom, Therese standing over her, her face blank and the LaLas laughing and orchestrating a viewing of Lucy's body under a sign that said "Lucille Jones 4 Loser Queen. Popularity status: DOA. Teasability: Astronomical."

Therese turned around to glance at her reflection. She touched the puffiness under her eyes with her fingertips in a way that reminded Lucy of the time when she'd walked in on her mother frowning at herself in the mirror. Therese reapplied her lip gloss, smacking and puckering her lips. Lucy wondered if Miss Winthrop's lips shimmered now. Lucy could see where tears had dried on Therese's face. Lucy was so much lighter than Therese and not nearly as pretty. Therese put her hands under the faucet and patted water against her cheeks.

"I heard about you and Angela," Therese said. "Her mother made her transfer schools."

"Oh," was all Lucy could manage.

"Yeah, 'oh,'" Therese laughed. "Nice job getting rid of her. You know, they say Coach Daniels had to pull you off her. Guess Angela didn't know what she was getting into when she took you on, did she?"

"She was always trying to start something with me. I don't know why."

"Don't you?" Therese asked, and she reached out to finger one of Lucy's braids. Lucy managed not to flinch. "She was jealous."

"Of what?"

"You don't have a clue how pretty you are. All this long, thick hair, plus you're gonna get taller any day now and that weight you're carrying is gonna drift to all the right places, and when all those things line up, you're gonna be a knockout. Another year. You'll see."

"I doubt it," Lucy said.

"You'll see," Therese said, and Lucy wanted to believe her. She wanted Therese to be a friend. She wanted to bask in her aura of coolness.

Therese pulled a pack of cigarettes from her bag and picked up the *Vogue* from where Lucy had set it down on the sink's edge. Said, "Hey, you ever think of cutting your hair?" Shook out a cigarette, lit it, and again leaned back against the sink, flipping through pages until she found what she wanted. She turned the magazine to Lucy. "You could absolutely wear your hair like this. You'd be adorable."

Lucy reached for the magazine. The pictures on the two pages were of models in 1920s-style flapper clothes. The model Therese pointed at wore her hair in a short, bobbed style with just a hint of wave in it. She was thin and angular, with her eyes ringed with black eyeliner, and she wore a shimmering dress that caught the light. She had a drink in her hand, and her smile was wide and bright.

"I couldn't cut my hair like that. My mom would never let me."

"You always do what your mom says?" Therese exhaled a long stream of smoke toward the ceiling, then looked at Lucy with a smile on her face that said, *You and me could have some fun.*

• • •

At lunch the next day, Therese appeared at Lucy's table and said, "Come on." Therese was ditching some class, Lucy was sure of it, but she felt honored to be seen with Therese. Everyone always stared at Therese with some sort of awe or at least respect. Lucy followed her out the side doors to the back of the school, where all the seniors and juniors held court. Overlooking the back baseball field, the area consisted of one stolen cafeteria table and a stack of mats from the weight room. Therese led Lucy past several small groups of seniors to the table and introduced Lucy to her friends, a couple of girls, one named April, a girl with bad acne across her forehead but with the loveliest brown eyes Lucy had ever seen. April patted the table next to where she sat, and Lucy hopped up beside her.

"So how did you two meet?" April asked.

"I told you, detention," Therese said.

"Can't I hear it from her, Therese?" April turned to Lucy and smiled.

"Detention," Lucy said. She glanced from April to Therese to April again, feeling like she was missing something. Therese frowned.

"So you're the one who fought Angela?" April asked.

Lucy nodded.

"We didn't get along with her really," April said, tapping the end of her cigarette into an empty Tab can.

"Hey, are you gonna help Therese get out of the tenth grade?" one girl asked.

Therese rolled her eyes. "I don't need any help."

"And yet you flunked. Seriously, how did you fail *art* class?"

All the girls giggled, and Lucy started to join in—until she saw Therese's face twist into a scowl.

The bell rang, and the girls started to pack their things.

April patted Therese on the shoulder. "You know we're just playing," she said.

Lucy grabbed her backpack and stood to leave, but Therese said, "Stay and hang out." Lucy had never ditched before. In fact, her next class was math, her favorite subject, but that day and the rest of that week, Lucy ditched with Therese. Each day Therese would come find Lucy in the cafeteria and bring her to sit among the older girls, and each day Lucy listened to them talk about the senior boys—even Therese did, and Lucy got the impression that no one else knew about Miss Winthrop. The girls liked to talk about what colleges their parents wanted them to attend and who was going to the lake that weekend. Boring, impossible stuff like that.

• • •

On Friday, detention was back in session. Lucy and the others sat in the auditorium watching rehearsals of *West Side Story*. On the stage, Mrs. Gould, their warden for the afternoon, was trying to get an adequate rehearsal out of her junior drama class.

They were supposed to do homework, and Lucy was trying to, but Therese sat next to her, flipping pages in the most recent issue of *Jet*, one with Janet Jackson on the cover, pointing out hairstyles she liked. They had their feet on the backs of the wooden seats in front of them. Behind them the boy with the airplanes seemed to have fallen asleep listening to his Walkman. Lucy caught herself humming along to the sound of New Edition's "If It Isn't Love" leaking from his headphones.

The LaLas were in the second row. They turned around occasionally trying to catch Therese's attention, but she never looked at them. Therese kept showing Lucy pictures until she stopped writing her paper and focused on Therese. They traded thoughts on hair extensions versus natural, short versus long. Therese was adamant that Lucy should cut her hair.

"You would be so cute."

"I'd be dead," Lucy said.

"Your hair'd grow back quick, though. You have good hair. You don't do anything to it, do you? Just shampoo and conditioner, right? You and Miss Winthrop both have good hair."

"Hers is nice—nicer than mine," Lucy said, thinking of the twist of curls that cascaded down Miss Winthrop's back. "But she's blonde. So much better than my brown."

"She colors hers. I helped her dye it once. But it's still good hair."

Lucy wondered how long Miss Winthrop and Therese had been seeing each other. Lucy said, "Really? It looks natural. Yours is nice, too." She reached out and touched Therese's long, thin braids.

Therese watched the people on the stage. "It's okay."

"You know, I could help you with your English homework if you wanted," Lucy said. Midterm reports would be coming out the next week, and Lucy knew Therese was worried about her grades, really didn't want to be a sophomore again.

Therese's mouth dipped into a frown. "I don't need a freshman's help to do my homework, girl."

"Okay, just thought I'd offer." Lucy sank lower in her chair and went back to doing her homework.

Therese raised her hand. "Mrs. Gould, can I go to the bathroom, please?" She nudged Lucy with her knee.

Lucy said, "Me, too. Please."

Mrs. Gould turned from her stage instruction. "Go." And when the LaLas tried to go with them, Mrs. Gould told them they had to wait.

In the bathroom, Lucy held Therese's tote bag while Therese lit her cigarette and then took apart one of Lucy's braids, fanning the still-wet strands out and combing her fingers through her hair. "See, if we cut it to right here," Therese said, tapping Lucy's shoulder, "I bet it'll curl up to just below your chin."

Lucy squinted at her reflection in the water-spotted mirror. She could sort of see what Therese was suggesting.

"You'd cut it for me?" she asked, hoping they were over her stupid homework offer.

"Sure," Therese said with a smile.

"I'd get in trouble."

"So tell your mom someone cut your hair at school. She'll be upset, but it'll be done."

Lucy handed Therese her bag and began to re-braid her hair. "My mom would be down here screaming at Mr. Allegretti. She'd have the PTA, the church, and the local news camped out on the principal's lawn at home if something like that happened to me. I'd have to tell her you did it, and you could be expelled."

Therese considered this, her nails tapping on the edge of the sink. "Maybe."

"Maybe? That's a huge risk, don't you think?" Lucy couldn't imagine what her mother would do if she was ever expelled. Lucy thought it would involve prison for herself or her mother. She twisted the elastic band around the end of her braid. She tugged both braids and smoothed the hair back from her forehead, checking for evenness between them.

"Some risks are worth it," Therese said. "What are you gonna give me for doing this for you?"

Lucy frowned. "Give you?"

"Payment, white girl. Money?"

"I don't have any money."

"Your parents do. Do they smoke?"

"My dad," Lucy said. Her voice sounded distant and small in the empty bathroom—a little girl's voice.

"I want cigarettes and money. Let's say forty dollars. Then I'll take the blame for cutting your hair. It's all risky, Lucy, but what's it worth to you?"

The bright orange dot of the cigarette's end bounced when Therese smiled at her. Therese pulled the cigarette from her lips and licked them once. Lucy thought of Miss Winthrop kissing those lips.

"Therese, what's it like kissing Miss Winthrop?"

Therese went still for a moment, then cut Lucy a look that seemed to say Lucy had gone too far, stepped over some invisible boundary line. Then Therese shrugged. "It's kissing," she said. "It's good." She put her cigarette out in the sink, picked up her bag, and gripped the straps tightly in her fists, almost as if struggling with it. Then she closed her eyes, and her face relaxed. She sighed and said, "It's like holding on and letting go. It's better than everything."

. . .

Lucy spent that Saturday on edge. She did her chores early and kept to her room with the copy of *Vogue* that Therese had sent home with her. She studied it and imagined her parents talking in their bedroom after she came home with shorter hair. Their hushed voices trickling down the hallway to her room, thick with concern. Should we take her out of school? her mother would ask. Private school? her father would wonder, putting out his cigarette in the ashtray on the nightstand. We can't afford it, her mother would say, unhappiness hanging in the air in competition with the lingering cigarette smoke. We could swing it, her father would say to make her mother happy. He would work more. They would both work more.

No, Lucy decided, she wouldn't do it. She went to bed that night haunted by the look of disappointment she knew her mother's face would wear.

But Sunday night, Lucy stood in front of her dresser mirror, folded the ends of her hair up, and pinned it back with a wide barrette so she could see herself with short hair like the model Therese had shown her. Lucy imagined dark eyeliner around her eyes, her arms thin, the baby weight all dissolved into the new figure of a woman, of a sophomore. Lucy tilted her chin upward to elongate her neck. Oh, she could see her, that other self, right there in the mirror. That was a cool Lucy. Any day now, she'd be that girl, just like Therese had said.

When she was sure her parents were in their bedrooms for the night, Lucy moved silently down the hall, avoiding the spot that creaked and not turning on a single light as she went. Nervousness had her fumbling her way until she reached the bookcase in the living room. Her mother hid the cigarettes from her father in an effort to get him to cut back on them. This week they were behind worn copies of fairy tales and King Arthur stories on the low bookshelf next to her mother's chair. The carton had five packs in it still. She removed one, lifted the hem of her Jem and the Holograms nightgown, and slid the pack inside her underwear, making sure it was snug against her hip, and then she replaced the books.

Her father's wallet was by the front door in the misshapen bowl Lucy had given him for Father's Day when she was eight. She shifted her fingers in between and over the pieces of paper in the wallet, taking the first things that felt like money. With that last bit of theft done, and she knew it was theft, felt the weight of it settle on her, she crept back down the hall to her bedroom.

In the moonlight that spilled through her bedroom window, she inspected the money in her hand. She'd grabbed a ten and a twenty. It'd have to do. There was no going back now. She removed the cigarettes from her underwear, pulled the tab to unwrap the cellophane from the top of the pack, and folded the money in half, then in half again, and slipped the bills down between the pack and the plastic wrapper. She put the cigarettes and the money in her pencil pouch and zipped it all away in her backpack.

In her dreams, they caught her leaving the house with the cigarettes. All her hair fell out at the breakfast table. Her nose grew Pinocchio-style when her mother asked her what she had planned for school that day. It was all ridiculous. Her mother would already have gone to work when Lucy left for school. Her father would still be asleep. They trusted Lucy to get herself going in the morning. They trusted Lucy, period.

At school the next day, there was talk in the halls about Miss Winthrop. Mrs. Dunlop was back early from her maternity leave, and Miss Winthrop was gone, effective immediately. Lucy looked for Therese in the hallways. On her way to fifth period, Lucy spotted Therese down the hall turning the corner into another hall, and Lucy sprinted after her, knocking into people, apologizing as she went. The final bell for class rang, the hallways emptied, and Therese was nowhere—she was gone. Lucy was late to math, and after ditching she was late turning in her homework, but still she wandered the hallways looking for Therese, peeking into classroom windows and sometimes calling for Therese softly. After five minutes, she gave up. She figured by the time she made it up the two flights of stairs, she'd be a full ten minutes late for class. She was already forming plausible excuses when Therese stepped out from the recessed alcove where the bathrooms were. They looked at each other, and Therese disappeared into the bathroom, and with only the tiniest hesitation, Lucy followed.

Therese was staring at her reflection in the water-spotted mirror over the sinks. Her eyes were red-rimmed. Lucy noticed she was wearing Miss Winthrop's silver bangle watch.

"I'm not staying, so if you want to do this, let's do it now." Her voice was low and miserable.

"Okay." Lucy fumbled in her backpack. Her hands shook. She thought she should say something to make Therese feel better. The bathroom they were in had no windows. The tiles seemed to glow yellow under the fluorescent lights.

From her backpack, Lucy pulled the cigarettes, money, and Therese's *Vogue*, handing them all over to Therese.

Therese slid the money out from the side of the pack and shoved it into her tight jeans pocket without counting it and set the cigarettes next to a faucet.

Lucy tried again: "Therese, I'm sorry she's gone."

Therese wouldn't look over. Lucy stood next to Therese and studied her reflection in the mirror, hoping to convey how sorry she felt for her. Lucy thought she understood what the absence of Miss Winthrop must feel like to Therese. Thought of Leroy in his school across town and the press of his lips against her own. At least Therese wouldn't have to see Miss Winthrop with another girl, the way Lucy had had to watch Leroy in eighth grade.

Therese opened the magazine and found the page with the model on it. She balanced the magazine on the edge of the sink.

"Look straight ahead," Therese said, stepping behind Lucy and adjusting her head in the mirror. "Keep looking ahead or it'll be shorter than we want."

She went back to her bag and pulled out scissors and set them on the sink's edge.

"You remind me of Elaine," Therese said. She took up the end of one of Lucy's braids with her left hand and began winding the hair around her hand, tugging hard with each successive loop of hair. "She's smart like you are. Too smart. She thinks I need help, too. She thinks I need more than she can give me. All I needed was her, though."

"Therese, you're hurting me," Lucy said.

"Don't be a baby." Therese took up the scissors with her

right hand, and Lucy saw something twisted and angry on her face.

"I'm not a baby, Therese—just stop," Lucy said, her voice just this side of a whine.

Therese yanked on the braid, and Lucy yelped in pain. "Shut up and hold still."

"No," Lucy said, afraid now. Lucy pulled away from Therese, backing up and pushing at Therese. Therese followed, her hand pulling harder now, the scissors edging closer.

"Stop it or I'll cut you," Therese said.

They both turned in the same circle, Lucy trying to escape and Therese trying to stop her. Their voices rose until Therese yelled, "Hold still!" and forced Lucy to kneel with her fist hard against the side of Lucy's head. Fat tears ran down Lucy's face as the scissors made their first cut just above Therese's knuckles.

"No!" Lucy said, her voice just a whisper.

With the last snip of the scissors, the length of hair pulled away from Lucy, and Therese straightened. "There," she said. "One side down and one to go. That wasn't so bad, now was it?"

The bathroom door opened, and Mrs. Gould walked in on the tableau: Therese with scissors in her right hand, the thick braid of hair in her left hanging like meat in a butcher's case, Lucy on her knees sobbing, her face in her hands.

"Ladies, what exactly is going on here?" Mrs. Gould asked, looking from one girl to the other.

Therese saw Lucy crying and said, "She wanted me to do it."

Lucy tried to stifle her sobs. The bathroom air was cool on her neck, and her head felt lopsided without the weight of her hair on her right. What was left of her braid began to unravel as she stood. She looked at herself in the mirror. A different Lucy stared back. A Lucy she didn't recognize. One that didn't match any version she had imagined. She wiped at the tears on her face.

"Come with me," Mrs. Gould said.

Mrs. Gould took the scissors and reached for the curl of braid still wrapped around Therese's hand, but Therese shoved it at Lucy, who took it and clutched it against her torso.

"It's what you wanted," Therese said. The *Vogue* lay discarded on the floor. Therese picked it up as she gathered her bag off the floor. She glared at Lucy, her arms folded, her eyes shiny with tears of her own.

Outside the principal's office, they sat on the white plastic chairs not looking at each other. Lucy's mother arrived first and gasped when she saw Lucy's hair.

"Baby," her mother said, and she pulled Lucy toward her chest. Out of the corner of her eye, Lucy could see Therese watching them. Studying them like Lucy had studied the girls in *Vogue*, trying to figure how to become like them.

PRACTICE

ALEX PICKETT

I instituted a rule. Since they weren't mature enough to both play freshman football and control themselves, they were to put their phones in a big canvas bag before practice. A rule about which they soon and often groaned. Then again, they groaned about everything.

On maybe the third day I realized the rule had potential beyond simply eliminating distractions. There was this one kid, Terry Hagadorn, on the offensive line who could not grasp the concept of snapping the ball "on two." Frustrating for so many reasons, but foremost because the nature of the penalty meant that the play couldn't be run, meaning practice kept grinding to a halt. After about the thirtieth time, when I snatched off my visor and was about to ream him out, I noticed our equipment manager—Jonathan, a pimpled, standoffish yet very polite farm boy who was far slower physically than the players—standing on the sideline with the canvas bag slung over his shoulder, watching me as respectfully as my beloved cocker spaniel, Betsy, would before I'd let her outside.

The fact that there were all those phones in that bag gave me an idea. I put my visor back on, cleared my throat, walked over to Jonathan, and pointed at the bag, which he handed to me without word.

"The next time anyone moves a muscle before that ball is snapped," I said, "I will take their phone out of this bag—" I held up the bag "—and text whatever I want to whoever I want."

Everyone laughed except Terry Hagadorn, the kid who couldn't remember the snap count, who I, of course, was glaring at. The other kids began saying, then shouting out, the names of various girls to text on Terry's behalf. They were energized if nothing else.

The next play, Terry kept to his stance like a rock. Well after the ball was snapped, he remained still, finally getting knocked on his ass by the second-string nose tackle, who might have hit him for the sheer fun of it. But hey, after the day we'd been having, I'd take that. And no one made a mistake for the next four plays, which was maybe a record for us, until our tight end—Eric Duoss, a giraffe-tall kid with hands that had a knack for grabbing and holding on to overthrown passes—jumped early.

"Jonathan?" I said, without really wanting to punish Duoss, who, again, had a dedication any coach would love.

Still, I called Duoss over and asked him to find and unlock his phone. A smart kid, too, this Duoss. The type you have on a team only now and then, the kind who succeeds because they understand the game.

In fact, smart as he was, he complied with a little grin on his face, like he was curious to see where this was going.

And worse, I didn't have a next move. I certainly wasn't going to text a girl like the team wanted me to. Get the student body involved in this and you have no idea where it's going. There was a lot of hooting, so I milked the suspense by taking my time figuring out what to do. I hemmed and hawed as I scrolled through his contacts. Then, on the screen, I saw "Dad."

I clicked that. The texts between them were logistical. Arrival times home and dinner consumption. Anyone else—Terry Hagadorn, for sure—and I would've grilled him and let him off the hook without sending anything. Or maybe written Jim Hagadorn something like, *Hi Dad, I jumped offside twenty times today and wasted everyone's time at practice. Especially Coach's, who has better things he could be doing. Apparently I don't know the difference between going on one and on two. Maybe some extra chores would help me learn?* Jim and I could have had a laugh about it at his hardware store.

But Eric Duoss wasn't Terry Hagadorn. Eric Duoss was a *player* and a solid kid, and he didn't flinch when I glanced up at him. Maybe he was doubting my ability to follow through. Maybe he sensed I knew nothing about his father. Since he wore glasses and was in the honors program, I pictured his dad working at a desk, calculating, making a lot of money, a microbiologist or a college professor. Anyway, Duoss and I maintained eye contact, and as we did, his smile deepened.

Finally, a decent zinger hit me, and I nodded at him as if to say, *Don't underestimate me.*

Then I typed, "Dad, I love you." And hit send.

I handed him the phone. As soon as he read the screen, his smile disappeared.

"What in hell?" he shouted. "Coach, you can't do that!"

I'll be honest, I did question myself about this right then.

But no way was I going to back down. No one can show weakness on a football field, definitely not a coach at practice.

"*Listen* next time," I said, as though this was a normal teachable moment.

He stared at me with his mouth open for so long that the tittering of the rest of the team died down. Then, as he handed Jonathan the phone, an uncomfortable silence fell upon the field and beyond.

Back in the huddle, he must've told the rest of the offense what I did because they all raised their heads and looked at me in horror.

I clapped my hands and yelled, "Let's go! Clock's ticking!"

They got their asses in gear after that. All the rest of practice we had only two more false starts, easily the fewest we've ever had in an hour and fifteen minutes.

And those two kids who jumped—I texted their dads as well.

• • •

That night, while I was sitting on my porch grading take-home tests and drinking some Keystone Light, worry crept into me. Because now I was thinking about worst-case scenarios, like maybe one of the kids' fathers was dead. I would've heard about that, though, I told myself. After all, it was a small school. But even within father-son dynamics in families who were alive and well, something about what I'd done felt itchy and vaguely obscene.

Okay, I told myself, but it wasn't like I'd sent one of their mothers a picture of my johnson. Though maybe, given the choice, these three kids would've preferred that. In any case, I couldn't put my finger on why I felt on edge. Maybe because I had never told—and never planned on telling—the same thing to my own father?

But my father leaned toward being a lying, bamboozling son of a bitch, and most of these kids came from good families.

Right then Betsy began scrambling back to the porch, barking her head off. She'd been out there in the woods horsing around, and she'd emerged from the pitch-black covered in mud and leaves and a couple twigs, running toward me like she'd stolen something. She scratched at the door and did a little let-me-in dance, but I was curious about why. She knew the deal with me, that I wouldn't open the door at all if I didn't right away, so she gave up dancing and crouched behind my chair, knocking the table and spilling my beer.

"What is it, Bets?" I asked, laughing a little.

She whined, set her ears straight back, and lay down with her chin between her paws.

I turned away from her and faced the woods, a little scared about what or who might come running out also, but nothing else emerged.

"You're just a scaredy-cat, aren't you?" I asked Bets.

She whined.

"Just a widdle scaredy-cat," I said.

• • •

The next day the team was dressed and on the field before Jonathan, with his usual wide-eyed reticence, handed me my whistle. Being on time was highly unusual for my ragtag squad.

To make sure I'd start in total control, I said loudly to Johnathan, "Got the phones?"

He grinned and shook the canvas bag like he was riling up a bunch of hornets.

I wasn't convinced I should continue with my new policy until I saw that every kid was doing his best to please me. And at that point, in fact, I expanded the use of the punishment so it included other offenses, some of them arguably not even related to football. I'd text the father of the player who came in last during sprints and of anyone who swore. I texted two more fathers during the first water break because their sons had merely pretended to hydrate.

And it was during that break, while Jonathan and I were setting up cones for a round of Hamburger, that Duoss approached with the grim look of an emissary from a tiny country recently aggrieved by a neighbor with nuclear capability.

"Coach," he said, looking me in the eye. "I don't think the texting punishment is fair."

"That so?" I said, handing Jonathan a cone.

"It was super awkward at home last night," Duoss said. "My dad asked me if everything was all right. He told me he'd thought I was in a car accident, that I'd been on life support and only had enough time left to send one text. He also smelled my breath to make sure I wasn't drunk."

"What did you tell him?" I asked, curious about how such an interaction would go.

"The truth, that, you know, I jumped before the snap. And that, instead of having me run laps or something, you texted him that I loved him for some reason no one on the team can figure out."

"What did he say?" I asked.

"Basically nothing—he just kind of, like, groaned a little. I mean, he might have been hurt a little that it hadn't been for real. He spent the rest of the night alone in his study. It was really awkward, Coach."

"All the more reason to keep the snap count in mind, I guess," I said.

He sighed, obviously dismayed. "Can we at least just keep it to false starts and offsides?"

You know you have them once they start trying to cut a deal.

"Seemed like everyone had an extra bounce in their step during conditioning today," I said. "You guys ran harder than you ever have before."

"I mean, you know that Stewart has asthma so he can't help coming in last during sprints. I don't think it's right that he was punished."

That was true about Stewart. Level-headed Eric Duoss—he had a point there.

"Just make sure you're hydrated before we start back up again," I said.

Then, after a round of Hamburger and then Oklahoma drills, we separated the starters from the scrubs to run through some plays. The tension was palpable. Before each snap they nodded at each other gravely, like soldiers before battle. But on both sides they held firm. For a while I thought this was how it must feel to coach the New England Patriots. But just as I was figuring how I could parlay my new method to coach at some small college where I wouldn't also have to teach, or even how I could live off speaker's fees at coaching clinics, Duoss, of all people, jumped early.

I shrieked my whistle and called him over. Jonathan fished the phone at issue from the bag. Duoss wasn't walking over. He was hanging his head, his hands gripping his face mask in frustration. I blew my whistle again.

"Ah, come on, Coach," he said softly when he finally walked over and faced me. His voice was shaky.

Jonathan thrust the phone at him almost violently. Jonathan, apparently, was growing some balls.

"I won't do it," Duoss said. "I'll quit before I do it. This isn't fair."

"Go on now," I said with genuine sympathy, surprising myself. "Just go on and unlock it. You friggin' jumped."

"I know, but it isn't worth this. It's just practice, Coach. It's just football played by a bunch of no-name high schools."

"Go on!" Jonathan shouted, shaking the phone. I touched his forearm to calm him.

Duoss turned toward the rest of the team.

"This is crazy, right?" he shouted. "He can't do this, right? And we can all just . . . walk out. He needs us more than we need him, man. Without us there isn't anyone for him to coach."

"You're only digging yourself deeper," I said calmly, confident that no one would join in his revolt. "Just go on and unlock it. It'll be over with before you know it."

He glared for a moment at his cowardly teammates before he allowed his shoulders to slump. He studied Jonathan's face intently, not necessarily threateningly, but intently, then took the phone from him and unlocked it.

This time I knew what I was going to write:

"Hi Dad. Remember when I told you yesterday that Coach sent you that text? Well, I lied. It was me. I was just embarrassed to admit it in person. It's easier to text about these kinds of feelings, I guess. Anyway, just know that I do love you but that if you ask me in person about this text I'll deny writing it and give some weird excuse like that Coach did it to punish me, as though that makes sense. Coach is a good guy though. I shouldn't have put the blame on him."

After I sent it, I reached the phone toward Duoss, so he could read it. He took it but merely turned it off and handed it to Jonathan, then slunk back toward the huddle.

• • •

That night, back on my porch with my Keystone Light, I kind of wished I had some papers to grade. A hot night, even sultry. Betsy had not yet come in from the woods, though it was well past her dinnertime. Without her around, I couldn't help but wonder what was going on at the Duoss's right then, if maybe Eric and his dad were playing a game of cribbage or Mastermind before heading off to bed. Or maybe Pops was helping Eric with his advanced-level homework, a hand resting on his gifted son's shoulder.

I grabbed another cold one from the mini fridge I keep on my porch. I stood and peered into the darkness, listening for barking or whining or rustling. By the end of practice, almost every player's father had been texted once, and three had been texted for a second time. Oddly, one of the only boys to escape punishment was Terry Hagadorn, the kid whose ineptitude had started the whole deal. At some point, I admitted to myself now, I had gone too far. The adrenaline that had flowed had turned into frayed nerves, the players snapping at one another for no apparent reason and getting into fistfights on the sidelines.

"Betsy!" I yelled into the darkness. "Dinner!"

Nothing.

Maybe, I told myself, I should call my own father. Not, of course, to profess my love, or to get advice, but just see how he was doing. I had spoken to my mother the previous Sunday, as usual, and she'd called to him loudly, very loudly, as usual, to let him know I was on the line. His voice had carried from the living room: "Tell him the Packers need a safety who can tackle." My mother chuckled and said, "Got that?" And I laughed and said, "Yeah, got it."

"Betsy!" I now yelled again, louder this time. I stepped down from my porch to the edge of the illuminated portion of the lawn. "Betsy, for Chrissake, it's time for your chow!"

I listened for a long time then.

I heard nothing.

And I heard and saw no sign of her throughout the rest of that night and all of the next morning while I took my time getting ready to go to work.

• • •

At practice that afternoon, players were sitting on their helmets when I arrived on the field. I held out my hand for my whistle, but Jonathan was nowhere to be seen.

"Where's our man Jonathan?" I asked the team as a whole.

They all turned their heads toward Duoss. He stood and spoke as though from a prepared statement.

"When Jonathan came to collect the phones, Coach, we refused. Then he went back inside and came out with this yardstick and started reefing on Stewart, so we had no choice but to put the canvas bag over his head. He kept fighting us so we kept yanking it down until we were able to tie it around his thighs. We might have gone a little overboard by dragging him into the shower, but we told him we were just doing him a favor by cooling him off. But really, Coach? We were just tired of him. Now we know it was wrong."

"Is he still in the shower *now*?" I asked, trying to keep calm but feeling my voice waver.

"He's in the shower *room*, still tied in the sack last we saw him," Duoss said. "But the shower itself is no longer on. He was thrashing around so much we didn't want to touch him anymore. He kicked Kurt so hard he broke his pinkie."

Kurt, just behind Duoss and a bit to his left, held up his hand, displaying a gruesomely dislocated finger.

"Kurt," I said, "go to the nurse before she leaves for the day." I doubted Kurt's family had good insurance and wanted him to get whatever free health care could be provided, even if only a rudimentary splint and some tape.

"Westrick and Ostertag," I said to our two middle linebackers, "go to the locker room and make sure he's out of the bag. And make sure to apologize to him before you free him, much as he probably deserved what he got. His bad was mine—he thought he was only doing his job."

Westrick and Ostertag got up and jogged toward the school building.

"I know this week has been difficult for a few of you," I said to the rest of them. "Though we *have* had fewer false starts and offside penalties than ever before. All told, I guess we all learned that it's difficult when those improvements come with a change in personal relationships."

I had written and memorized that last line during sixth period while my students took a pop quiz. Now the remaining players shifted around, trying to get comfortable, apparently.

"But this change in personal relationships was a desired effect," I continued. "I have never told my own father I love him. He has never said those words to me. I thought this tactic would not only cut down on penalties but improve your lives and those of your dads. It's best if things like this are taken care of early, while you guys are still young."

"Then why don't you do it?" Duoss chimed in. "If the experience was so important for *us*, why didn't you just text your own father? You're still kinda young . . . and your father . . . from the sound of it, he's apparently still alive."

"Three laps," I said.

A vexed look came over Duoss's face, but then, as if everything made sense, he took off running.

As he rounded the bend back toward us, the three boys returned from the locker room. Jonathan was sopping and still holding the yardstick. He sat on the sideline bench closest to me and bowed his head in shame. "They wouldn't give them over," he said to me breathlessly. "I tried to make them, but they shoved me into the sack."

I nodded kindly by way of apology. I couldn't verbally admit wrongdoing. In the unlikely case that charges were brought against me I wanted my union rep to have a fighting chance.

"The lesson here is about sports and life," I was finally able to say. I looked down at my feet as I continued: "Normally the only times you send texts like those are when you're on the verge of death or under extreme duress. That you were able to send them without suffering any physical harm or significant regret is akin to how, in football, you're able to inflict and endure pain within the confines of a sanctioned activity. Though it now might appear to some people that perhaps I went too far, I see no reason why you should go through all this practicing on this field if there aren't any real-world upsides to having done so."

I looked up and noticed most of the kids were watching the cross-country runners practice.

"One day," I continued, going off script, "when your father is on his deathbed, you will be thankful that I sent those texts. Also, in the short term, your fathers will be proud that you aren't committing stupid mental errors on the field. I'm telling you now that, no matter what they tell you at home at dinner or wherever, they are embarrassed as hell when you mess up like that."

I needed to wrap up my lecture, I told myself. Not only was Duoss almost finished with his laps but I was losing my train of thought. I was, after all, exhausted, I guess because of lots of things.

"Now does anyone have anything to share about the texts?" I asked. "About how your father reacted or—if he did *not* react—how that lack of a response made you feel?"

To a man, they were all staring at the cross-country athletes now. Despite cross-country being the most boring sport to watch.

"What I was wondering," came a voice so close I almost jumped, "was why you didn't text my father anything."

It was Jonathan. He was looking up at me, his eyes now not only wide but decidedly forlorn. "Is it because I'm not really on the team?" he asked.

Before I could answer, another kid, James Thomas, my best slot wide receiver, said, "Consider yourself lucky, bro. My dad was so happy last night he made me go fishing. I got poison ivy rash all over both my hands now."

In order to encourage future contributions, I resisted pointing out that, as someone who often caught the ball, it might be best if James wore gloves from now on.

"At least he said something about it," my only field goal kicker said. "My dad wouldn't even *look* at me last night. My mom had to work late, so we heated up some lasagna, and he didn't say a word the entire meal."

"You should get Coach to text him again," said my QB, one of the kids whose father I texted twice. "It was uncomfortable the first night, but whatever Coach wrote yesterday really calmed my old man down. He still didn't say anything, or make much eye contact, but he gave me two hundred bucks for no reason."

Duoss finished his laps and stood there huffing at the edge of the group.

"What are you guys talking about?" he asked between gasps.

"Two more laps," I said, because, as I saw it then, the rest of us were doing fine without him.

And true to my hope, after he took off again, more kids piped up about their experiences. Our left starting guard, who everyone called Tommy Pumpkin, said that, just the previous night, his father got really drunk sitting at the kitchen table, then later, in Tommy's bedroom, while Tommy pretended to sleep, stood unsteadily over Tommy for twenty minutes without saying a word or doing a thing. Then he simply walked out of the room. Our safety said his father told him a story about his time in Iraq, about how he shot and killed a civilian once because the civilian wouldn't stop his car driving through a checkpoint. Apparently it was the first time the father had ever mentioned the war in front of this kid. Then Stewart, the kid with asthma who didn't exactly have a designated position, mentioned that his father hugged him for several minutes as soon as he walked through the door after practice. Stewart explained that his father's father died last year, and guessed that the text and subsequent hug maybe provided a release for his dad and him both.

Duoss had rejoined us halfway through Stewart's story but was apparently too tired to add his two cents. I hoped hearing the very end of what Stewart said would put the experience into perspective for him, and maybe it did, since he merely stared at me while catching his breath.

Then I clapped my hands and said, "Let's go! Clock's ticking! Starting offense and defense team B on the field! We'll skip conditioning tonight."

They let out a rousing cheer at not having to run sprints. Then everyone who was supposed to line up got into position. On the first play I called, Terry Hagadorn jumped before the ball was snapped, and I whipped off my visor in frustration. But I did not tell Jonathan to fish out Terry's phone. Instead I thought about how Betsy had run away, probably for good, and I yelled, "Terry, you were just messing with us, right?"

THE DOG

NATHAN ALLING LONG

I've spent so many hours on Greyhound buses, if I cashed them in for nickels, I could buy the state of Tennessee. My friend Billy always said he'd rather hitch than ride the Dog—that was his word for it. But for me, to hell if I'd ever stand in the cold and sleep out at night, just to get from one job to another. I have always traveled respectably.

Once Billy and I had to go from Myer's Orchard in Washington State to Southern California to harvest lettuce, and we decided to race—me in the Greyhound, him on the road.

"Why waste your money?" Billy said at the station. He'd gone with me to get my ticket. "Get there the same amount of time using your thumb."

"We'll see," I said back. It was a hot day, early summer, and the station's air wasn't running yet. The doors were wide open, and you could hear each bus pull up, the hiss of brakes, and doors opening and closing.

"Ray," he said, "there're places you can't get to by the Dog."

"No place I want to go," I said. You have to be pretty down and out to stick to the road, I thought. But I didn't tell Billy that. The guy had had it rough—lost two toes to frostbite in the past year. And he'd drink till his nose got purple.

He was probably drunk when he lost his toes, but I never asked him.

We looked around at the passengers sitting in the plastic seats and standing in line.

"Nicer people on the road," Billy said. He had a hard time letting a thing go. "I mean, if they pick you up, it means they like you. I mean, you're *chosen*."

"But these folks know exactly where they're going," I said, and I headed for the end of the line, Billy following me to say goodbye. "It's written on the ticket in their hands."

• • •

You meet the damnedest people and see the wildest things on the bus. People fuck, take drugs, steal. It's entertainment, I told Billy. Better than those grocery store newspapers. Once, I saw someone in the back pull out a gun, though he didn't shoot. At the next stop, the cops came on and hauled him away. And in Oklahoma one time, a guy punched out a side window with his fist, yelling about not getting any fresh air. They kicked him out right there on the side of the road.

I remember last year seeing a shaved-headed man boarding the bus outside of Asheville, North Carolina. He wasn't tall but he was well-built, with arms like river rocks, hard and smooth. He sat behind a white woman with brown hair in a feather cut, though her bangs hung heavily. He was a black man, but about as light as they get before they look white, the color of ash. What you really noticed, though, was his eyes. He had the eyes of a husky. Pale blue, as though the whites had bled into the center.

The man was fresh out of a penitentiary—you could tell

from the blue issue shirt and pants. I don't think the feather-cut woman could tell, though, or else she didn't care. They started talking the way people do all the time on the bus. I couldn't hear much, a little here and there. "Florida," he said to her at one point. "To the west coast, near Fort Myers, where my family is. How far you going?" She was twisted around, looking over the seat. I couldn't make out what she said.

Then, later: "*Why*?" he said. "Because bald men are the best lovers. Don't tell me you never heard that?" He slid his hand over his shaved head.

"I never heard that," she said.

"No one's ever told you that? Where are you from?" he asked. Then she got to talking all about her growing up. I looked out my window: We were crossing the Georgia line.

Later, when I looked back, his hand was brushing through her hair. "No, I like it like that," he said. His words were sounding sweet, but I kept staring at those arms. There were tiny white scars in his skin. Two stops later, when the bus pulled out of the station, I noticed that she was gone. Maybe it was her stop, I thought just before I realized that he was gone, too. Then I saw them out the window, walking up into a cemetery above the town, holding hands. Lucky them, I thought. It can happen that quick, on the bus.

• • •

One guy, in a diner just outside the Dallas station, offered to pay for my cup of coffee—he was a bit funny, I think, but I was broke and stoned and he was loaded: wore a two-piece suit, lots of rings, slicked-back hair. It was late at night, but he was eating a steak-and-egg breakfast. A business guy, I figured.

As I waited for the coffee, he asked me where I was going.

"Idaho," I said. "Potato season."

"You want a lift?" he asked without looking up from his plate.

"I'm taking the bus," I said. "Already have my ticket."

"You know," he said, turning to me, "there's no way I'll ever ride a Greyhound again. I rode it once, from Boston to New Orleans."

"That must have been one hell of a ride," I said.

"Well, I guess you could say I've been *grey-hounded*." He paused and really stared at me. "That's a verb," he said—as if I wouldn't know.

The coffee came and I took a sip. "Well, I've ridden them everywhere," I said. "I like who you meet."

"See, I'm not saying Greyhounds aren't important. No, I mean, my God, they're classic." He dropped his napkin onto the rest of his food. "I figure one day they'll have a museum for them. It'll have uncomfortable seats in the auditorium, and the whole place will smell like exhaust fumes and piss."

He was laughing.

I didn't say anything. What could I say? He went on a bit, about that Greyhound museum in the future, and kept looking at me like he wanted something. But I couldn't give him anything. He was the one with money.

• • •

I won the bet with Billy, by the way, though Billy didn't think so. I made it to Escondido before him. It took me a while to get out to the actual fields, but that's because the farm trucks were late picking us up, and Billy'd gotten a ride straight there. He said we were counting from site to site, but I said no, what counted was from region to region. He started fussing. I mean, we'd only bet ten dollars, and I wasn't going to fight over it. Not worth losing a friend. I said maybe it was best we both kept our money and called it a draw. He didn't say anything to that.

After picking that lettuce, I headed to Mississippi for oranges; Billy stayed on out West. Next spring, we hooked up to thin apples, up in Washington again. It was probably our eighth year out there together, Billy and I.

They say thinning is unskilled, but it's skilled. If you snap the wrong ones off, they could lose half their crop. You have to snap them off with a twist, so you don't end up tearing the bark. There's a lot of ladder-moving, too. And you can damn near break a leg tripping over the fallen fruit.

The best job is at Myer's, near Spokane—they're the largest in Washington State, and we always show up there early, get the best cots in the barracks. They let us leave stuff there, too, for when we come back in the fall to harvest. Not that we have much to leave.

. . .

It was that spring after the bet that Susie showed up at Myer's. Billy and I had been working there for about a week when he spotted her one afternoon. She drove one of those golf carts managers drive, and she had on tight jeans and a white shirt that wasn't tucked in at all.

Billy had just repositioned his ladder. He said to me, "Ray,

I think Eve just showed up." He was always talking about the Myer's grove like it was Eden, because of the apple trees, I always thought, and the rolling hills, and the lake. I turned around for a look.

Susie had this curly hair tied back in a ponytail. It was all gold in the sunlight. And her face was just like the skin of the best Georgia peaches when they're too ripe to pick to sell and you have to eat them right there under the hot sun.

"That's *my* girl," I whispered down to Billy.

"You fall for them all the time," Billy said.

"No, this one I'm serious about," I said. "It'll happen."

"Start praying," Billy said, laughing at me.

Just then the foreman came out of nowhere. He watched us for a couple minutes, inspected our tree. By the time he had gone, Susie's cart had disappeared too.

• • •

Susie had a special job, sawing off the dead limbs and treating them with black tar to keep the trees healthy. She worked by herself but sometimes ended up at the same tree I was working at. I remember the first time she came to my tree, looking for any dead parts. She circled it twice, then set her ladder up near mine.

"Found a bad one?" I said, grinning.

"Yeah," she said, and started sawing. Behind her was the lake.

I wanted to give her something, but all I had with me was a joint. The limb fell to the ground and looked like a stiff hand lying in the grass.

"Want to get stoned?" I asked.

"Not while working."

"After, I mean." I reached far in the branches to twist off an apple.

"I better not, thanks," she said. "It's hard enough getting up on time."

"Maybe on Friday," I said. I leaned back so I could see more of her.

"Maybe." She had cut another branch and I watched it drop to the ground. There's so many good limbs left, I thought. If she could just stay here to cut them all off, we could talk for hours.

When she pulled out the tar can, I said, "You like doing this work?"

"It's all right," she said. "I like being outside. What about you?"

"My friend Billy there says it's Eden." I pointed to him working away in the next tree.

"What do *you* say?" she asked, and she grinned.

"Feels that way at the moment," I said, and for a while then, I let my face show how happy I felt, something I hadn't felt in a long time.

"Well, good," she said, and she began tarring the ends. It was then that I saw Billy shake his head at me. Susie didn't see him, though.

"What?" I said to him, after she had gone.

• • •

The conversations were always short like that, but over the weeks, I felt we were developing a rapport. I asked Billy if he thought so.

"Keep dreaming," he said. Billy could be about as sour as anyone I knew. Even more than he'd been about losing our bet about whether Greyhound was faster. But like I said, he didn't have it so easy. It was no wonder, with his putting half his money into booze, that he couldn't afford to ride the bus.

"What do you know about these things?" I finally asked him.

"And what are you, Albert Einstein?" he said.

"No," I said, "but I do pick up a lot of stuff on the bus, things you'd never learn while you're hitching."

Like once, I told him, in Nevada, I sat next to this girl heading to Mount Shasta. She wore one of those Indian cotton dresses and sandals. She was a looker, but nothing compared to Susie. Her name was Star, or Moon or maybe Venus—I can't remember. The whole trip she spent telling me about vortexes, said they were centers of energy that existed all around the world. The Teton Range was one vortex, and Devil's Tower, South Dakota, was another. And Glacier Park, and Big Rock Candy Mountain—which, in her mind, was in Idaho. She said vortexes were sites aliens had picked out long before humans came. Later, certain natives figured them out, like the Aztecs, who built a temple on one of them. She said she was visiting all the sites, to collect the best energy in the world; it would prepare her to be a warrior for life somehow.

She believed all this.

She was something.

She couldn't have been more than seventeen.

On the bus, I realized years ago, you're not quite resting on the earth; you're suspended above it, so all kinds of things can seem real: vortexes, alien centers, energy for life battles. Why not?

Not to mention that while riding the Dog, I've learned about how to hook a phone up for free, why that helicopter fell into Crater Lake, how to heal wounds with lichen, and how weather satellites are heating up the planet. You could pay to read all about that stuff in a grocery store newspaper, but by riding the Greyhound, it's free.

. . .

I didn't get to see Susie often, only every few days. Each time she seemed just as beautiful, even though she wore jeans and carried that leather tool belt around her hips. It hung down on the right like a gun belt, and everyone kidded her about looking like a cowboy. Me and the others, we didn't have belts. All we had was our hands.

"Where you from, originally?" I asked her once.

"Maine," she said. "Well, I was born in Vermont."

"That's pretty . . . up there."

I snapped off a few apples and let them thump against the ground. I felt like God just then, dropping those apples to the earth.

"So, you'll be here next year, then?" I asked.

"Maybe," she said.

"Why not yes?"

"I'm trying to get a real job."

"Real?" I asked. "Like what?" I looked down at all the golf-ball-sized apples I'd pulled, then out over the trees, at the lake. All of this right then seemed real pretty to me.

"I'm going to be a carpenter," she said.

I looked at her mouth, and there wasn't any smile, so I knew she was serious. Still, I couldn't believe it. "A carpenter?" I said. "Why you want to be a *carpenter*? Why not let a man be a carpenter, and you can have a house?"

And as soon as I said it, I wished I hadn't.

"What man?" she said. "I want to be a carpenter."

"Just because you got a saw?" I said, joking.

"No, not just because I got a saw." She shook her head. Her being mad, though, didn't really take the sunlight off her hair or make her skin look any less like peaches.

"I bet you'll be a good carpenter," I said.

"Yeah."

She stepped down her ladder until her feet were on the ground.

"See you," she said.

• • •

The next morning I spent a long time thinking about Susie while I was in the showers, imagining she was in the spray of water with me. I started singing that old Kris Kristofferson song about the carpenter and the lady taking a chance on him and having his baby.

I knew the words didn't fit right, but it didn't matter. It had carpenters in it, and it was a love song. I would have gone on like that all morning, but Billy came in and told me to haul my ass out of there, I was late.

Billy left, then came back a few minutes later to say the last truck was about to take off for the site. "You miss it, you won't get paid for the day."

I hopped out and dressed fast. I didn't want to lose any

money. I have to admit, Billy was good at reminding me about things like that. Better than anyone, actually.

• • •

I think Susie has to be the most beautiful person in America. Once when she was leaning over to snip a branch, hanging from a ladder just a few feet from mine, I looked down her shirt, and I could see one of her tits, the shape of a strawberry, the color of a plum. It was perfect. I nearly fell over staring. She reached out and steadied me, her hand on my arm, just for a moment. That was all I needed. I snapped apples the rest of the day, imagining I was twisting her nipples.

Going on the Dog, I've probably seen more people than just about anyone has, except maybe the drivers. So when I say Susie is the most beautiful person, it means a lot more than someone saying that about their wife, or daughter, or high school sweetheart.

Her hair was somewhere between red and blond, and so frizzy when it wasn't held back that light would thicken it.

"It's like a halo," I said once. It was near the end of the season. We had two days left. The foreman had stopped coming out to check on us.

"Well, I'm no angel," she said, with that grin of hers. She was on the ground, inspecting all the limbs she'd tarred up during those past weeks.

"Prove it," I said. I watched her circle my tree.

She smirked and came back around to my side. "What do you plan to do with yourself?" she asked.

I have to admit, I was surprised at that. I stopped picking

a moment and wiped my brow. I used to think about plans. Then, after a couple years of following the seasons—planting, pruning, picking—it got hard to think about it.

"I like moving," I said to her then. "Seeing the country." I could tell she wanted more, so I said, "I like working with my hands, too, like you."

Susie nodded, gave me a warm look. "That's good." She gathered her tools. "This tree's done," she said.

"See you later," I said as she got in her cart, but she didn't say anything back.

I didn't see her again that season. I hoped she'd be there in the fall, when Billy and I came back to Myer's to pick, but the foreman said she wasn't due back until spring. I thought of her all the time, though, while I was in the trees, filling bushels. As I worked, I'd sing the carpenter song to myself, but loud.

Billy then would hit me on the head with a bad apple. "Your singing is about the worse-assed thing I could think of for a hangover, Ray."

I laughed. I liked Billy for that, being honest like that.

"Well, now we've both got headaches," I said.

"Look at us," he said. "We don't have nothing."

And this time, I realized, he was right.

• • •

It was nearly November when I left Washington State and took the Dog to Phoenix, to pick cotton. Most people don't know it, but that county around Phoenix grows a lot of cotton. For some reason, they don't like black folks picking it, so they give it to us and Mexicans to pick.

I was waiting in the Flagstaff station for a connection, drifting off to sleep, sort of stoned, when a man came up and said to me, "Hey, Ray."

I didn't recognize him at all, but he said he'd met me a year ago, in that same place.

"You a picker, too?" I asked. I could tell he wasn't by his hands and by how clean his glasses were.

"No, I'm hiding," he said, and he sat down and slapped his thighs with both of his hands. "The police are after me, the whole town, really. It's hard. Especially if you have bankers after you. Then how do you get your money, Ray? Tell me that."

"I don't know," I confessed. This man, I thought, isn't all there.

"My home," he said, looking at the floor, "the bankers sold it."

"I'm sorry," I said, and I thought about Billy, wondered where he was just then, what he was doing, whether he was with anyone.

"Tell me, Ray," this guy who'd come up to me said. "Tell me something about yourself, so I know you're not a banker."

It was Sunday and I had nothing to do but wait for the bus, so I told him a little about farmwork, and even about Susie, because I'd been thinking about her. I said we'd met in Washington working apples.

"I live by the I-10 bridge," he said. "But you know, Ray, they're kicking us out and building a Wendy's." He stopped suddenly and slapped his lap again.

"That's awful," I said. I didn't know what else to say.

"Yes it is, Ray," he said. He looked very worried. "Awful

is exactly what it is. But there's just one thing I want to know, Ray."

"What's that?" I asked.

"Well, Ray, what I want to know is why there're not more housing duplexes for all of us? Why do they keep building Wendy's and not duplexes?"

"I don't know," I said.

He slapped his thighs harder, laughing this time. "Of course, you don't. That would be too simple. You have to ask Susie. Ask your friend Susie, the carpenter."

He talked as though he knew her. It made me think about back when Susie asked me what I planned to do. I felt then that I actually did have a plan. I would go back to Myer's, ask Susie to join me. Together, we would build buildings. Hell, we could build duplexes, if we wanted. Then maybe we'd get married and build a house together. She'd probably like that.

I fell into that dream then, with that guy sitting beside me in that depot. Like you do when there's some story they read to you in fourth grade, about living happily ever after—a story you never forget.

• • •

I got through that winter and the early spring, traveling from crop to crop, always taking the Dog. Finally, it was late spring and I was heading back to Myer's from the East Coast, to thin apples again. I hadn't seen Billy since the fall. He'd be there if he wasn't drunk in some ditch. I sensed Susie would be there for sure. I would tell her about what the Flagstaff man had said, and she would see that we were meant to be together. I would even let her be the lead carpenter, I told myself.

There were the two days crossing Missouri and Kansas. In Pueblo, a young guy from Minnesota named Joel sat beside me. I was hoping to be by myself, to sleep all the way through to the next stint, but then I figured he might have some weed to share. I'd been out of weed for a week. I now can still remember waking up as we pulled into Grand Junction, Colorado. The sky was layered with purples and blues, and I wasn't certain if it was sunset or dawn. Even after I stumbled into the station and stood there a moment, I couldn't tell. The clock read six forty-five. It was cold, but when Joel asked me if I wanted to take a walk, I thought, Sure. Yeah. Here we go.

Joel and I stood behind a brick wall along some dirt road—I swear they don't pave the roads in Colorado if they don't have to. Joel loaded the pipe and handed it to me. When I flicked the lighter, I saw that the bowl had a face on it with eyes made of small green stones. Those eyes stared right at you, and the mouth was stretched out along the stem, as if it was smoking you.

"Mean pipe," I said.

"I made it myself," Joel said.

"It looks like the devil," I said, and I took another hit.

He smiled at that. "It's just a face I came up with when I was high."

"I bet," I said, and I took another drag before handing back the pipe. We smoked a long while. Joel kept looking at me funny, but maybe it was the dope. If it was daytime coming on, I thought, I wanted to be stoned, to get through the flat lands that were ahead of us.

. . .

Back at the terminal, we tried to warm up, walking back and forth between the restaurant and the lobby. If I'd had more money, I'd have bought coffee. Joel finally sat in one of those TV chairs and took a nap, and I went over and stared at the map of the U.S. on the wall.

All the roads looked like veins. I got to thinking of a woman at some hot springs outside of Eugene, Oregon, who had varicose veins so bad her legs looked like the hills of West Virginia. That got me to thinking about all the hippie chicks who'd be all naked in this pool fed by one of those hot springs. I'd spend the day hanging out at that pool, sweating half to death, just so I could watch those girls with their ratty hair and their tattoos and their rings in their noses. Sometimes rings in their nipples, too. There were some damn nice girls hanging out around those hot springs, but none got close to Susie.

"God, this is good shit," I said to myself, meaning the dope. I looked away from the map a second and out the windows. It was pitch-black, so I finally knew we were going into night. I went back to staring at the map, and the highways began to lift off the paper, like they were 3D. They looked like wire mesh I'd seen in a warehouse window once somewhere. Chicago? I thought. Yeah, the South Side, just outside of the station on 95th Street. I remembered the driver there had said don't leave the station, that a man had had his face cut in two a week before, near a church just a block away. But I walked around anyway—what did I have to lose?

In my mind I was still there, in Chicago, when some voice said, "Which way you heading?"

I nearly jumped against the chairs behind me. Standing in front of me was a short man who wore a black cowboy hat drawn down to his eyes. I must have stared at him a minute before I said, "West." And then I thought some more and said, "And you?"

"I just came from there," he said. He was rocking a bit and steadied himself with one hand on the wall. "You going through Salt Lake, or up through Idaho?"

I could smell whiskey at the end of his question, and it made me think of Billy.

"Idaho," I said.

"That'll be fifty, then."

"Huh?" I said.

"Route 50, that's it right here." He jabbed his index finger at the map. I was surprised it landed right on the line.

"Loneliest highway in the world," he said.

"Why do you say that?"

"That's what they call it, that's all."

Then he tilted backward a bit, walked off, and dropped himself into a chair.

• • •

When our bus came, it looked like it was going to be crowded. I took the back seat, hoping to get it all to myself, but Joel asked to sit there, too, and I couldn't say no after he'd given me smoke. The bus lights went out and we jerked forward.

At the corner I saw a Wendy's and thought of the Flagstaff guy, him warning me about bankers. We passed the building where Joel and I had smoked. I was going to say something to him, but he already looked asleep. In a few minutes his head began dropping toward my shoulder, like his neck was an old door hinge. But I didn't care. It was almost nice, and I was so high, and when it was especially dark, I could imagine he was Susie. I leaned farther back, and he did too. In my head, I began singing those Kristofferson lyrics.

I was thinking about Susie's hair, the warmth of the sun on those days, and of course I was thinking about what I'd seen down her shirt the day she'd bent over to clip that branch. I guess that's why I didn't do anything when I felt Joel's hand fall into my lap. It moved a bit, and then some more. Soon, he was rubbing, and I didn't know what to do. I hadn't stopped him when I should have. So, I imagined it was Susie again, her hand touching me. Joel was about her size.

And we were in the back, so no one could see. And at the time it was as dark as anywhere in that bus. I'm not that way, so I guess I was just too stoned to stop him and too tired to care. I remember feeling like I wasn't inside the bus anymore. I was soaring above it, like a large bird, a hawk or something. There was all this wind around me. I saw the bus below, like prey, traveling on the highway. I thought of vortexes then and wondered if we were headed toward someplace special.

The city was far behind us, and not even a farmhouse light shined in through the tinted windows. The small golf-ball vent above us was blowing air on my neck. Like Susie's breath, easy, floating there in the night air, with Susie saying in my head, *Baby, I want you.* She was right there in front of me, her lips like every fruit I'd ever picked, and I kissed her and kissed her, and then I was no longer a hawk, but something smaller and white, like a dove.

Or just a feather floating away.

• • •

After we stopped at a town just in that corner of Utah you go through before you hit Idaho, Joel got up and changed seats. I guess he knew not to stay beside me. It had been five or six hours, and we'd both slept right through them, and I was definitely coming down. I had never guessed him to be that way; if I had, I would've figured out a way to keep his head from resting on my shoulder. I was in the last seat by myself now, alone, and I couldn't fall back asleep. I kept wondering if it had really happened, but I knew it had. Maybe he'd gotten me high just so he could do it? It was better not to think about this, I realized. Instead, I tried to think of Susie, but no image of her would come.

When I reached Spokane, I stepped off the bus, not realizing how stiff I was. I just wanted to be at the site. I was running late this year. I walked around the town, waiting for the Myer's truck to pick me up. A young Asian guy wanted to sell me a quarter bag for a hundred bucks. He must have been desperate, though, because I talked him down to fifty, the last of my money. It was a deal.

When I got to Myer's, I went straight for the barracks. I saw Billy lying on a cot.

"I tried to save you a good one, pal," he said, "but no dice."

"That's all right," I said.

"Welcome back to Eden." He laughed.

"Is Susie here?" I asked, throwing my bag on the last free bed.

"Haven't seen her. Think she'll show?"

"I have a feeling."

Billy had been hiding a bottle by the foot of his bed, and he lifted it up for a swig.

"Keep praying," he said, and I wanted to punch him, but not really.

The next morning we got up with the others and worked through the day. I kept looking around for Susie, but she didn't appear. It was one of those rare cloudy days during late spring. That meant we could work later, without the sun killing us, but Billy and I were talking so much we still barely made quota.

That night we sat off by ourselves, Billy and me, near the campfire they light every evening, him getting drunk and me getting high. I was keeping the quarter bag in my shoes; there were over forty guys there in the barracks, and I trusted maybe only about three of them. I mean, if your stash is stolen, you can't really go to the foreman and tell him about it.

Billy said he'd slipped by his folks' house for a while, in Arkansas, then gone to Michigan for a job. To get to Myer's, he'd hitched across Montana. It had taken him four days. I would have told him how it'd have taken half the time by bus, but there was no point.

That night he went through a liter of Beam by himself. Around eleven-thirty, I stood up to go to bed and nearly blacked out. I was stoned good. Billy said he was going to take a walk, which meant going into town for more, and when I watched him head off toward the road into town, I wondered if it was him or me who seemed to not be standing up straight.

. . .

We were all awoken by sirens at two in the morning. For a second I thought we were being attacked. But then I got up and peered out the window. Three cop cars were parked at different angles, like they never learned what a straight line was, and five cops stood in front of them, talking to one another. Our foreman was there.

Just about everyone in the barracks had some reason to be afraid of the police. A few Mexican fellows talked rapidly at the end of the building. They were probably talking to Jerry—their white buddy who spoke Spanish—about what they should do. One Mexican unlocked the window above his bed and looked out to see if they could escape that way. I thought about the quarter in my shoe, then looked around and noticed Billy's bed was empty.

Finally, a cop came in with a flashlight, sweeping it back and forth like it was a sword.

"Sorry to bother you gentlemen," he said. He walked slowly around the room. I get suspicious when a cop acts friendly. It means he wants something and if he doesn't get it, he'll just switch tactics. Once a cop told me he'd found a bag of dope laced with arsenic and was just trying to prevent people from killing themselves—did I know anyone who had tried to sell me some recently? I said no, kept saying no, and by the time I figured out that wasn't the answer he wanted, he'd already thrown me on the ground, searched me, and found a reason to put me in jail for a week.

"Does anyone know a William Denton here?" the cop asked.

Billy.

"He was found on the side of the road with blood alcohol poisoning, barely breathing, and the foreman said some of you all here might be his friends. We just need someone to go down to the hospital and answer some questions."

No one said anything. It was the questions that scared us. Besides, everyone was sleepy and didn't want to miss work. Me, Billy was my friend, but I couldn't go. I felt bad, but I had enough grass in my shoe for them to get me good. There's no reason they'd search me, but you never know how things can turn. And I wasn't going to leave the quarter there in the barracks. It was all I had. Plus, what good could I do?

"If your foreman has to go, he'll be pissed," the cop said, and he began shining the light in one face after another. I saw it coming, he was shifting over to being mean.

No one stepped forward. A couple people looked over at me. I felt like a dog for not speaking up.

"I guess we'll have to turn on the lights," the cop said, "and check everyone's ID."

"I'll go," a guy said in the back, where it was dark. The cop shone his light down that end so the guy could walk up. It was this older guy named Jerry. He already had his shoes and clothes on.

"Thank you, buddy," the cop said. "Good to see there's a decent man in the bunch."

A couple guys rolled their eyes.

I said, "Thanks, Jerry," as he passed.

Once the cops and Jerry left, I checked my shoe and went

back to bed, but I couldn't sleep, worrying about Billy. I felt bad, but again, what could I've done? What could anyone have done?

. . .

The next day I didn't see Billy or Jerry. I had a dope hangover on top of the interrupted sleep. And I was worried. Everyone was, I guess. I would've asked the foreman about Billy, but he knew we were best friends and I didn't want him asking me why I hadn't volunteered to go to the hospital. Work was slow that day. I'd pretty much given up thinking about Susie because she hadn't shown up.

That evening, by the fire again, Jerry showed up and everyone gathered around him to hear. He held a loose fist up almost to his mouth, sort of grabbing his jaw, and he was looking into the fire.

"He's not going to make it," he said. "He went into shock this morning, and a doctor said his liver was crumbling into little pieces like an old sponge."

Some guys were asking questions, but I just walked off. It sounds strange, but hearing what Jerry said made me want to drink. Just that night.

To, you know, get as drunk as Billy would and maybe feel a little of what he'd been feeling.

. . .

I was late for the crew the next day, missed the second truck run and had to walk across the orchard to the site. The grass was wet and all the clouds had disappeared; there was only a line of pink along the horizon. On the way, I thought a long while about Billy, lying in a hospital bed. I wished that, way back, I had paid him the ten bucks for that bet. Then I thought about how he would have just spent it on booze.

The air was cool still. Walking between the trees, I breathed out—glad I was alone. I could see for quite a distance rows and rows of trees, and I thought how Billy called Myer's Orchard Eden. What a joke.

I saw the foreman walking toward me, one row over. He was carrying a wrench and a bucket. When he was near enough he said, "You're late, Ray."

"I know," I said. He passed me without expression. He was an ordinary man, I thought. Nothing special.

For a moment, I almost ran back and asked the foreman about Susie, but I knew what his answer would be. She wasn't coming this season. Meaning she might never be here again. It made me sick then to think Joel's hand was the closest I'd ever get to her. She was probably off becoming a carpenter, making good money. And here I was, still in this orchard.

Instead of heading to the site, I went down to the lake and looked out into the water. A couple of spring apples had rolled down to the edge, and I tossed them, one at a time, across the surface of the lake. Then I turned and went back toward the barracks. I wasn't going back to work. Instead I'd walk into town and say goodbye to Billy. Then I'd take off somewhere new, somewhere the Dog couldn't go.

THE BRICK

NANCY J. FAGAN

"Are you Ben Cutler's mother?" the officer at my door asked. My stomach clenched even though I'd long expected a visit like this.

I heard myself answer—*Yes*—and then it all finally came tumbling down on me: *I'm sorry to have to tell you he was found dead in the front seat of a car registered in your name. A woman we're guessing was his wife was found beside him. Deceased, too. I'm very sorry.*

I felt guilt about my gratitude that Ben and Paula's nightmare with drugs had finally ended in death, but then I heard the officer going on: *A boy who we think was theirs was found in the back seat. He's alive and we believe he goes by the name Jazzie*—and I thought, *A boy?*—and wished my husband was alive to steady me. *A boy?*

But it wasn't until two days later—after I'd identified Ben's and Paula's bodies, after I'd signed everything I'd needed to sign for Ben's cremation, after I'd endured the phone call from Paula's mother, who I'd never met—that my eyes, imperfect as they were, confirmed it for sure:

Yes, there was a boy.

And when I first saw him, he was sitting on the floor beside a social worker named Felix Marquez, doing nothing but slurping from a box of orange Hi-C. He would not look up, and certainly wouldn't look up and over at me. For his part right then, Felix held my eyes with his and said, "I'm sorry about your son and your daughter-in-law."

"I appreciate that," I said.

Felix cleared his throat, turned to the boy, took hold of his hand. "Here she is, Jazzie. This is your grandmother."

The boy had a yellow Lego brick in his other hand. He tapped the brick repeatedly with his thumb, clenched his fingers around it. He was wearing a long-sleeved T-shirt with a yellow Mack truck blazed across its front and pajama bottoms with trains on tracks that ran in diagonals. His nails were bitten to the quick, and he had a half-inch-long scar under his right ear.

I stepped toward him, held out my palm, and said, "What do you have there?" and he squeezed the brick even harder and held it close to his chest. "Is that your favorite?" I asked, and he turned away from me.

A tower of red and blue and yellow Legos stood in a large clear zip-top bag beside him.

"Should we rebuild your building?" I asked him, for lack of anything better.

He held up his hand and looked off.

"Okay," I said. "We'll wait."

He untangled one leg from beneath his wiry body, opened the zip-top, pried one brick after another off his tower with his stubby thumbnail.

Head cocked as he watched along with me, Felix said, "It seems like a ritual for him. The way he separates them methodically."

I had nothing to say. How could I care for a child who

didn't speak? Let alone who didn't seem to care whether or not I existed?

Felix touched the back of my hand and said, "I think it's best to follow his lead. Let him make the first moves." He bit at the corner of his moustache, and I preferred looking at him to looking at Jazzie.

Soon Jazzie was banging the Lego tower against the floor, breaking it down completely. "More of the ritual," Felix said, and Jazzie began sorting the blocks according to color, reds and blues to one side, yellows to the other. He picked up a fistful of yellows, let them fall to the floor. He rocked back and forth and began stacking them, but that one yellow brick, the one he'd had in his hand when I'd walked in, remained directly beside him. He'd glance at it now and then.

"I'll help you pick them up," I said, but again he faced away from me. He grabbed his collapsed juice box, held it out toward Felix, who gave him more Hi-C, this time a box of fruit punch.

"The nurse gave him some mac and cheese," Felix told me. "He gobbled that down."

"So what happens now?" I asked, clutching my pocketbook—I had to admit, the only reason I cared about this troubled boy was that, according to Social Services, he was my grandchild.

"We grant you temporary custody until we can find parents for him."

"But why me?" I said. "You saw—he clearly doesn't like me. And I'm guessing he has no idea what a grandmother is."

"You're all we can find, Mrs. Cutler."

"Really?" I said. "No one in his mother's family is willing?"

"Not a one. From what I gathered, they're not in a position financially or otherwise. And there's no one else, really. The only reason we knew about you was your name was on the car's registration."

I felt bad for the boy but uneasy. "So the custody with me would be temporary?" I asked.

"Yes. I mean, we *could* put him a group home. At his age, though, I wouldn't recommend that. He's impressionable and needs a lot of attention right now. Our plan is to keep looking for two young parents—which might not take all that long. He's definitely young enough for placement."

Jazzie turned and looked sideways at me. His hazel eyes took on a gray cast, as if he knew what I felt and felt the same.

"You really think," I said to Felix, "that at my age . . . "

"It's temporary, Mrs. Cutler. So, yes, I do think you can."

He stood, stepped over to his desk, took from it a clipboard on which were two sheets of paper and a pen, and handed it to me.

I glanced at the forms. I tried again to offer my hand to Jazzie. "Hey, Jazzie, I'm your grandmother," I said, but he turned to the wall, more defiantly this time, and began making clicking noises with his tongue.

Felix nodded. "He's done that a few times. My guess is that, for him, those are words."

"Does his head look smaller than normal?" I asked.

"I'm not sure that matters," he said. "He seems to know what's happening around him. His most glaring difficulty, if you ask me, is that he apparently can't speak. Or at least, you know, like we do."

Yet more fear flooded into me. "So then how, *really*, could I take care of him?"

Felix made sure his eyes were level with mine. "You can try."

Slurping the last of his fruit punch, Jazzie lowered his right hand toward his crotch, then squeezed it.

"Do you need to use the bathroom, Jazzie?" Felix asked loudly but gently.

Jazzie peed right then, his pants darkening.

"Jesus," Felix said. "He *knows* what to do—he went earlier. He's just upset; this is definitely not a habit." He walked to a closet, took a pair of brown sweatpants from it, held them up to see if they'd be a decent fit.

"There's really no one else?" I asked, realizing that, a while back and for quite a few years, I'd wished for more children than Ben.

• • •

From my compact kitchen in my over-fifty-five apartment building, I watched Jazzie open his zip-top bag of loose Legos, pour them onto my glass coffee-table top, and begin to build with focus. He turned each brick over and back, rotating yellow ones as if in search of something more than interlocking bumps and holes. Then he worked intently until a building appeared with extensions on two of its sides.

I sat on the couch with my hands in my lap. "What is that, Jazzie?" I pointed. "A house?"

He kept his eyes lowered. His blond lashes, like his unevenly cut hair, contrasted with his nearly black eyebrows. He picked at a scab near the top of one ear, twirled a finger around in a nostril, then wiped what he'd found on the truck on his shirt.

The clock on my wall had me wondering about his bedtime. "Would you like to see where we'll sleep?"

He stood and, as if suddenly fearless, followed me into my bedroom, where my husband's and my twin beds had remained since my husband's death. I grabbed some fresh sheets from the closet, went to work making my husband's bed for Jazzie, patted the white fleece blanket and told Jazzie he might need it if it got cold.

He said nothing. Not even a click. He was looking away from me again.

"Bathroom," I said, and I pointed toward the bathroom doorway. "Would you like to take a bath?"

His chin rose, moved slightly in my direction, a question on his face.

"I'll help you," I said.

Looking away again, he shook his head fiercely. I stared at his fingernails—little boy nails with dirt under them.

"You can bring the Lego bag with you. How's that?"

He walked to the bathroom, looked at the tub, clicked as he pointed at it.

And then, after I'd drawn the bath and as he splashed in the sudsy water, I thought about the horrors of the past few days. The doctor had said Ben and Paula had likely lived in their car, the car that I'd bought for Ben before he and Paula disappeared. Whose idea was it to live that way, his or hers?

Jazzie dunked his head and let me pour clear water over his face. But he recoiled when I tried to wipe his face with a washcloth, so I left it. Three dark bruises dotted his lower back; a scar on his right arm glistened with a white sheen. He ran a finger along the length of a blue brick. His toes were long and agile enough to pick up each brick and place it on the edge of the tub. But the whole time he bathed, he clutched that yellow brick, his favorite one, the one he'd rarely let go of for longer than a minute. With his other hand he dipped another Lego, then another into the bubbles, clicking as if naming each. His lips mimed conversation but made no sound. Felix had given me a bag of mismatched pajamas, a pair of jeans, and a T-shirt, and I offered the pj's to Jazzie; he took the pants but shook his head no to the Sponge Bob top. He grabbed his snotty truck shirt and pointed at the bed.

"Yes, that's yours," I said, hoping my tone sounded reassuring.

. . .

That first night, he slept with his bag of Legos, his necessary yellow one in a fist next to his nose. I watched him for an hour, then slept too, if fitfully. When the memory of the previous day shook me wide awake, his bed was empty. I found him in the kitchen peering out the window, his yellow Lego in his hand, others on the table behind him.

I put down a bowl of cereal without milk, and he nibbled at it, taking one oat ring at a time. He dipped some in a glass of milk I brought over and started building a Lego tower with his free hand, using only yellow bricks.

And each morning from then on, he followed the same ritual: kitchen chair, oat rings, milk, yellow bricks. He communicated with simple clicks, buzzes, and grunts.

Ben had not been that predictable. One day he'd begged me for Count Chocula, stirring the leftover brown milk for an hour after he scarfed up cereal and mini marshmallows.

"I like this," he'd finally declared.

He'd repeated that declaration for days but then refused to eat Count Chocula or any other cereal again; a dozen different cereal boxes sat uneaten on a shelf in the cupboard. He'd never played with toys the normal way; instead he'd kicked at them until they'd scatter. His temper had flared easily. I have a scar on the nape of my neck where the edge of a glass hurled in anger split my skin. After each time he'd hurt me, I'd tried to convince myself he was going through a stage and that it would get better, but it never did, really.

I pressed my fingers to my forehead and tried to remember a single time when he'd sat quietly to stare out a window like Jazzie was now. I could not. Maybe this time, with Jazzie, things would be different.

• • •

I took the box out of my closet. Its top was covered with dust, which I brushed with my hand into the wastebasket in the bedroom. I hesitated before going ahead. Then, there, inside, some of Ben's things seemed to be looking up at me: his birth certificate, a baby book filled with carefully written entries until halfway through his first year, and a 4" x 6" photo album of his childhood. I studied the photo of him holding his favorite toy—a Mack truck, its modern replica on the shirt Jazzie was wearing.

Tears flooded my eyes. "Look, Jazzie, here's your daddy. Look at that big truck."

Jazzie glanced briefly at the photo and might have smiled, but the expression disappeared as fast as it came. The truck, a gift to Ben on his third birthday, stirred a strong memory for me. We'd lived in a fifth-floor walk-up downtown then, close to my husband's supervisor job at the NYC Port Authority. I'd carried that boy up and down those stairs every day, even in the brutal heat. Ben's face in the photo mirrored Jazzie's. They both had one eyebrow arched: Ben's left, Jazzie's right. I noticed similar complexions despite Ben's dark hair and a shared darkness beneath their eyes. Jazzie was now rotating his hands like a whirlybird as he looked down at the photo, and I remembered Ben doing the same thing, a helicopter-like hover over toys or food.

Ben had torn apart his coloring books as a child. Tantrums had come in waves, so I couldn't take him to the grocery or anywhere without the threat of one. I'd tried my hardest to love him. I did love him. When he'd misbehave, we would try any of the 1980s punishments—a time-out in a corner, or we counted to ten, or any number of others. I would stroke his self-esteem by telling him he did a "good job" on his schoolwork and compliment the rare times he cleaned his room. When those methods didn't prove effective, I would spank him. While I did so, I'd remember how my father had swatted my bottom, and how I'd never lied again. But with Ben, spanking seemed to make matters worse.

"He needs medication," my husband once said. "Lots of kids go on medication."

"Okay, if you think that's the right thing." I hated the notion, though. Why couldn't I be a better parent? Could pills change the essence of our Ben?

Ben's pediatrician then prescribed Ritalin and suggested a course of positive reinforcement with a star chart. Things finally seemed to change when we gave him his toy Mack truck as a reward for earning ten stars. He sat for hours on the floor and rolled it back and forth over the burgundy braided rug in the dining room. This occupied him long enough for me to do housework and laundry. We took it away if he acted up and gave it back when his behavior changed for the better. Life did finally seem easier for a while. Though rough days did follow.

One morning, on a day when Ben decided not to follow any rules, he wanted the truck. He refused to eat his breakfast and dumped his plate of eggs and sausage in the trash.

"You have to earn truck time," I said, and he sat at my feet and pouted.

To make extra money back then, I'd taken up sewing. On that day, I was sewing our neighbor Mrs. Markham's curtains. Ben pulled at my pants leg and then hit the floor pedal on the sewing machine to get my attention. I shook him off time and again, then finally said, "Benjamin, I must finish these curtains for Mrs. Markham. Right now, she is more important than you are."

He continued to whine, so I promised him that if he sat quietly for five minutes, I'd let him play with his truck. He stayed quiet as a mouse for a minute, but soon his hands began moving in large circles, an omen of agitation, and he slapped me on the leg—hard. According to every book my husband and I had read, I should have withheld the truck even longer to correct the behavior, but my work needed attention too, so I went to the closet and brought down the truck. I knew trouble would come by the look on his face, but still, I let him have it. He wheeled the toy to the living room, and I left him there while I sewed. He banged that truck back and forth against the wall, but I kept sewing.

Then I heard the scream. It came from Mrs. Markham—she'd been walking down the sidewalk below our open window. Ben had thrown the truck through the screen at her, and it had missed most of her, but the crane on it had sliced open the side of her face, leaving a slit that required twelve stitches.

• • •

Jazzie ate a hotdog every day for lunch. I soon learned that he preferred ketchup over mustard and relish. Once, he grabbed a raw onion and took a bite before I could stop him. From that day on, I fried his hotdog in a skillet with chopped onions I'd prepared the night before as he'd slept. He would plop himself down at the chair by the window, and I'd watch him out of the corner of my eye, his little body at attention as he stared down at the passersby and traffic below. His fingers would twist and untwist from around one another. He'd kick at the air and whirl his hands when he'd see a cab. He was growing used to watching life through a pane of glass, and those moments when he was excited endeared him to me.

The cause of his silence remained a mystery. Had he inherited the condition? Of course, I could not account for his mother, or for her family, who'd been at the memorial service for her and Ben but hadn't returned my calls since.

"You shouldn't change his first name; it's what they called him, his legal name—it's on the birth certificate they found in her wallet," Felix explained at our follow-up meeting. "He's vulnerable, and we need to be careful to change his environment in gradations rather than radically."

A sparkle in Jazzie's eyes told me Jazzie was listening to us closely.

"I think he understands you," I said.

Felix frowned, as if frustrated with me, and continued in a loud whisper: "We have no idea what he's seen or what's been done to him."

"You mean abuse?" I whispered softly.

He nodded and turned to look down at Jazzie. "All we know is that something happened. Maybe abuse, maybe he had a virus or something. Could be his diet—malnourishment." He motioned an open palm toward Jazzie. "Would you like to play something?"

Jazzie nodded and grabbed the bucket of Legos Felix handed him.

"We can talk in the next room while he plays."

Felix led me around the corner and motioned to a chair upholstered in a subtle floral print. On the wall was a one-way mirror we could watch Jazzie through.

Felix spread his hands open on the desk. "Trauma can cause muteness. We can assume he suffered some sort of what we call an 'insult' to his development. At four, he should have at least a thousand words, and obviously, he can't express any. Though he does seem to understand what's said to him. And he makes his sounds, and his hearing appears to be fine. Once we determine the cause of his disability, we can begin targeted treatment."

"The cause is drugs," I said as I swallowed. "Heroin. Cocaine."

Because Ben and Paula had never hid their drug use from anyone. They'd visit me and my husband when they were high, pacing back and forth through the living room, rubbing their noses, scratching at their faces. They'd tell us they needed money for electricity, for food, for various medicines to help them get sober. My husband had always handed them what was in his wallet, though that added up to only a few twenties now and then. Sometimes, they'd stopped over to sleep on the couch but left before we woke. Once, they joked about the people they met in their drug dens—about how they felt closer to them than actual family. In fact, my husband died shortly after that conversation. His coworkers at the Port Authority thought the devastation that he witnessed on 9/11 caused the heart attack, but I believed the unrelenting strain of being Ben's dad was the reason. Ben did not come to the funeral. My friend Louise, the minister, and I stood on either side of the gravestone. A few church ladies stood at a distance, then murmured their condolences as we passed them.

But what broke my heart, too, and what I think about more often, is the time Ben and Paula disappeared after an Easter dinner with me. They'd paced around that time also, eaten maybe a few bites, then left the large ham congealing on the table. They told me they'd made another commitment at "a friend's house." I asked the name of the friend and Ben said, "Doesn't matter." Paula saw me wince and added, "It's no one you've ever heard of before," and then, a few days later, I noticed that my sapphire-and-diamond bangle was missing.

After that, I had a locksmith change my locks, and after that, I never saw Ben and Paula again.

And year after year passed without a word from my son.

• • •

The first time I opened *The Cat in the Hat* for Jazzie, as we sat on my couch, I remembered reading the same story to Ben. I tripped over the rhymes as I read to Jazzie; the book now sounded political to me, a rebellion against "the man," and I wondered if it had added to Ben's unruliness. As I read, I noticed Jazzie's clenched fist, his blanched knuckles. When his bottom wriggled against the couch cushion, I remembered that Ben rarely sat still for a book either. Worse for Jazzie now, his truck shirt was tumbling in the dryer, temporarily replaced by a green sweater. He kept eyeing the dryer, and I knew that as soon as the buzzer sounded, he'd click until he could wear the shirt again. I'd learned that any delay by me after that buzzer buzzed resulted in a full-blown tantrum, and it occurred to me that there must be a gene for tantrums.

But Jazzie did tolerate certain things. He let me sing to him while I cooked his meals, and he walked behind me like a duckling when we went shopping. He wouldn't let me hold his hand; instead he tied himself to me with an invisible string and weaved behind me holding that yellow Lego inside his fist. He could sit for spurts when I read a few pages of books he tolerated, but he looked away if I pointed out something on a page that was apparently too much for him to absorb. He definitely liked to be tucked in under a heavy blanket in his bed at night no matter the temperature, and he needed to keep his socks and sneakers on during the day. He never would permit a hug, never—I'd tried three times, and he'd buzz-clicked and pushed me off each time, with both hands.

• • •

As that summer progressed, the prospect of preschool loomed. The preschool teacher assigned to Jazzie was smart and upbeat, a special education teacher who was also quite young. Two years out of college and eager to change his world, she called me in August to introduce herself, then weekly to check his progress. "I'll send you a worksheet," she explained toward the end of one call. "So he can get used to the format we use."

The worksheet she sent then sat on my kitchen counter, next to the canister of flour. One morning, when I had a bit of extra energy, I showed Jazzie the shapes on the sheet and asked him to name them. He took the sheet, examined it, crumpled it with his left hand, and dropped it to the floor. I asked him gently to pick it up, and he battered my ribs and chest with his arms. Though quieter than Ben's, his tantrums happened more often. I picked up the worksheet and smoothed it out, but he never as much as glanced at it again.

As September approached, Felix had a speech therapist visit our apartment every week. This therapist persisted despite her ineffectiveness, and assured me that repetition would help.

"Ba-ba-ba, pop-pop-pop," she'd say to Jazzie, coaxing him to mimic her.

He'd looked down and stare at the floor.

"What word does the chicken use?" she said once during a visit. "Brwaack *brwaack*."

Nothing.

"Moo says the cow, neigh says the horse."

He took his Lego out of his pocket.

"No, Jazzie, make these *sounds*!" she said. She held the cow closer to his face and said, "Moo moo moo!"—and he spun away from her. She touched his shoulder and gradually turned him toward her.

She was not unkind, just misdirected. I knew what would happen and watched it unfold to let someone else in on what I dealt with. Once, after he'd batted the cow out of her hand, she picked it up and mooed once more, and he grabbed her arm and bit her, his jaw holding on until she dropped the cow.

I gave her an alcohol wipe then, as well as a pink-skinned Band-Aid, and of course I apologized. She told me it was her fault—"I shouldn't have taken his Lego," she said.

But the next week, she stacked her own bag of Legos beside some new animals, jungle animals. He had no interest in those either. I suggested that instead of animals she use a cab; he seemed to like cabs, I explained. She looked through her bag but found no cabs or cars, no vehicles of any kind, certainly not any yellow ones.

"Jazzie, you can play with the Legos after you make the 'rawr' like a lion and the 'wheet' like the bird," she said, and he stared at her and blinked.

She pressed a plastic lion into my hand and told me to help him practice three times a day.

"I'll give you a tip," she said. "Take it out only when he's quiet."

"Great advice," I replied, sure she was doomed for failure, but before she left minutes later, she gave me a thumbs-up.

• • •

The next afternoon, my phone rang, and I saw Felix's name on the screen. Jazzie clicked and slid off the couch and headed for the bedroom.

"Hello, Felix," I said, and as usual, Felix began with formality, saying something about hoping I was well.

Then he said, "It's been nearly two months that you've had Jazzie, and of course we both know you agreed to do this temporarily. And you've done fine work with him so far, but, well, it looks like we have a permanent foster for him."

I found it hard to breathe. I'd been tired all day, but now I felt worse. "Permanent foster? What does that mean?"

"It's something like an adoption except it gives the foster family a way to change the situation if need be. It's not the optimal arrangement when it comes to life-long permanence, grant you, but the couple *is* young, and usually these things work out."

The thought of Jazzie leaving me at this point was making my hands tremble. "But is now the right time?" I asked. "School's starting soon, he's already met his teacher—"

"I'm not sure if you remember, but officially speaking, the time frame for temporary custody is two months. You can file for an extension, though, if you're interested. Though as I recall when you first met Jazzie, you weren't quite sure you'd be able to handle him."

"But that was then—we're getting along better now," I lied.

"So you'd like to file for an extension? You should probably know this before you answer. Between me and you, if you do want . . . well, let's put it this way: If you pass up this opportunity for him with this young couple, I'm not sure there'll be another."

I tried to picture myself a year from then, still taking care of Jazzie. I felt so exhausted I doubted I could last another week.

"And again, this decision is of course yours, Mrs. Cutler, but it's probably not a bad idea to factor in that he'll be growing bigger and stronger, with more ambitions as it were than he has now."

"You're saying you think I'll become too weak to deal with him?"

"You know the answer to that more than I do. It's a question of physical strength, of course, but there's also the emotional component. You've raised a son; I think you know what I mean."

And I did know, much as I didn't want to think about Ben right now. I also knew I felt as if I'd aged ten years since I'd taken in Jazzie: the lack of sleep, the stress, the ups and downs—when I'd look in the mirror most mornings, I'd feel terrified.

"But if you want an extension," Felix said, "I can make that happen. It's just that this couple is interested in Jazzie *now*, and that could change quickly."

"Because . . . why would that change?"

"Because the longer you make them wait, the more likely they'll find another boy."

Jazzie was standing beside me right then, yellow brick in hand, clicking every three seconds or so. I scratched the top of his head to get him to look up at me, but he wouldn't. He was occupied enough by the clicking.

"Could I have till tomorrow morning?" I asked Felix.

"How 'bout this?" he said. "I'll tell the couple he's theirs, and that they can pick him up from my office tomorrow at ten. If you wake up tomorrow and feel compelled to adopt, you'll adopt—and they'll simply have to move on. Either way, I'll be at your place at nine. For you to sign the adoption papers, or for me to drive Jazzie to my office."

I felt a pang then, at the thought of saying goodbye to Jazzie. Would I hug him and smother him with kisses? Or, to keep him from suspecting what was up, would I simply act as if Felix was taking him for a walk?

• • •

I slept in the next morning, and not intentionally. It was as if my body was telling me, *No. You're worn out. You'd be lucky to last another day living like this.* Worse, I kept thinking about how old I was, my life expectancy, the fact that I believed my husband's death had been hastened by our having raised Ben. I wasn't Superwoman, and when I got out of bed, I felt this in my bones.

Worse, Jazzie wasn't exactly having an angelic morning. His aim at the toilet when he'd peed upon waking had been casual at best, and while he ate his oat rings, he'd dip every other one in his milk but then toss it at the kitchen window. The more I'd pick up the oat rings and tell him to stop, the faster and louder his clicking, and when he got up from the table and kicked the couch, I knew a tantrum would follow.

And one did. And it was bad. While I stood looking on at him, I noticed that he was indeed growing physically, and that maybe, if I was being honest with myself, this tantrum was more violent and angry than the ones he'd had when I'd first taken him in, and the thought of this itself made me feel faint.

"Jazzie, please?" I said, but he raged on, kicking himself down into a blob, flailing, rolling back and forth on the floor. I tried to give him his brick, but he batted it away, sending it up toward my face so hard I covered my eyes with my hand. "Jazzie!" I said. "Stop!" He kept thrashing. "Jazzie, do you *understand*? If you don't stop now, you can't live with me anymore! No more me, Jazzie! No more *me*!"

And he did stop that tantrum, but not for at least another fifteen minutes. And of course fifteen minutes feel like fifteen hours when your own flesh and blood is making it so clear that, despite all you've done for him, he's miserable.

So even after he'd stopped, as we'd sat finishing our breakfasts, I knew. Knew it in my body and mind both. I was unfit to go the long run with him. I had me to worry about, and even when it came to what was best for him, I wasn't enough, because he needed a mother and a father both, and in any case, he needed someone stronger than I.

• • •

As it turned out, Felix didn't arrive until almost noon, and before he'd arrived, Jazzie had napped on the couch, snoring lightly, his yellow brick back in his hand, which was yet again pressed against his chest. Green snot had appeared in one nostril, and I dabbed it away with a washcloth while fearing I'd wake him and he'd get upset again. He didn't wake then, but I knew that there was nothing to do but forgo adoption, and that as soon as he'd leave, I'd take a long nap, too.

And I did take a long nap after he left. Sleep didn't overcome me immediately, but I did sleep, and deeply, and for a long time.

But before I fell asleep that afternoon, alone in my room on my twin bed, I thought about Jazzie's goodbye to me, which happened minutes before I nodded at Felix to say, *Yes, take him now.*

Jazzie had been sitting beside my kitchen window then, gazing out at the traffic below us peacefully and contemplatively, as if he knew this was his last look at it from up there, and I stepped over to him, lay my hand on his shoulder, and without word, kissed the top of his head.

And he didn't react, not gratefully, not angrily, his eyes taken by what he was seeing out there.

Then, as if the kiss had finally registered in his mind, he pointed at a cab while looking up at me. "Yellow," he said clearly. "Yellow."

YOU DON'T HAVE VERY FAR TO GO

FRANCISCO URIBE

Sharleen left.

She packed her bags and poured my beer down the drain while I was at work. I'd been hauling concrete slabs all day that day and now smelled like horse sex. I'd strained my groin with those God-danged slabs. On the drive home, all I could think about was putting a cold one right between my legs. But neither a single beer nor Sharleen Honey could be found inside the house. This wasn't the first time she'd pulled a stunt like that on me. But this time, I knew she'd had enough and wasn't coming back.

Sharleen Darling. I'd no longer be able to bury my face into her fine, forty-inch-wide behind, and that knowledge had me feeling down, so much so that I went out, bought a case of Old Milwaukee, along with a bag of ice and several Lotto scratchers. The best time to play scratchers is when you're at your lowest—reason being, ain't no other way but up.

When I came back home, the sweat on my back and chest had dried. But my shirt had latched on, so I peeled it off and threw it against a wall. I turned up the volume on Merle Haggard. His *Big City* album sounded nice as it blared out of the woodgrain speakers. The beers and ice I put inside a cooler, which I then carried and placed on Sharleen's side of the bed. I went to my knees and searched under the bed but found nothing belonging to her. I kept rummaging around, rifling through the drawers, looking for her favorite mug in the kitchen and everywhere, delving into the closet. Nothing at all—except, at the bottom of the hamper, one unwashed pair of panties, her pink G-string, the one she herself decorated with magenta sequins. Every time she'd worn that thing, I'd gone wild. So of course, the hopeless romantic in me believed she'd left it on purpose—something for me to remember her by.

After shutting the blinds, I closed the curtains all the way and fell onto the bed. The mattress squeaked, my head spun. The G-string brought me a great deal of comfort, so much so I placed it on my chest. I reached into the cooler for two cans of Old Milwaukee and wedged the colder one between my nutsack and my sore groin. The other I popped open. Once the beer intensified my godforsaken feelings to an unbearable degree, I began singing along with ole Merle.

Shit. I just couldn't live without her. I thought about shooting myself in the head with the G-string hanging around my neck. That was the state of mind I was in while driving down to the Book Exchange. I'm the kind of person who reads books when I'm in the shitter. That's what I do. At four most afternoons, I'm in the stinking stalls at work, pushing out my morning's breakfast and reading a good yarn about some poor shmuck who has a certain flair for failure. When I finish at both ends, I'll flush, light a match, and think, Good God almighty, at least my life isn't *that* fucked up.

It didn't help now that inside my pickup's glove compartment was the .22 caliber revolver I'd been using at work to shoot down rats, pigeons, sometimes snakes, and once a cat that had been mauled by a coyote. I checked the .22 to make sure it was still loaded, and it was.

So walking through the aisles of the Book Exchange with the revolver in my pocket and Sharleen's sullied underwear around my neck, I kept my eye out for any book that could dig me out of the hole I was in. On the bargain rack, I spotted an old Avon copy of *Autobiography of a Flea.* A dirty book about a filthy bug who likes to follow and suck the blood out of a young, pretty harlot, who in turn likes to suck the spunk out of older men. Some people liked to get screwed over and over and over, and it was good to be reminded of that, so I grabbed the cruddy book, its yellowing pages coming apart at the spine.

The old woman behind the counter had on a pair of oversized glasses with a chain attached. She was also wearing an itchy-looking grey sweater that matched the coarseness and color of her hair. Sewed onto the sweater were these small, deformed cats—obviously, she'd knitted the sweater herself. I kept eyeing those cats, and she kept eyeing the pink fabric dangling around my neck. Once she realized what it was, the wrinkles around her eyes and forehead grew meaner looking.

I dropped the book on the counter, counted all the loose change I had, but was still short three pennies. I pulled out the .22, placed it next to the book, fished around inside all my pockets for more coins. Upon seeing the .22, the old woman froze. She could only press her lips together, the edges of her mouth turning white. Her hands started shaking. To show her I meant no harm, I handed her the money, down to the exact change. That seemed to calm her a bit. Her lips returned to their normal shape and color; whatever tremors she still exhibited seeming to be due to her age only.

She took a good hard look at the book I was purchasing. On the front cover was a young woman—in soft focus—standing in front of a full-length mirror, red hair curly and coiffed, her outfit only a pearl necklace, white stockings, white heels, and a garter belt. Her dainty hands covered her breasts. It was like an advertisement for a classy '70s porno flick starring Annette Haven. Glancing away from the book, the old woman made a face as if the book or I had farted. She grabbed the book using only her fingertips and dropped it into a brown paper bag. Annoyed by whatever she might be thinking, I said, "Lady, you're the one who stocks and sells this smut!" And I left.

I thought about her as I drove home. It was good not to think about Sharleen. Pulling up to the curb in front of my house, I hoped to see Sharleen's rusted old Mercury in the driveway. But no. She wasn't there. Not her, not her car, nothing.

I stayed inside my truck for a good while, reading *Autobiography of a Flea*, drinking, smoking, inhaling the faint musty odor Sharleen's underwear still offered. On the radio, Stevie Ray did his thing, causing the sky to cry by stressing his guitar's strings right up to their breaking points. I messed around with the .22 revolver—unloading it, bullet by bullet, then loading it, bullet by bullet. She loves me, she loves me not.

I'll be honest, taking that first step through the front door that evening was tough enough. Sharleen's absence could be felt and seen all around. But what helped me was Merle. Before stepping out, I'd rigged the stereo so he'd be playing when I came back. He'd never stop singing, and that made things a little easier.

While restocking the cooler, I heard Tito's wife from across the street. She was squealing, and I imagined her in her faded lemon-yellow, crosshatch-patterned apron with curlers in her hair, waving a rolling pin above her head like they do in the movies. Tito was making his way on over for a visit, and he was paying for it by getting an earful from her. She didn't like me very much, and she shouted real loud about that. She also squalled about her *viejo*'s lack of money, his drinking too much, and his need to stay away from that dirty, drunken redneck *gringo* from across the street.

"He's no *bueno*. That's why his *vieja* left him . . . fuckin' drunks!" she said.

"Why *did* you leave me, baby?" I whispered into Sharleen's pink G-string.

The doorbell rang, and I wanted to yell out, "Go away!" so I could be left alone to read *Autobiography*, scratch my scratchers, and listen to ole Merle. But I felt bad for Tito. He'd gotten into it with his wife and risked sleeping on the couch on my account. He'd heard the big bad news and come to check on his good pal Larry. God bless that brown-skinned fella, all five-foot-three of him.

Bullshit. I knew better. The truth was that Tito thirsted after my beer. His wife forbade alcohol, kept their home as sober as a dry county on a hot summer's day. Sharleen had tried that shit too from time to time, but it had never worked. Not on me. I was no pushover like Tito. Not one bit. Still, I had nothing against the guy. He at least still had a woman.

I opened up, and there he was, Tito jammed into a sea of denim and flannel glory. A dirty trucker hat on top of his head. "*Hola*," I said.

He swooped right past me and made himself comfortable on my couch. I closed the door with a hardy thump and slouched next to him.

"Ey *compradre*, where's the *cervezas*?" he asked.

I pointed.

He commenced to drink and drink and talk and talk, and although I tuned him out for good portions, I couldn't ignore him altogether because it's in his nature to be annoyingly inquisitive.

"Good God, Lare, why does it stink so bad in here? Is that why your *vieja* left? She couldn't stand the stank? But really, Lare, what'd you do to Sharleen? Did you smack her? I saw her taking out some of her things the other morning. Did she tell you she was leaving? *Dios*, you guys were together . . . for how long? Three, four, *five* years? Hey buddy, this isn't all the *cervezas* you have, is it, pal? Yo, *hombre*, what's that around your neck?"

I lifted Sharleen's underwear and said, "This . . . this is real love."

"It looks like your *vieja*'s dirty panties to me."

He walked over to where my cassettes were scattered on the shag carpeting, next to the stereo system. He knelt beside one of its three pieces and scanned my collection of Mexican folk songs. I was more than likely the only *gringo* he knew who could sing along to Vicente Fernández's "*La Ley del Monte*." Tito picked up a cassette and turned off Merle so he could start playing Vicente's "*El Rey*." I was more than tempted to pull out my .22 and tell him to put Merle back on. But Tito would sing along with Vicente if I let him, and that would be better than him probing into the whys of my life, so I remained passive.

And Tito did sing along. And drank my beer, one after another. At some point while he did this, I rubbed Sharleen's G-string with my fingers and noticed that the tag hung by a thread. Many of the sequins had fallen off, too, but that didn't matter. The way Sharleen's behind looked in that piece of nylon and cotton had always made my mouth water, and now was no exception.

"Jesus," I said.

About seven years ago, before she and I had moved in together, she'd come to my place and we'd take these long naps together in the middle of the day inside my red-walled bedroom. At the time, I was nineteen and living with my pa. He'd be out of our trailer house, doing his regular nine-to-five. I'd be in bed, lying next to Sharleen, hard and trying hard to get her to take off her jeans or shorts or skirt or whatever she damn wore. Even back then, she liked to tease. My face would be a mixture of tears, sweat, and frustration, and I'm guessing seeing me that way was some kind of boost to her fragile ego. Not that she had an extremely fragile ego, but at eighteen then, she was still young, and anyone young is fragile no matter what they say.

Fuck, fuck, and fuck. With those memories swirling around in my head, I began to cry. But only a little. Tito made as if he didn't see me, and I got that. It's an awkward thing to witness, a grown man crying.

"Dang," I said softly.

"*Que?*"

"Nothing."

"Listen, Lare, it's okay. I'm your pal. You can talk to me. What happened? Do you have another piece on the side? Sharleen found out? That's what happened, wasn't it? It's okay, we're only men, it's natural. But hey, Lare, don't worry 'bout it. You're still young. Take it from me, who's much older, you'll do just fine. You'll get over it for sure. You're, what do you *gringos* from your neck of the woods say, a tall drink of water? I'm not coming on to you, buddy, but you're a good-looking guy. You're what? Six-two, six-three? And built like a thoroughbred. And sure, maybe your hair is starting to go thin and your hairline's receding, but under bad lighting, it's hardly even noticeable."

I narrowed my eyes at Tito, got up, rubbed a cold one against the crotch of my blue jeans, moseyed up to the gold vein mirror above the stereo. The tops of the speakers were covered with filmy rings of residue from never having seen coasters, and Vicente's booming voice was shaking the mirror. Staring at my own reverberating reflection, I agreed partly with Tito. I was indeed built like a thoroughbred. And I had hair on my chest. And my body was muscular, firm, you might even say hard. Sharleen would miss this, right? It was surely gonna be her loss.

Then I leaned forward to take a better look at what the hell Tito was talking about in regards to my hair. I ran my fingers through it a couple of times but couldn't figure out what it was he was seeing, so I turned the volume up on the stereo, hoping he'd get the cue and quiet down.

But he kept poking me with his talk. Irritated and resigned to feeling that way, I reached for my Lotto scratchers and was about to go at them when Tito asked if he could try one of them first. Shoving the scratchers toward him, I said, "Go ahead. But keep your damn thoughts to yourself."

"*Orale*, Lare. Sure thing." He dug a penny out of his pocket and got to scratching. "Nothing on this one, pal. This one, no winner. Oooh, *ticket*; that's five *dólares*. Can I keep this one, Lare? Next one. Nope, not a winner."

Then he scratched one but didn't say anything for a while. He held that scratcher close to his face.

Then: "Oh, *Dios*, five hundred!" He stood. He hollered, "Lare, we won! We *won*! God damn, we gotta celebrate, man! What damn luck! What damn, stupid luck! *Oye*, Lare, listen, just listen. Mike Tyson fights tonight, and I got this bookie friend we can call. We can increase our money real easy tonight. What luck! Tyson fights that bum Douglas! Easy money! Tyson is a forty-two to one favorite! A sure bet if we ever seen one!"

"You mean one to forty-two."

"Whatever."

"At one to forty-two, we'd only profit like, what, twelve bucks? For risking five hundred bucks? Why would we do that?"

"Because it's *sure money*, man! Because our cash will be growing almost instantly!"

Tito was insane when it came to gambling—this was now clear. Anyone who bets anything knows you never go on an odds-on favorite, because favorites lose more often than people think. Everyone knows this yet a good number of gamblers, most of them in the case of this Tyson fight, would still bet on favorite after favorite, assuring their financial demise over time.

"Come on, man," Tito said. "Let's do it. Let me call my bookie and do it."

It's not even your money, I thought to say, it's mine. But I didn't want to say that right then. How could I? Right then, beside the panties, Tito was all I had.

"Why the hell not," I said. "But we'll bet the five hundred on Douglas."

"Good one, Lare," Tito said.

"I'm not kidding."

"Lare, Tyson's *not going to lose*. He won't lose. He *can't*."

"That there is my money," I said, and from its hiding place beneath my couch, I pulled out my .22. "Make the bet. Five hundred on Douglas."

Tito looked me in the eyes. He gripped the winning scratcher, not ready to say goodbye to what it meant, even if I might not give him any of it. I cocked the gun and his eyes went big. He had this real scared look. "Lare. Come *on*. Who are you kidding? Five *hundred* on Douglas?"

I pulled the trigger, shooting the Naugahyde recliner beneath him. Six shots, six bullet holes, Tito's face now whiter than mine.

Within minutes his voice quavered over the phone as he said, "*Quinientos para* Douglas." When he hung up, he looked my way and said, "*Adios, dinero.* Now we just gotta find a place to watch the fight. And drink some more. But before that, Lare, could you please do me a favor? Could you please go take a damn shower? Because if you shooting me doesn't kill me, your stench definitely will."

He was right, I knew. And a shower always made me feel better. So I jumped into mine with three cans of beer. And it felt good, really good, the warm water hitting my chest and sliding down my back, the cold beer going down my throat and into my belly, the piss running down the drain as my eyes watched the yellow swirl away.

Though when I came out of the shower, I felt refreshed, sure, but I still missed Sharleen, so I put her underwear back around my neck.

And I'll say this: Standing naked in the bathroom with my neck encircled by that G-string made me feel closer to her, so I stood there for a good while before putting on any of my clothes.

Then, from near the stereo, I heard, "Lare?"

"What," I called.

"Let's go, man. Fight starts in like twenty minutes."

Outside, Tito jumped into my truck and slid onto the driver's seat. He was less intoxicated than I was, so he wanted to drive. But seeing he was brown, the chances of us being pulled over by the cops were higher if he drove. "Scoot over," I told him, "I'm driving."

He looked at me for a second, studying my reddened face. I pointed at one of his forearms, and he frowned, then moved to the passenger side without saying a thing. I sat behind the steering wheel, turned on the ignition, put the loaded .22 in the glove box, and kissed Sharleen's underwear in the same manner he'd kiss rosary beads for heavenly protection whenever he was about to take a long drive.

Then he and I kept passing a can of Old Milwaukee back and forth like it was the last cigarette on earth. After taking the last gulp, he pointed me to a rundown, one-story place called La Playa Bar. Inside, there was nothing but Mexicans, with more Vicente Fernández playing on the jukebox. Vincente was their Johnny Cash and Hank Williams rolled into one, and all the men in the bar sang along to a tune about some poor dope who ripped his veins to shreds because of a love gone wrong. That much I understood. That much I sang along to loudly.

The place's floor was covered in sticky grime, and my steps toward the bar sounded like Velcro coming apart. The patrons themselves had vomit on their breaths. You could smell a vinegar-like odor. From one of the place's dark corners, you could also smell piss. The place was small and the men were old, their spider-webbed eyes red around the irises. Mostly, they wore cowboy hats, cowboy boots, big belt buckles, and denim jackets. They tended to lean to one side but never fell. The young ones who were scattered about stood with their arms crossed, legs far apart, allowing them to scratch themselves rarely but well.

At the far ends, women sat on stools and laughed with ease and stretched their legs in a friendly manner. They wanted to show their magic, it seemed. Tito got in my ear and said, "You see those *legs*, man?" And he headed toward one of them before I could answer.

"They're gonna take everything he's got," I said to myself, and I maneuvered myself toward the lady serving the drinks. She'd been a beauty in her heyday, I could tell. I gave her a good eyeful and began imagining her in Sharleen's G-string. A passing of the torch, if you will.

But neither she nor anyone was paying any real attention to me or to the G-string, which I continued to wear like a necklace. Everyone was too busy looking at the three large monitors mounted on the walls, next to posters of girls in bikinis holding frosty bottles of beer and the 1986 Mexican national soccer team.

I myself kept looking at the bartendress whenever she walked away. I decided she was the Latin version of Sharleen. A bit on the shorter side, with darker hair and darker skin, bigger eyes, a bigger bust, sharper penciled-in eyebrows, okay, but her behind was just as plump, and she moved it from side to side as if she were on a conga line. When she came to me, I tried a line or two on her, but she didn't respond, so I backed off, never being one to beg. But I thought this: Women have no idea how much we need them, their bodies, their skin, their warmth. A touch from any of them can revitalize any soul and bring any man back from the dead. If only they could learn to love us unconditionally.

Then the fight was all set to begin.

No one at the bar was taking Buster Douglas seriously. Even his opponent, Iron Mike Tyson, was looking loose and cool, his arms, chest, torso, and thighs appearing yet again as if they were about to be forged into steel. Walking around the ring, he reminded me of a caged tiger ready to devour a small boar. Everyone in the world was certain he was going to KO Douglas in a matter of seconds.

But Douglas had other ideas. Showing no fear, he jumped on Tyson from the get-go, and with every passing round, Douglas only grew stronger. He showed good lateral movements, popping Tyson with jabs, hitting him with one-two combinations that became more and more earth-shattering. In the fourth round, Tyson had the same look I had when I came home and realized Sharleen was history. The crowd in the bar couldn't believe it, and I couldn't either, but then it really started to sink in: Tonight and tomorrow and the day after, I'd be sleeping alone. Tears were rolling down my face. Fuck, not again, I thought to myself, and a few brown eyes fell upon me, and I began hearing whispers about the *gringo* who bet a small fortune on Tyson.

Over at the far end of the bar, Tito was hugging a pock-marked yet gorgeous woman in a red dress. He bought her a drink with three cherries. He was grinning and cheering wildly, overjoyed by what he was seeing on the TVs.

"Fuck, these things just don't happen," I said out loud, but no one cared.

I began feeling sorry for Mike. He'd never known defeat. He'd always won, just like Sharleen had always come back. That was how it was supposed to be, so in that way I needed Tyson to knock the shit out of Douglas and win. That would set things right, I believed, back to their proper course. If Mike did what he always did, Sharleen would be back in my bed tonight.

In the eighth round, a miracle happened—a Tyson up-percut knocked down Douglas. I jumped, smiled, pumped my fist in the air. Who cared about $500? Sharleen was coming back!

But in the next round, Douglas was steady on his feet, popping the jab, keeping Tyson at bay. And I'd really broken down by then. Tyson was a goner. I just knew it. Sharleen was a goner, too.

In the tenth round, Mike fell and hit the canvas hard. The ten-count started. The ref, in Tyson's face, yelled, "One! Two!"

The ref's fingers matched his words. Tyson, flat on his back, gazed up at the ref in disbelief. How could this have happened?

"Three! Four!"

Iron Mike no longer appeared to be carved out of iron.

His body looked human as he rolled to his side and got himself on all fours. The ref expressed *five* and *six* with his fingers and shouted words out. Tyson had four seconds to get back up, but he needed his mouthpiece, which had been punched out and lay on the mat. Tyson clawed at it. The ref's fingers went from seven to eight. Tyson wasn't going to quit. He had every intention of keeping on. Finally, with the mouthpiece back in place but hanging like a pacifier, Tyson raised himself up, but it was too late. The count had reached ten, the ref waving off the bout. The ref even hugged poor Mike Tyson, who looked punch-drunk and miserable.

Tito yelled, "Yes! Yes! Oh, *Dios*! Yes!"

A voice said, "*Mira, como llora el gringo.*" It was a guy who'd noticed I was sobbing.

Real quick, it got real quiet, and I could hear the talk.

"*Porque esta llorando?*"

"He must've bet on Tyson."

"I wonder how much he lose?"

"He probably bet the whole house. Poor *hombre*."

"His *vieja* is going to kill him. *Lo va a mata*."

I wiped the tears away using Sharleen's underwear. An old-timer with wrinkles that made me think of aerial photographs of the Grand Canyon straight-out asked, "*Oye, amigo*, how much you out?"

Then it began like a chorus: "*Una cerveza para mi pobre amigo*." And, one by one, Mexican guys were buying me drinks. Even two of the women came over and put their arms around me and twirled my hair around their painted fingernails. They were going to make it okay, they thought. They were going to raise me from the dead with their skimpy outfits, their hugs, their kisses.

Then I heard whispering in my ear, but it wasn't from either of the women. It was Tito, saying, "Man, we gotta get out of here."

"Why?" I asked.

He moved his mouth closer to me and said, "Because if it gets around that we won rather than lost big money, you and me both are gonna get our asses kicked."

"Then don't let it get around."

"I won't. It's you I'm worried about, bro. Because you're *plastered*, Lare. You're all wobbly and crying and shit—who knows *what* you'll say or do next. Seriously, man, I can just see you telling Lupita if she gets you in one of those dark corners."

"Who's Lupita?"

Tito pointed at the woman with the pockmarks. "That one," he said, and she raised her eyebrows even higher at me.

"Then let's go," I said. See, it was still all about Sharlene.

I thanked several of my new friends as we were heading out the door. In the moonlight out there, standing in the parking lot, as I tried to key open my truck's driver's side door, Tito said, "No-no, Lare. I'm driving. You drive and we'll get pulled over for sure."

"But you're Mexican, man. A cop sees you behind the wheel and you're sleeping in jail tonight."

"Doesn't matter, Lare. You can't even stand straight."

And Tito was right: I was wobbly, weaving. Not exactly like Iron Mike before he hit the canvas, but all those drinks were catching up with me.

So I let Tito drive. Shit, what other option? There was no calling Sharlene, that was for sure. And calling Tito's wife? That was out of the question.

For about a quarter of a mile, Tito drove perfectly, with no signs of cop cars ahead. Then, sure enough, he hit the brakes—because a cop car was parked in the emergency lane ahead, its blue and red lights making a big deal out of the fact that they represented the *law*.

"Make a U-turn," I said.

"You *are* plastered, Lare." Tito said.

"What do you mean?"

"Me making a U-turn would be like asking a cop to shoot me."

"Well, then we'll shoot him back," I said, and I tried to open the glove box, but Tito grabbed my arm and yanked it down.

"Don't be stupid, *compadre*," he said. "Try to pretend you're not so drunk."

"Fine," I said, and I noticed Tito had taken his foot off the brake, my truck rolling forward, toward the cop car, outside of which were *two* cops.

"What are you doing, man?" I asked Tito.

"Going for it."

"*You're* drunk."

"Maybe so. But sometimes you gotta be confident."

And he let the truck continue to roll ahead. One of the cops, white as hell and thick-headed, was questioning a guy, shining a flashlight in his face. As we grew closer you could tell the guy was both scrawny and Mexican, and the other cop had a flashlight too, which he was shining at us. Still, Tito pressed on, even slowed down to let the second cop study us as we passed, which that cop did, keeping his eyes on Tito as long as Tito was in his line of sight. There was hatred on that cop's face, too—hatred for Tito, I was sure. In this cop's eyes, I was fine, even though I wanted to use the .22 to show him who was boss.

Either way, he didn't gesture or point to have us pull over.

"Confidence, baby," Tito said after we were well in the clear.

"Or luck," I said.

Then he turned onto a road that headed west even though our neighborhood was south of us.

"Where you going?" I asked.

"The bookie's," he said. "If there's one thing I know, *hombre*, it's you collect your big winnings as soon as possible. Otherwise these bookies—they leave town, sometimes for good, or they say they forgot about your bet and never wrote it down. Or they tell you *they* were just arrested and that you and they both have to lay low. Or they *were* arrested and you *do* have to lay low. And how're you gonna collect twenty-grand-plus from a bookie who's in jail? Go to the cops and say, 'He owes me?'"

Tito went on even longer talking about how to collect winnings from bookies, but to be honest, things got fuzzy from then on. If the drinks had been kicking in just after we'd left the bar, they were now taking me to blackout territory. I do *kind* of remember trying to take the .22 out of the glove box, but Tito saying, "No, man. If anyone's using that gun, it's me." But that comes back now as hazy. The next thing I remember for sure is we were in the bookie's house, which, as it turned out, was a trailer. It stunk in there, too, though mostly from bacon grease. And the bookie, an old guy, maybe half-Mexican, maybe an Italian who'd spent lots of time in the sun, was yelling at Tito, "WHERE AM I GONNA GET TWENTY-ONE GRAND?"

"I don't know, man," was how Tito answered. "You're the bookie—that's your problem."

"Not exactly," the bookie said. He was drunk also, slurring his words. "If I don't got it," he said, "I don't got it."

"Oh, you got it," Tito said, and he pointed a gun at the guy's face—my .22.

"Tito, there's only like eighteen K in my kitty," the guy said. "Swear to goddamn Jesus Christ. But I tell you what. If you agree to call it even at eighteen grand, I'll give every last dollar of it."

And that's when the arguing in Spanish happened. I remember a few choice cuss words—*joder, coño, carajo*—and at one point, the phrase *que te den por culo*, but other than that, I was too drunk and they were speaking too fast for me to know what they said.

And then, from what I remember, we were behind the bookie's house. This was when I realized his trailer was only a single-wide but his backyard was an entire desert. We must be fifty miles east, I kept thinking. I also kept thinking, But living out here is smart when you're a bookie? For his part, the bookie had a steel shovel and was digging all these holes in the stony sand. He kept saying, "It's here somewhere. Maxwell House. One of those newer blue plastic ones. You know, for the French roast."

At one point, out of breath from digging, he stopped and looked at me and apparently noticed Sharleen's G-string around my neck. He seemed all set to comment about it when Tito jabbed the .22 even closer to his face and said, "Keep digging, *pequeño*."

"But I just wanted to ask your pal something," the guy said.

"*Dig*," Tito said.

It was after Tito fired the second bullet that the guy dug up the blue plastic can. Very soon after. And the guy handed over three wads he assured Tito was eighteen grand "at least." Tito flipped through them clumsily, keeping the .22 aimed, then crammed all three wads into his pocket. He kept the .22 aimed at the guy as the three of us walked around the lit side of the guy's trailer to what I figured the guy called his front yard. Kept it aimed decently as we got in my truck. Handed it to me and told me to keep it aimed at the guy, then started my truck, and we sped off, spitting gravel.

I remember being sure, as I pointed the barrel at the center of my truck's rear window, that any second the guy would shoot my tires flat, if not me. Then shoot both me and Tito dead and take back the cash and bury it again in the plastic can, after he'd buried us first.

But then, after I could no longer see the guy, I remember thinking about Sharlene. About how bad it would be when I'd get home and she—again—wouldn't be there. How hollow my footsteps on my floor would sound, all that.

But then I realized what would be even worse: If she *were* home, and she learned I'd won eighteen grand in a bet, and she and I ended up together.

Because you'd always suspect the money was why, I thought.

You'd try to believe *you* were why, I thought.

But you'd always know the money was.

Then I remember Tito pulling up to my house, taking the wads of cash out of his pocket, handing them to me.

This was as I was studying my house with all its lights off, without Sharlene's Mercury parked in my driveway, without Sharlene anywhere in sight.

"You don't want half?" I asked.

"It's your money, Lare. I mean, you bought the scratcher, and you said to bet on Douglas. I don't want to be an asshole about the whole thing."

And what got me even more right then was that it was clear, from the drunken look on his face, and from the fact that he'd kept my truck running even though it was in park, that he wanted to keep sitting there, talking with me. That he didn't want to face his wife, not anytime soon, not with her thinking he was now even more of a loser when it came to drinking and gambling and life in general.

And for a while right then, as I put the .22 back in my glove box, I again believed that, maybe, somehow, Sharlene might still come back.

So I handed the cash back to Tito and said, "I want you to have it. All of it. If you don't want it, give it to your wife. So she'll see the time she spent with you was a good investment."

"Seriously, bro?" he said, and he was trying to act as if he wasn't excited, as if he didn't want all of it for himself or for her, as if he didn't believe it might fix what was still left between them.

But I knew he was excited, and I knew what he believed. And I still believed I'd see Sharlene again. So there I sat, beside him, in my gas-guzzling truck, saying to him, "Yes, my friend. Seriously."

AURAS

ELIZABETH P. GLIXMAN

I was not a natural beauty like Farrah Fawcett in *Charlie's Angels* or my friend Muffy. I had to iron my hair to make it straight like that English model Twiggy's hair. My nose was too wide, and my lips were too thin. I saw the way guys looked at beautiful girls. They didn't look at me that way.

My mother said, "Lisa, you are beautiful in a Rubens way." She was referring to the painter Rubens who lived in the sixteen hundreds. I knew she was trying to make me feel better, but in my mind, those women were fat. "Large," said my mother, but to me, there was no difference. I was a large, fat girl.

Worse, for me, school was boring. The dress code at the school my mother paid for left no room for self-expression. It only added to the bleakness of the daily routine. We were not allowed to groom ourselves to attract boys. All three hundred girls, ages six to eighteen, wore gray wool skirts most of the school year and dresses with proper necklines that showed no flesh and hemlines that were no longer fashionable, especially during the warmer months. Dangling earrings and nylon stockings were not allowed. Anything three-dimensional that felt, looked like, or smelled like it had power to awaken the senses and dull the intellect was banished from any and all school property.

To make life even duller, school days started off with a Bible reading or a quote from a person few of us in upper school study hall had ever heard of. For example, the week the school was celebrating the virtues of moderation, our headmaster, Mr. Bingford, started the day by saying, "Girls, moderation is the key to success in all aspects of life. Remember the words of William Cowper the poet: *With caution taste the sweet Circean cup: He that sips often, at last drinks it up.*"

And since my world had long ago proved imperfect, I, along with my classmates, had to sit in uncomfortable starched blouses and scratchy dry-cleaned skirts, listening to this guy. I would pretend to listen while I daydreamed about what smoking marijuana would be like, or about whether Frank Zappa was a God or not, and how I could get my mother to let me wear nylons to the next school mixer.

Lucky for me, I had my one good friend, Muffy. Muffy had a thing for tall guys. She'd given away her *Mamas and Papas* album to a guy she'd met at an amusement park when her family was on vacation in Florida—she always took her records and a portable record player on family trips, as it was the only way her mother could get her to join the family.

"How could you give *California Dreaming* away?" I asked her after that trip. "And to someone you knew for only a few minutes!"

"He was six-two," she replied, like that made it okay.

I guess we all have our *things*, as my mother put it.

My thing was auras. I started seeing colors around people

after my father died, way before everyone started talking about auras or colors.

In any case, the thirty girls in our class were divided into several cliques. Muffy and I were in a group all our own. We weren't cotillion material, and our parents didn't have summer homes at the Vineyard, Nantucket, or the Republican coast of Maine. We weren't descended from the Mayflower. But one thing we did have was bucks—we were, as one girl in our class put it, "nouveau rich." My mother and I lived on the settlement we'd received after the death of my father in a freak industrial accident, the horror of which had made us even wealthier. Muffy's parents' money had come only from making investments. Maybe because we sensed we were being judged about this, Muffy and I were the most rebellious of all the girls. You could say we were juvenile delinquents, or close to it.

Soon after our freshman year and all the way to senior year in high school, we were nicknamed "The Terrible Two" by Mr. Bingford, who always wore a little red bow tie and a tweed jacket. And we *were* terrible, I'll admit now. We acted immaturely. In fact, in the middle of our junior year, Mr. Bingford said to us, "I have never seen two more disrespectful young ladies in my entire career at Putters. No one has ever wrapped the teacher's rest room in toilet paper before, and no one has ever hidden at the boys' school after a mixer, making their classmates wait three hours on the bus until the girls in question were found drunk in a crew boat on the river. You girls are a *disgrace*. I'll have you know you're confined to study hall for every free period for the next six months, and you won't be able to attend another mixer for the rest of the semester."

With that, he walked away from us, looking like he was on his way to a stroke.

"I guess we're kind of in trouble this time," Muffy said.

I grinned wholeheartedly, and we both laughed.

Then Muffy puckered her lips into a small, round hole as she imitated him:

"*You*, Ms. Monfford, are definitely the worst of the two. Because you're the gang leader. Which is probably because your ancestors are from Northern Ireland."

From then on, Muffy said she'd use this statement in her defense if things got worse at school. She'd taped that whole conversation with Mr. Bingford on a small recorder she kept in her blazer pocket. Muffy had always been prepared; there were several lawyers in her family.

By then Muffy knew that I believed in auras, so she asked me if I saw any around Mr. Bingford. What I saw was bad news for him. His aura was fading and gray. He was sick and he didn't know it, I said. The last time I saw that color around someone—my fifth-grade dance teacher Mrs. Simons—she'd died three months later.

• • •

Because Muffy and I knew we were under scrutiny at school, we decided, after that meeting with Mr. Bingford, to do our indiscretions off school property. We had to let it rip somewhere.

On our way home from school that day, we stopped at the corner market so we could tease Jason Ridley. Jason Ridley went to public school, was seventeen, and had a blossoming case of acne. His face turned bright red whenever Muffy and

I bought sanitary napkins right in front of him, the redness of his face making his zits look worse.

"Let's see if we can make those zits pop!" Muffy whispered to me after we'd arrived at the market that day. She went in, and I followed her, and she yelled, "Where are the *Stay Fragrant* Napkins?"

I leaned on the cash register counter batting my overly mascaraed eyes. I smiled at Jason flirtatiously.

"My friend wants to know where the Stay Fragrant ones are," I said.

Jason's mouth dropped, and he began to stutter. Then he walked away and, in a minute or so, returned with the right napkins, which we paid for before we walked out of the store laughing.

"I'm going to pee in my pants," Muffy said. "Did you see how *red* his face got?"

And that was just one little thing we did. We also decided to read D. H. Lawrence's *Lady Chatterley's Lover* on the phone to each other at night. It was like listening to soap opera installments on the radio. Mr. Bingford had told us about the hours he'd spent listening to Hardy Boys mysteries on the radio when he was a boy and how it had shaped his life, so we wanted to shape our lives too, so we read to each other after we'd complain about not knowing any boys except for Jason.

"This is pathetic," Muffy said one night. "No boys, how are we going to learn anything?"

She'd also often complained about her mother making macaroni and cheese again for dinner, and about her father going away on business trips to Singapore. As she put it, "My mom keeps slamming doors—she is *not* a communicator."

In any event, to get in the mood for our nightly readings, we would dress up like loose women, or at least what our idea of loose women was. We wore our bathrobes over our outfits in case either of our mothers pushed open one of our doors to check in on us.

"What are you wearing?" I said to Muffy one night before she began to read.

"My fishnet stockings, a black garter belt, and a slinky pink satin bathrobe. You?"

To make my outfit sound as vulgar as possible, I said, "I have on red nail polish and pearls."

"Big deal," Muffy said. "My mother wears that to go shopping."

"Hang on," I said. "I'm also wearing a leopard skin see-through bodysuit with a plunging neckline that shows my ample cleavage, and I have super-long eyelashes, and fat red pouty lips, and there's *glitter* on every other one of my nails."

"What about the shoes?" Muffy asked.

"Black three-inch kick-em-in-the-butt stilettos," I said proudly.

"Not bad," Muffy said.

I'd been poring over Fredrick's of Hollywood catalogs under the covers when I was supposed to be studying French. I always wanted to impress Muffy with my knowledge of womanhood.

And our nightly readings did help feed my demanding imagination, but I needed more. Sometimes I wore nylons under my argyle knee socks to school. When school was over, I'd go to this tree across from the school parking lot, whip off my socks, put on the high heels I stashed in my locker, grab a cigarette, take the number six bus, and go downtown to walk around and feel like a woman. I walked and wiggled and used my eyes to flirt shyly with every passing man, young or old. Claremont was a small town, population six thousand. There weren't too many strangers, but I was sure no one recognized me. Years later, Mrs. Gowan, who ran the Swiss Chalet Donut Shop, told me she and her husband saw me wiggling about the streets in the afternoons—and that they didn't tell my mother, and that they got into fights about my behavior.

But that was years later. Now, with Muffy and I in high school, we began to think we had some kind of deviant sexual disorder.

"Seriously, how many seventeen-year-old girls think about sex so much?" Muffy once asked me.

"A lot," I said, and I quoted statistics from *The Journal of Adolescent Psychology*. My mother's sister was a psychologist, so I had sources. The statistics made us feel better—about deviancy.

Finally, we graduated. Mr. Bingford, who was quite sick by now, his aura getting weaker and paler, was ecstatic. He sent us cards and gave us each a copy of *The Oxford Book of English Verse*. "Get some poetry in your souls," was the message in the card I received. "Good luck to my favorite Putter girl."

"You'd think he was fond of you," my mother said when I showed her the inscription. She added, "But we know better, don't we, Lisa?"

• • •

Muffy then went to BU to major in drama. I went to a liberal arts college well upstate in New York and majored in English. During my first semester at school, my libido was submerged under the weight of achieving. I wasn't a social butterfly like Muffy. When I'd been with her, I'd become another part of myself. Left alone, I studied, apparently programmed to please my mother. That meant I would be successful in school and then pay my way through life, alone if necessary, like my mother.

Anyhow, Muffy and I didn't talk on the phone anymore. Neither her parents nor my mother trusted us with a credit card. Her mother had found the clothes she'd ordered for our nightly readings and said no more access to things she couldn't handle. Her mother and mine had a hard time accepting that we were on the verge of womanhood.

"It isn't S and M," I said to my mother over the phone, after she let me know *she'd* been aware of my secret wearing of slutty clothes. "It's lingerie. You wear lingerie around the house on Sunday mornings."

"That's not lingerie. Plus what do you know about S and M?"

I ignored the question, knowing this would drive her nuts.

"Go figure adult thinking," I then wrote to Muffy in a letter. "Adult thinking has no logic to it."

"Adults are afraid of raw passion," Muffy wrote back. "Maybe they think we'll catch it like some kind of virus that will eat us alive!"

"It's too late." I wrote back. "We've already caught it."

And I tried to sound self-assured in that letter, but in reality, I knew far less then Muffy about passion.

And pigs knew more about soap than I knew about lust

and sex. I'd kissed only one boy in my entire life, in the third grade, when my mother had made me do so in thanks for a valentine.

Then came winter break of our freshman year in college. Muffy was coming home to visit her family for the holidays; I thought it would be like old times, that I'd break loose from being all academic and get wild with Muffy.

Instead, I listened quietly to Muffy's news. I'd gone to her house on Christmas Eve, and in front of the tree decorated with white lights and tinsel and gold-plated angels, she said, "I met someone." Her eyes sparkled and flashed like the blinking lights. She was gleeful. For my part, I had that familiar sinking feeling in my stomach, the same one I'd had right before midterm exams in high school. A sign that I didn't understand the material.

But what worried me most were the auras I saw around Muffy. Bright red halos of light flashed around her feet, and crimson streaks shot across her abdomen—pink and yellow every time she smiled. Lightning strikes also leapt outward from her hands.

What could this all mean? It didn't feel good.

"Tell me more," I said to her, even though I wanted to run out of the room screaming.

"Someone *special*," she said, and if you asked me, she looked dazed, as if she'd been on an ice floe in the Arctic without food for weeks.

"Wow," I said, faking happiness. I needed a cigarette. I'd started to smoke my second night in my dorm room. But of course here there was no cigarette in sight.

"He's so cool," Muffy said. "You'd just die if you met him."

I had visions of Muffy screaming, like young girls did at Beatles concerts.

"You would *die*," she repeated.

I was dying already, of course.

"He looks like Mick Jagger," she added. "But taller."

"No," I said calmly.

"Yes!" she screamed.

That did it. I bit my nails feverishly. Muffy had always gotten angry with me for doing that, but now she didn't notice—that's how into him and out of me she was.

"He goes to school with you?" I asked, trying to make polite conversation.

"No, no, no," she said dramatically. "I dropped out of school! I'm living in Maine! I'm living in an old farmhouse with Max!"

"That's his name?" I asked. "Max?"

"Yes! Max Von Schlemenheimer!"

Things were going too fast. Last I'd talked with Muffy, she was going to be a marine biologist.

"You're *living with* this guy?" I asked. "Your parents are going crazy, right?"

"His hair is down to his *waist*," Muffy said. "Can you believe it?"

I believed it all right. But mostly I was jealous. While I'd been studying whether or not it was good to use semicolons, Muffy had been learning about actual life. Had she done the deed? I wondered. Had she actually *had sex*?

I wanted to ask her this right off, but I didn't. And the look on her face assured me she didn't want me to either.

• • •

Instead, that winter break with Muffy was one long conversation about the wonders of Maine. In between her monologues, she went shopping with her mother or was on the phone with "Maxy."

But with a name like Max Von Schlemenheimer, I'd kill myself. And how cute could he be? He was probably short, with a mustache. He was probably a Nazi. How could Muffy do this to me?

After winter break, Muffy wrote me weekly and filled me in on her life. Max had dropped out of graduate school, and they were living off the land completely. He'd been at BU's School of Public Communication in hopes of getting into broadcasting, and she thought his choosing the land over school was so "pastoral."

I thought it was all so stupid. In my mind, people needed supermarkets. When it came to me, jealousy was rearing its ugly head.

"Everyone's dropping out of school," I wrote back.

Muffy answered, "Have you ever thought about it?"

I really hadn't. I liked to finish the things I started, and besides, my mother would've had a cow.

And as I tried to finish the semester, Muffy continued to write long letters to me. "He was lonely," she once wrote. "He needed a warm body to wrap around himself on those cold Maine country nights, when all you can hear is the sound of your boots crushing snow as you walk to the outhouse at two A.M. on nights that are nothing but cruel."

Parts of Muffy's letters, I have to admit, reminded me of *Doctor Zhivago*. The cold that brought frost to the lover's eyebrows and nostrils and hung like sparkling diamonds from cabin roofs. The shivering together when the coal was gone. The smoke rising and curling from chimneys, the sense of isolation, the passions that grew hotter when temperatures were well below zero.

Oh, the poetry of it all.

Yes, you could say that what I had was envy. What I really wanted, I didn't have—Muffy had it. She was getting to yield and quiver before I was; I was sure of this. Worse, she hadn't mentioned anything sexy about any of it, hadn't told any details to me, her best friend. In fact, in those days when we'd dressed like sluts in our separate beds together, we'd agreed that whoever did it first would tell the other immediately, within twenty-four hours, cross your heart and hope to die.

Was it possible she *wasn't* doing it? No, I told myself. Something *is* happening in their bed, something exciting and grand and mature.

So it was like she no longer "cared to share." Like she now thought I couldn't understand.

Somehow, though, alone and feeling sure I was way behind when it came to social and sexual development, I got through another semester of Great American Fiction, Western Civilization, English Comp II, Light and Science, and countless hours of loneliness. I ate pounds of lemon meringue pie, shepherd's pie, chocolate cream pie, Eskimo Pies. In fact, when it came to eating Eskimo Pies, I'd also want to feel the Maine cold, even if it was only in my throat. I would've eaten rough drafts of my papers if I'd thought that would make me feel better, but best were things that were cold or gooey, therefore somehow emotionally soothing. I was eating to rid myself of the thought that Muffy was experiencing what I was merely reading about.

• • •

Finally summer vacation arrived. Thanks to sheer boredom, I was eager to see Muffy. I got to Union, Maine, around seven-thirty one evening, after a hot, ten-hour bus ride. I had finished eating two apple pies, those small ones in the cardboard boxes with the see-through windows. I had not graduated to eating a regular size one yet. My mother had told me I'd do that after my first failed relationship.

"How can you be so sure?" I'd asked her.

"It happened to me," she'd said. "And statistically it happens to most women."

The bus rolled to a halt in Union at the U.S. Post Office, where the bus stop consisted of a small sign and a bench. Dressed in a loose-fitting, yellow-and-white checkered shift and barefoot, Muffy was there to greet me, her olive skin glowing with health. A lanky young man with hair to his waist and a handlebar moustache stood beside her—Max Von Whatshisname, I presumed. He had a huge orange aura swirling around his head. As much as I hated him, I noticed how his smile affected me; it made me feel as if I'd eaten one of those lemon jelly candies that were sweet and sour and satisfying. When he wrapped his arm around Muffy, his aura grew larger and pulsated. I felt like smiling when I looked at them. I decided to give him a chance. It was the end of August, and everything, not only the grass, was dry, dusty, and crunchy.

"No rain for the last three weeks," Max said as he grabbed under my arms and swung me off the bus, then round and round in circles while I clutched my knapsack in one hand and held onto him tightly with the other.

"This is Max," Muffy said, and Max put me down on the sidewalk. "This is my best friend, Lisa," she said to him.

In less than one second, his eyes scanned my body from head to toe. I blushed. To avoid his gaze I viewed the surroundings, including an oak tree with pendulous arms, its bark thick and tough, like a rhino's skin. Someone had carved hearts and lovers' names in it, and behind it was a red brick building with a wooden sign that read TOWN HALL, UNION, MAINE, 1702.

There was also the small post office, and three boarded-up buildings, a convenience store with a Budweiser sign and a clock in the window with huge numbers on it, and a hardware store with heavy-looking metal rakes on its front porch.

Opposite these buildings was a small, two-story cottage with dandelions covering the lawn between it and the street. Hanging from an aluminum beach chair in the center of this lawn was a sign that read *Wicker Furniture, T-shirts, and Card Readings*. And beyond the center of town there were woods and woods for as far as I could see, and to get a ticket out of town, Muffy had told me, you needed to drive to Waterville, an hour away.

"Paradise, huh?" Muffy asked me now. "No shops or bars—it's quiet, and it's home."

"But not exactly booming," I said, and Muffy not only didn't answer, she didn't even glance my way because she was busy being goosed by Max.

So it was then that I decided for sure that I didn't like Max. His orange aura, I decided, meant he was dripping with ill intent.

A horn beeped. In front of the post office was now a very

old pickup truck. Isaiah, Muffy explained, Max's best friend, was waiting to give us a ride to Muffy and Max's place.

Isaiah, it turned out, didn't speak much. When he did, you could see his toothless grin. He was a townie who'd lived in Union all his life.

In the fading light of day, we drove to the farmhouse that Muffy and Max called home. I watched the rolling landscape blur past with its rundown shacks, rusty tractors, and barking dogs chewing their skin raw. This area had once been farmland with families working the soil and proudly struggling to survive. That battle had clearly been lost. This rural America was beautiful, that was true, but like a cave down in the ocean, it possessed a coldness and indifference to human suffering. The rebels who now inhabited it—college dropouts, hippies, people who listened to "the beat of a different drummer"—would not stay forever; they'd leave it for hot and cold running water and toilets.

Max was sitting between Muffy and me in the back of the truck, one arm around each of us.

"We bought this baby for fifty dollars from Isaiah's father, Alton," he said. "He's the road commissioner," he added, and he squeezed me like I was an orange he was going to juice.

I gave him a dirty look, and Muffy said, "Relax. Max is harmless."

What am I doing here? I thought. *Why* am I here?

Then Muffy said, "Here we are, home." I removed Max's hand from my arm—it had traveled during the ride—and looked at the place, a farmhouse that was not only the sole building on the dead-end road we were on but was also in significant disrepair. Two front steps were missing; the other six leaned to the right. The windows had no glass, and only some of them were covered with plastic. One match to the dry shingles would've created the quickest house fire in history.

Smiling as if she enjoyed living in a dump at the end of a dead-end street, Muffy led me into the kitchen. I examined the black stove with cast iron frying pans on two of its burners. It was sturdy as an ox, this stove; if it could talk, it would have many stories to tell about the eighteen hundreds. I saw bright red zipping down across the kitchen like a comet, which I was sure meant more than one person had suffered severe burns here.

To change the subject in my mind, I asked Muffy, "So you cook on this thing?"

"Sometimes," she said, and right then a pair of flies began buzzing around my head. "We usually eat vegetables from the garden and canned meat and rice from the government." She opened the screen door, shooed out the flies. "You know," she said. "Surplus."

And right then, a goat walked into the kitchen, approached me, and attempted to nuzzle my crotch.

"How's my baby, Mabel?" Muffy said.

"Hi, Mabel," I said.

"Are you hungry?" Muffy asked.

"Yes," I said—just before she grabbed a carrot and gave it to Mabel.

Then she, Muffy, handed me a plate of cooked summer squash, from a pot that had been sitting on the stove. "Have as much as you like!"

I waited for an offer of chicken or rice or milk, but none came. Squash was even dessert.

And it was dry and tasteless, like the dust from the dirt

road that had blown onto my face during the ride here. "Thank you," I said after I'd finished.

All this time Max and Isaiah had been upstairs moving around what sounded like dressers and chairs.

"They're getting your room ready," Muffy said after the look on my face must've asked, *Now* what's going on? Then she took me upstairs to a room that consisted of an old mattress on a very worn hardwood floor.

There was a vase of wildflowers next to the mattress.

"Isn't this great?" Muffy said. "Look at the view!"

I looked past the curled-down plastic that was no longer masking-taped to the molding. Muffy was right. The view of the mountains was spectacular. The sun was setting, and the mountains were in rosy splendor with the trees silhouetted by the dimming light.

We listened to the sounds of the crickets. Even if all you ate for a month was squash, I tried to tell myself, it was pretty great to be here.

Muffy stayed upstairs long enough to say, "I know this isn't what you imagined, Lisa, but I can see you feel at home here. It's good to see you again."

And then she walked out of the room.

After she'd closed the door as far as it would close and was halfway downstairs, she called, presumably to me, "Good night."

. . .

I was tired. I decided to go to sleep. Within minutes of when I put my head on the pillow, I heard footsteps on the stairs, loud, heavy footsteps that sounded like the person had a large peg leg. A light went on in the room next to mine. The light went off, and the footsteps came closer to where I was sleeping. I smelled beer. In the moonlight, I saw a half-naked, obese man with a large belly and a Santa Claus beard.

"Who the hell are you?" I said. "Get out of here!"

"Oh," he said. "Sorry. Didn't see you there."

He had a turquoise aura, and I had no idea what that meant. "Did you hear me?" I said.

"Fine," he said. "If I'm not your bag, I dig."

He walked out and, from the sound of things, lumbered back downstairs, where Muffy and Max's bedroom was. For a while I heard nothing down there, or anywhere except far away outside, where anyone could hear crickets.

Then I heard Muffy making very loud noises, long and drawn-out moans, screams, and finally, sighs. Then I heard her laugh, and then I heard two other voices, Max's and apparently the bearded fat guy's. And then, after what seemed like a chair or small nightstand hitting the wooden floor of that bedroom, Muffy apparently quivering, then, again, moaning and screaming.

I covered my head with my pillow before I heard any sighs. I cried myself to sleep wondering what happened to our blood sister pact, and when I felt less betrayed, I began to wonder what was it like to quiver like that.

• • •

The next morning I woke early to see the sun rise. There really is nothing like the country in the hours before dawn. Dew on the grass, the birdsong, the clean air. Serenity was filling me with a sense of transcendence, the house quiet except for an occasional snore. Pink color was creeping up into the sky. Mabel, I noticed downstairs, was chewing the kitchen's screen door.

I put on my sneakers and headed out there. Muffy had written to me about a waterfall "down the road" where she and Max went swimming naked, and I figured it couldn't be far. This is freedom, I told myself. Take advantage. You need to clean up anyway. I went back inside, found soap and a towel in the bathroom, went back out and began down the road.

The road was flat for several hundred feet and then took a dive downward, twisting and turning. To keep from falling, I focused on my feet. I was a warrior walking fearlessly to my goal. I looked up often enough to see I was passing birches with their silver-green leaves, purple and blue asters, goldenrods heralding the coming of fall. A rabbit whizzed by. I could see an end to the road and a hunter's cabin, where Isaiah was standing, caressing his long black beard. He saw me and waved. He had this look on his face that promised he was harmless.

"I'm looking for the waterfall," I told him.

"My brother can take you," he said, and he pointed at a stand of trees north of us. "He lives over there."

And right then, appearing inside the stand of trees, was a man who, in my eyes, had an aura of pure gold. This man looked at me and asked, "Can I help you?"

"You can tell me how to get to the waterfall?"

"I can do better then that," he said. "I can take you there."

His green eyes landed on mine, and I was shocked—because I already knew I would follow him anywhere. I walked behind him silently and serenely, even though my legs felt weak. His legs took powerful strides, his feet meeting the ground squarely, his long arms swinging along like an athlete's. At one point he bent down, picked up a blade of grass, and chewed on it.

"I like to stop and hear the wind," he said. "It can teach you a lot."

That was it—I was now all his.

We walked ahead, veering off the road and into thick woods. I felt like a rabbit or fox, in any case a creature that longed to live with a mate in a cavern. After our path dropped toward the waterfall, I felt joy like I never had. The man was silent, but I could hear his thoughts. The gold became tinged with indigos and violet. This guy, I told myself, is his own light show.

"Last one in is a monkey's uncle," he said, and he pulled his T-shirt over his head, unzipped his pants, and, naked, dove headfirst into the deep, heavenly pond.

I stood watching as he surfaced and swam around. His long hair was flattened against his head and shoulders. He did the crawl in circles, water droplets on him catching the morning light, and again he was back to pure gold.

"Come in," he said. "The water feels even better than you'd think."

He encouraged me with a gesture of his arm.

"Don't be afraid," he said. "Nothing in here can hurt you."

I watched his aura for a few moments: still gold. I dropped my jeans down on the woods' pine-needled floor. I pulled off my jersey, tossed it onto a branch of a nearby bush, then glided into the water like a clumsy swan.

"Here we are," he said. "Here's an apple."

He pretended to throw an apple, and I pretended to catch it. Pretending to hold it, I said, "Now what do we do?"

"Toss it back," he said, and he pretended to catch it and take a bite from it.

"Just call me Eve," I said, and as he swam toward me, he grinned.

A SCARAB FOR NORMANDY

GERALD ELIAS

Harmonicas? Sam Shanowitz thought. Why would Facebook bombard him with ads for harmonicas? Ads for hair growth and for women available through Platinum Singles—those made sense. But harmonicas?

Then he vaguely recalled the conversation he'd had while waiting in line at McDonald's, with a total stranger who mentioned having played the harmonica when he was a boy. *That's* why, he thought now, and he had no doubt his phone was an eavesdropper.

And then there was the unsolicited third-class mail, congratulating him on being "pre-selected" for credit card eligibility, or for AARP membership, or urging him to fill out a survey to express his outrage against the opposing political party, or begging donations to any of dozens of worthy and not-so-worthy philanthropic organizations.

And the emails that unaccountably forged their way through his spam protection from Eastern European women promising to satisfy his every sexual fantasy.

Disgusted, he powered down his laptop. He poured the rest of his coffee down the sink, put on his jacket, grabbed his phone, and left his apartment, double-checking to make sure it was locked behind him.

As he did most days since Laura's death, he stopped at the McDonald's on the corner for his breakfast combo meal to go. The line today was long, longer than usual, and he arrived at the museum barely on time. Priding himself on never being late, he vaulted up the stone steps two at a time. He was out of breath—but right on time—when he stepped into the office.

"Morning, Sam."

"Hi, Harriet."

Harriet was the person he knew best at work. She was attractive for her age, bright and always kind, but light years away from replacing Laura. She handed him his lanyard with its attached ID tag: HI, I'M SAM. WELCOME TO THE MET.

"Catch your breath," she said, and she pulled a lacy handkerchief out of her sleeve where she always seemed to have one, and handed it to him.

"Thanks," he said, blotting his forehead. "I'll launder it by tomorrow."

"Keep it," she said. "I've got a bunch. Happy to share." She smiled at him. Was it suggestive? Probably not—by now she must've figured out he was a hopeless romantic for the woman he'd married back before people had all fallen in love with their phones.

He smiled at her somewhat wearily, walked up the steps to the Egyptian Antiquities Gallery, where, since Laura's death, he'd been a guide. When he'd started, he hadn't needed the money as much as he did now; work back then had simply been a way for him to pass time since there was no Laura to look forward to eating with, sleeping with, and doing pretty much everything with.

"Don't you slip now, brother," Freddie, one of the custodians, said. "It's still wet."

"Thanks, man," Sam said. "Have a good one."

That morning's first tour group—they were from France—was early and full of questions. It wasn't long before one of them asked the question he heard almost every day: "How much is Cleopatra's scarab worth?"

His answer was rote, but as usual, he tried to make it sound spontaneous:

"You know the Queen of England's Crown Jewels? Well, that's costume jewelry compared to Cleopatra's scarab."

After the *ah*s of incredulity dissipated, he continued, this time using the script he'd committed to memory.

"It is indeed a breathtaking piece of two-thousand-year-old jewelry. In ancient Egyptian religion, the scarab, in the form of the dung beetle, was an important symbol. The beetle's hieroglyph was also used to write the name *Khepri*, a divinity who the Egyptians believed rolled the morning sun over the eastern horizon. Because the scarab hieroglyph also refers to profound ideas, like those of existence and growth, the beetle itself was a favorite form used for amulets for centuries of Egyptian history."

And then it came, the mildly cynical follow-up question: "How do you know the scarab was actually Cleopatra's?"

"Well, we can never know with one-hundred-percent certainty, of course, but when you look at the precious materials that were used to make it—the gold, the lapis lazuli, and the carnelian—those were the materials that only the pharaohs owned. Then there's the exquisite workmanship, which suggests a royal commission. And there are frescoes, admittedly not contemporary, showing her wearing the scarab, and documents referring to it. And archaeologists broadly agree this particular scarab is contemporary with Cleopatra's life span, from sixty-nine to thirty B.C.—so, well, among those in the know about these things, there's essentially no doubt."

With no more questions, the group thanked him politely, then followed him and listened quietly as he led them through the rest of the exhibit, then shuffled off to the Italian Renaissance.

Sam passed time best he could before the next group of tourists arrived, then the next. It was almost lunchtime when a small man wearing a smart-looking suit and fedora approached him, a man Sam recalled had been in the French entourage.

"Your presentation was highly informative," the man said.

"Thank you."

"Let me introduce myself? I am Ouchard. If I may ask one more question?"

"Certainly."

"What can you tell me of the provenance of the scarab?"

"The museum has owned the piece since 1913, I believe."

"And before?"

"I don't know, really. Why?"

"Well, to be sure it is authentic, one would have to trace ownership from the present day all the way back to Cleopatra herself. But that would be an absurdity, of course."

"Of course."

The man looked behind him, then to his right, then to his left. Voice lowered, he asked, "Might it surprise you to know that when the museum purchased the scarab in 1913, they bought it from someone who had stolen it from its rightful owner?"

"I guess it would. Are you telling me the museum engaged in an unscrupulous transaction?"

Several visitors entered the gallery, and Ouchard took notice of them.

"This room has an echo, monsieur," he said quietly. "May we talk about this over lunch? My treat. I think you will find the subject interesting . . . and to your advantage."

"I don't think so, thank you."

"Even if what I have to tell you will add a new dimension to your presentation? What have you to lose?"

The man's eyes, bearing down on him, suggested that he, too, had endured his share of loss. And Sam had to admit he himself was hungry. But it was mostly just for kicks that he said, "Okay."

• • •

Sam handed his lanyard to Harriet on his way out.

"Back in an hour," he said.

"Don't be late," she joked poorly.

Outside, Ouchard was waiting at the bottom of the stone stairs. A cold late-autumn drizzle encouraged them to walk briskly. They went to a tucked-away French bistro called Little Normandy on a quiet side street. It had been Laura's dream, unfulfilled, to visit the famous Bayeux Cathedral in Normandy. Maybe this choice of restaurant was an auspicious omen, Sam thought. Ouchard ordered baked oysters and a glass of Pinot Gris; Sam, steak frites—Laura's favorite—and a fine Bordeaux. With Ouchard paying, why not?

They engaged in small talk: weather, politics on both sides of the Atlantic, what's the world coming to? Once their meals arrived, Sam's curiosity got the best of him.

"So, what's this all about?"

"If I provided you with documents proving that the museum illegally obtained the Cleopatra scarab," Ouchard all but whispered, "what would you say?"

"I would say many things. One, I don't know you from Adam. Two, even if I did, the documents would have to be analyzed by experts for their authenticity. Three, I would wonder why you're coming to me instead of to the museum board."

"Yes, yes," Ouchard said. "Of course those things. But, you tell me, how often does a museum like this admit they acquired a treasure by deceit?"

Point taken, Sam thought to say, but instead he nodded, though barely. "But, still," he said.

"For the sake of argument, my friend, let us assume you were convinced the documents I have access to were authentic."

"Okay. Then what?"

"Then would you not want to see justice done? Would you not want to see the scarab returned to its rightful owner?"

"Hypothetically, yes. I mean, we've seen 'justice done,' as you say, with Peruvian and Native American patrimony—artifacts, ancestors' remains, returned to their rightful owners."

"So, you do understand!" Ouchard said, his eyes slightly

wider. "And what if you and I took the one step from the hypothetical and into the reality?"

"Meaning?"

"What if we returned the scarab to the rightful owner?"

Sam pushed himself away from the table. "Mr. Ouchard, I think I've heard enough cloak-and-dagger for today. Thank you for the lunch." He stood, nodded, and turned to leave.

"Mr. Shanowitz?" Ouchard said. "I beg you. Please sit down."

He knows my whole name? Sam thought. How? he wondered, but then he knew how—probably because of his damn phone.

"But why should I?" he asked. "This is all so . . . ridiculous."

"At least hear me out, Samuel. I will tell you the full story. Then, after you consider its ramifications, you'll decide."

Sam sat down, then folded his arms over his chest. "All right," he said. "But I want no part of this. Anyway, who, may I ask, is the rightful owner?"

"Why, haven't you guessed? The government of Egypt, of course. And I represent, let us say, a go-between assisting them with its retrieval."

"Why a go-between? Why doesn't an Egyptian bureaucrat talk to one here? Apples to apples."

"They have tried, sir, to no avail—believe me. They have made good faith offers to buy it but have been rebuffed at every turn, stonewalled by supremely wealthy and politically influential persons on your side, greedy persons who refuse to do what is right. Which places the Egyptian government in a position of extreme delicacy. And given the precarious political situation in the Middle East, Egypt cannot be seen to be connected with this enterprise in any way, for fear of damaging the goodwill between it as a nation and yours."

"So, why come to me? What do I have to do with all this?"

"Very simple, my friend. For several years we have admired your sincere affection for these Egyptian antiquities, and have appreciated your apparent desire to do what is right and just."

"How would you know about that?"

"About what?"

"My desire to do what is just."

Ouchard removed his phone from a pocket inside his suit jacket, set it on the table. "We have our ways, Mr. Shanowitz."

"Okay," Sam said. "Fine. Could you please just get to the point?"

Ouchard assessed Sam intently, almost threateningly. "The point is, Mr. Shanowitz, we would like you to remove the scarab from its pedestal and give it to us."

"That's absurd, Mr. Ouchard! I've never been . . . a *thief*. That's what I'd be, wouldn't I? What I should do is call the police right now. In fact, give me one reason why I shouldn't."

Ouchard sighed. Again his hand went inside his suit jacket, this time toward where a holster might be. Sam stiffened.

"Please don't be alarmed, Samuel," Ouchard said with a sympathetic smile. From a pocket inside the jacket, he removed an envelope, then placed it in front of Sam.

"This, good friend, is for you to keep. All of it. It's documentation—copies, of course—of the scarab's proper ownership going back to the eighteenth century. That is as far back as we could trace it before the trail ended. It's also fifty thousand dollars in cash—all for your time spent simply reading the documents. No strings attached, though we would appreciate your discretion."

Sam tried to keep his voice low and steady:

"And after I read the documents, then what?"

"It is simple. If you successfully help us return the scarab, a million dollars will be deposited into a Swiss account in your name."

"A million dollars? You have a million dollars?"

"Not I. The anonymous donor whom I represent has *vast* sums. But, let me assure you, the funds we will deposit on your behalf will have been completely legally obtained."

Sam stared at Ouchard's face, then looked off, at everyone but.

"This is a trap," he said. "You're from the Feds. You're trying to root out the bad apples."

"A reasonable concern," Ouchard said. "But, I assure you, I am not in the least an agent of that sort. Besides, if I were, we would be after someone with a dubious track record, whereas yours is spotless. It would be a waste of our time."

"But why me? If you want the scarab stolen, why not go to a professional? Someone who . . . rips off museums for a living."

"These questions of yours convince me that we have found the right man in you, Mr. Shanowitz. Because we asked ourselves the same ones and ultimately came to the conclusion that a professional thief—even the most successful—will have a history, a traceable history, and we cannot afford a trace. You have a clean background. Furthermore, who understands the insides of this exhibit better than you? Yes, there may be art experts with pedigrees, but for what's in that gallery, you are, because of your job, a master of sorts, and may I add, are not paid nearly what you are worth. Would you care for another glass of Bordeaux?"

Sam shook his head no. "How do I get in touch with you? I mean, when I've decided. I mean, if there's any way at all I'd do this, I'd certainly first need some time to think."

"I will call you tomorrow evening," Ouchard said. "I have your number. Mine will be untraceable. You understand that we must be discreet. Now, if you don't mind, you will leave first. You still have ten minutes before you must be back at the museum. I will have coffee and perhaps dessert. Adieu, Monsieur Shanowitz. Don't forget your envelope, please."

. . .

Sam spent the afternoon in a daze, avoiding visitors when possible, answering questions politely yet quickly when he had to.

"Sam," Harriet said on his way out.

"Yes?"

"Your lanyard, please. Are you okay? You look a little . . . pale."

He removed the lanyard and handed it to Harriet.

"Tired. Busy day."

"I hear ya. Well, have a relaxing evening."

"Yeah. You, too."

After a brisk walk home, Sam found himself in the somber comfort he'd lived in for the past thirty-two years. Thirty-two and a half, to be exact, the first twenty-six with Laura.

They'd always felt happy here. Modest, yet happy. With her, having a small one-bedroom had never bothered him. With her, for a Manhattan apartment, the place had always felt as if it had more than enough light. Yes, she'd always wanted to travel, but still, she'd always seemed as happy with him as he'd been with her.

Now the apartment felt not only too dark but shabby. The frayed fabrics on the furniture, the dusty walls, the limp houseplants. And the faucets dripped and two of the small windows would get stuck. In the winter, the heating was erratic; the air conditioner made a racket in the summer. Yes, someday he wanted a new air conditioner.

Not to mention, face it, he was getting older. Until just now, really, he'd never thought squarely about planning for his last years. Social Security, savings, which might be sufficient but might not—would that, without his pay from the museum, be all he'd need for the rest of his life? Suddenly, he felt as dilapidated as his apartment.

And if he agreed to do it, which was a big if, there were two issues: how to steal the scarab, and more important, how to not get caught.

Hypotheticals, he thought.

A mental game.

No commitments—just read the guy's documents.

And the documents, he had to admit, did appear genuine. The earliest ones handwritten, later ones typed on a typewriter. But what did he know about things of this sort? He googled the names of the various authorities on whose letterheads the documents were written, and the names of those who'd signed them. Those that he could find on the Internet were legit.

He thought about googling "successful art thefts" but realized that could be seen as incriminating evidence at some future date. He might already have left a trail by googling the names he had. Or was he being ridiculous? Maybe, he thought, but those computer experts, he was convinced, could trace everything. No, if he was going to do this, he would need to devise his plan without Google.

He slept fitfully that night, but the next day he was back at the museum as if everything were perfectly normal. Elementary school groups noisily paraded through the gallery, excited to be away from the classroom.

"Where's the mummies?" one third-grader shouted out.

"And where's the daddies?" Laughter.

"Did King Tut have a pointy head?"

It was that kind of day, but the hyperactivity was not unwelcome.

And afterward, Sam rushed back to his apartment. He didn't want anyone to hear the phone call. He waited, and after an hour or so, wondered if Ouchard would even call. Maybe it was all a hoax. But no, the fifty thousand in cash looked real.

He fixed himself an omelet and toast and turned on cable news. He turned it off five minutes later, unable to concentrate. He opened his computer and went to Facebook. Now they were trying to sell him vacation packages to Egypt and the pyramids. Had his phone overheard his initial conversation with Ouchard in the museum? Or was it simply because he *worked* at the museum?

His phone rang, startling him. He looked at the number, POTENTIAL SPAM, and answered it anyway. It was a recorded woman's voice selling air conditioners. He hung up.

He felt more trapped in his apartment than he ever had. He paced. He rearranged the books on his bookshelves, separating the ones he'd read from those he hadn't and would probably never get around to.

He was in the shower when the phone rang again. He managed to answer on the fourth ring. Again the caller ID read, POTENTIAL SPAM.

"Good evening, Monsieur Shanowitz," he heard. "I was starting to worry that you weren't going to answer."

"Listen, I can do it, but it'll probably take about a year."

"Why the delay, sir?"

"Well, the exhibit goes on tour in a year. And as I see it, when they're packing it up to ship—that's the only time it might not be under ideal electronic surveillance. There'll be a lot of stuff coming and going. With any luck, I can be there to help."

Ouchard chuckled. "To help indeed."

"Not to mention the year will give me the time I need to set things up. I've got an idea. It starts with—"

"At this point, sir, it would be better for me not to know the details. How certain are you that your plan will work?"

"Not certain at all, but if it doesn't, it's my skin, not yours, right?"

"I'm glad that you see the reality of your having accepted the fifty thousand. And that, if you get caught, we must disavow having anything to do with you."

"Couldn't you then say that my attempt to steal the scarab proves the need for it to be returned to Egypt for safekeeping? It would be a win for you, no?"

"You're a creative thinker, Monsieur Shanowitz. But I doubt we'd do that. In my case, I trust you, though, and I have the authority to give you the go-ahead, which I now do."

"What if I need to get ahold of you between now and then?"

"Do not try, please."

"Then, how—"

"A week before the exhibit departs for this tour you speak of, I will visit daily the restaurant we first met in. I will continue lunching there until you bring me the scarab, at which point I will hand you an envelope with your new bank account number. I will be patient for a number of reasons, a small one being the fact that the food there is very good. Goodbye, Mr. Shanowitz. And good luck."

• • •

Even though Sam had a year to put everything in motion, there was no time to waste. After breakfast, he walked to the nearest branch of the New York Public Library. Using one of their computers, he googled a few background-check sites to find out what he could about Harriet. He would have tried Freddie, too, but he'd never learned Freddie's last name. Harriet's was Wexler. After a half hour of research, he had her date of birth, her address, and her phone number. He even discovered that she'd once been arrested, then not convicted, for shoplifting.

Another surprise was that she lived less than half a mile away. This concerned him, so he walked to the subway station and took a train to Brooklyn. There, he went to a post office and rented a box under the name of Harriet Wexler, paying $180 cash for one year. He then went to a phone store nearby and, again paying with cash, bought a cellphone, creating a new phone number and registering it under her name and her new mailing address. Then he went to a neighborhood branch of the city library and, using their computer, established an email address for her. Next, he went to a branch of the Chase Manhattan Bank that was open on Saturdays until 2:00 and filled out an application for a checking account in Harriet's name. He was momentarily stymied when Kristen, the friendly New Accounts manager, informed him that Harriet needed to sign it herself.

"Can I take the application with me, have her sign it, and mail it in?" Sam asked.

"You'd have to have it notarized in that case," she said.

"Jeez, I wish she could. But, see, she's currently bedridden. Because of her chemo. I don't know when . . . "

"Oh, I'm so sorry. Just have her sign it, then, and when she's feeling better she can come in and we'll finalize the details."

"So you'd be kind enough to open the account now?"

Kristen nodded.

"Thank you so much," Sam said.

"How much do you want to deposit?"

"Five thousand dollars? Is cash okay?"

"Good as ever," Kristen said with a smile.

They completed the transaction, and he was halfway out the door when she called out, "Sir!"

"Yes?" Had his plan already hit a dead end? "What is it?"

"You forgot Mrs. Wexler's temporary checks. They've got the new account number. She just has to write in her name and address at the top until she gets the permanent ones with her information on them."

"Thanks," Sam said. "She'll appreciate that."

Back at the library and using Harriet's name and all her new contact information, he set up a Facebook page and Twitter and Instagram accounts, all with an accurate profile but with flight-of-fancy handles that would distinguish the accounts from ones the real Harriet might have. That was enough for the moment, he thought.

With a bounce in his step that he realized had been missing since Laura's death, he returned to Manhattan and sauntered up to 59th Street, where he enjoyed a Sabrett hot dog and a knish. *Just like the old days*, he mused, his loneliness rekindled. He strolled through Central Park, considering his next moves.

Over the next few days, now that he had all the information that they required, he applied for credit cards in Harriet's name. He started making fictitious but innocuous comments on her Facebook and Twitter pages about food *she* liked or disliked—Italian yes, Indian no—what kind of clothes and music turned *her* on, places she had been, cuddly pets she loved, books she recommended. He downloaded from the Internet photos of sunsets, flowers, and food, and posted them on Instagram with thoughtful comments about how much she adored these things. Nothing political, nothing controversial.

As he expected, over the next few weeks and months, the new Harriet acquired hundreds of friends and followers who enjoyed communicating with her. Better yet, the marketers had begun posting ads on her social media, first in a trickle, then the flood he knew so well. When she wrote about flowers, she got ads for heritage nasturtium seeds. For to-die-for footwear, stiletto-heeled shoes. For bucket list travel dreams, glamping destination packages.

Sam chose carefully and frugally, purchasing through the new Harriet's credit cards those items that would reflect the profile of a tasteful, unmarried woman. Where to have purchases shipped initially brought him up short. If he had things sent to the post office, he might need to sign for them, in which case, after a while, he'd be recognized. And then there were some retailers who required a street address and wouldn't deliver to a post office box. For a few days, he explored some of the seamier neighborhoods of upper Manhattan. He discovered an abandoned brownstone where he imagined a delivery left on its front doorstep might be absconded with within twenty-four hours. He used its address as her shipping address. One of the first things he ordered was a lovely set of six monogrammed handkerchiefs embossed with the initials *H.W.* Someone of meager means would make use of all but one of them.

Every Saturday he went to the Brooklyn post office to gather the new Harriet's mail, and when bills arrived, he paid them dutifully using "her" checking account or the Venmo account he had set up on "her" new phone. Gradually, her credit limit increased. Little by little, he purchased items she might need on a long vacation: sensible shoes, sunglasses, evening wear, a luggage set.

In the meantime, he continued his work at the museum. Nothing changed. McDonald's breakfast meals. *"Good morning, Harriet." "See you tomorrow, Harriet." "Hi, Freddie." "Don't worry, I won't slip, Freddie."* Boisterous school classes, gaping tour groups, asking, joking, making noisy comments or staring in awe. All status quo, just the way he wanted it.

• • •

THE EGYPTIAN ANTIQUITIES GALLERY WILL BE CLOSING ON OCTOBER 1.

In smaller print, the sign explained that the exhibit was going to be taken on tour to major museums around the country for the next three years. Copies were posted everywhere in the museum.

"Looks like I'm gonna be out of a job," Sam said to Harriet.

"They're not keeping you on?"

Sam shook his head no, feigning deep disappointment.

"No exhibit, no work. Cost-cutting. You know the drill."

"I'm sorry."

"I'll survive."

"Good. Well, then think of it as a vacation. A well-deserved one?"

"I suppose. Six weeks and I'm outta here."

"So you're going to be helping them get the exhibit ready to move?"

Sam nodded. "I offered and at first they said no. But then they said I could be an extra security guard of sorts."

"So much stuff! I'll bet they'll be glad to use a helping hand like yours."

"I'm just glad I'll be around here as long as I can."

The packing and crating began at 6:00 P.M. on September 30. Supposedly it would take two weeks to complete. There were literally thousands of items, from stone statues of the deity Horus that weighed tons to minuscule gold hairpins—all inventoried, all accounted for. Sam showed up daily with his McDonald's breakfast meal, lending a hand whenever asked, all the while keeping his eye on a small numbered wooden crate. He memorized its number, 2170. Leaving for his lunch break on October 6, he rummaged through a heap of discarded crating near the loading dock and took a few scraps with him. That evening he fashioned a crate that looked identical to the one containing the scarab and numbered it accordingly.

Then, the waiting game. In a few days, he imagined, teams of workers with dollies would be coming and going to the loading dock, where a forklift would transfer the larger crates to waiting trucks. Though there was never a moment when the gallery was empty of workers, on October 9 came the moment when all backs were turned. Sam removed his homemade crate from his McDonald's bag and switched it with the one containing the scarab, which he placed in the bag. On his way out, he dropped Harriet Wexler's laundered handkerchief on the floor.

Though far from relaxed, he walked in a casual manner to Little Normandy. He found Ouchard, a cloth napkin tucked into his shirt collar, eating soup at the same table as before. Spotting Sam, Ouchard pulled an envelope out of his pocket and placed it on the table. As Sam held out the McDonald's bag, Ouchard was almost unable to repress a smile. Sam placed the bag next to the envelope, which he transferred into his own jacket pocket. Then, after making sure no one was looking, he sauntered out of the restaurant.

• • •

It didn't take long for Harriet Wexler to be arrested for the theft of Cleopatra's scarab.

Four days after leaving New York City, the crate was opened at the Cleveland Museum of Art, the exhibit's first stop on its national tour. Inside was a well-wrapped garden stone, almost the exact weight of the scarab. A massive investigation began immediately—involving multiple levels of city, state, and federal law enforcement—to recover the priceless jewel and track down the thief.

Everyone along the chain who'd had a hand in preparing and delivering the exhibit was interviewed. The first bit of incriminating evidence was the handkerchief found in the now empty Egyptian gallery, which Wexler readily admitted was hers, though she denied ever being in the gallery during the packing.

"My office isn't even on that floor," she said.

The investigators, spurred on by Wexler's prior arrest for shoplifting, dug deeper and discovered her hidden checking account, which had suddenly been closed; her post office box, the rental agreement for which had just expired; the credit card accounts with her alternate mailing address; her social media posts, in which she wrote, among other things, about her passion for travel, antiquities, and fine jewelry; and the cellphone, with fingerprints wiped, buried in a dumpster outside her apartment.

The authorities had particular interest in her online purchases, only months before, of luggage and other assorted travel items, which she'd had delivered to a bogus address, no doubt in order to elude discovery. Again, she denied knowing anything about any of those things.

"Tell us about your one-way plane ticket to Tunisia."

"I don't know what you're talking about. Why would I want to go to Tunisia?"

"Because it has no extradition treaty with the U.S., perhaps?"

They offered her a plea deal if she confessed and told them where the scarab was. No matter how much she professed her innocence, they didn't believe her. The KLEPTOPATRA TRIAL was in the headlines for months, garnering almost as much notoriety as the O.J. Simpson trial in '95. Sam was called as a character witness and testified on Harriet's behalf. He said he couldn't believe she could have done such a thing. No, they hadn't really been *friends*—not like *that*—but they had been friendly. He said she'd never done anything to make him believe she was anything but a totally honest and ethical human being.

It didn't help.

There was so much circumstantial evidence.

Harriet Wexler was convicted.

• • •

Sam, of course, continued to keep a low profile. Once the trial ended, and recognizing that the appeals process could linger for years, he started sprucing up his apartment, but only a little bit at a time. Nothing extravagant. Nothing to call attention to himself. He had the plumber in, then the painters. A few months later, he had new windows installed, windows that would open easily.

He wondered when, if ever, the Egyptian government would announce the return of the scarab. Maybe, if they did, it would help get Harriet off the hook. That would be nice.

Would a proclamation be made with great fanfare, or would it be subdued so as not to ruffle any ally's feathers?

Or was Egypt even the scarab's true destination? Maybe Ouchard's middleman was in reality an end man? Maybe the end man was Ouchard himself? It was possible, Sam realized, that the scarab would never be seen in public again. Regardless, he needed to stop making it his concern.

After a year, he decided to splurge and do a little traveling. The occasional pangs of guilt he initially felt were disappearing. Was it really his fault that the cops were incompetent enough to peg the wrong person? That Harriet's defense attorney wasn't capable of convincing a jury that the evidence was merely circumstantial, and that his client was obviously an honest woman? He had told the truth at the trial, hadn't he, that Harriet could never have done such a thing?

What more could he have said?

And wouldn't anyone in their right mind grab at the chance for a million-dollar Swiss bank account?

No, he had little to feel bad about.

He bought a round-trip ticket to Paris, and from there rented an inexpensive Renault to drive to Normandy. He wanted to dine on steak frites there, in Laura's honor. He was sure being in Normandy alone would at first make him feel nostalgic, even sad, but after a while, it would feel better than all the money in the world.

Whether he'd get a one-way ticket to Tunisia and from there let it be known—discreetly, of course—that it wasn't Harriet who had stolen the scarab was something he'd decide down the line. He was still mulling over this and the prospect of Normandy, though, when he made a left onto the Rue du Beau Site and noticed a milk truck barreling toward him. He would've been killed instantly if the truck's driver hadn't already braked, swerving and plowing into a cluster of cardboard boxes, crushing some before he stopped a mere foot from Sam's bumper.

The driver glared at Sam as if to say: *You*. Are an *idiot*.

No, Sam thought. I am lucky.

A MOTHER'S LAST REQUEST

R. C. GOODWIN

My mother didn't know I was a lesbian until I told her, emboldened by a large amount of alcohol, two months after my nineteenth birthday. Never underestimate the power of denial.

The evidence had been there. My tomboy childhood, my disdain for the frilly and dainty, my wardrobe devoid of pastels. My fascination with my brother Eric's toy trucks and adventure books—dolls bored me. My unconcern with dating (although I did go out with boys, rarely, a bone tossed to appearances). Whenever Mother spoke of my inevitable wedding, and how beautiful I'd look in white, and the joys of life with a husband and children, I fought to keep my eyes from glazing over.

At times I thought she *had* to know. If so, it put her in a bind. Mother was a child of the 1960s and 1970s. Not a full-fledged member of the counterculture, but on its fringes. She liked to tell Eric and me of her youthful days with no bra beneath her tie-dyed T-shirts, her braided dark brown hair falling past her shoulders. Of staying up all night as she and her comrades talked of love and revolution, of passing around joints and jugs of hearty burgundy while listening to the Doors.

This was her life before my father—six years older, practical and settled, a Delta Airlines pilot who voted for Ford—brought her back into Middle America. But not all the way. She still fancied herself the freethinker and free spirit, with a peace sign on her Subaru, just as one had adorned her orange-and-gold VW. She was given to hypertolerance, especially in matters of sexual freedom.

It was therefore okay in principle for a woman to be with other women. She may well have engaged in such adventures herself. *To add it to my book of life experiences*, she would have said. One of her favorite phrases. Her own book of life experiences contained some interesting pages. Hearing Martin Luther King's "I Have a Dream" speech at the Washington Mall in her teens. Backpacking through the Pyrenees, crisscrossing between France and Spain, although she spoke no French or Spanish. Having an overheated affair with her philosophy professor at the University of Massachusetts. Writing a vegan cookbook before rediscovering BLTs and pot roast. And those were just a few of the ones I was aware of.

But in her eyes, if it was okay for women to be with other women, her daughter's case was different. This became clear to me when I came home from college one winter weekend. Mother had a recipe for glögg, a Swedish drink, and insisted we try it. Glögg consists of brandy, red wine, and sherry, garnished with orange peel and slivered almonds. It's like the fake Polynesian concoctions served in tacky Chinese restaurants. You're unaware of the kick until you try to stand and find your knees have liquefied.

Mother and I sat alone in the kitchen. Father was flying to Frankfurt, and Eric had a date. We were each on our third cup.

"I'm worried about you, Claudia," she said somberly.

"Why?"

"Because your college experience seems so . . . *limited*."

"*Limited*? I have a 3.8 average in a very tough field"—I was majoring in microbiology—"and I'm a varsity tennis player and a literacy volunteer. What else do you want me to do, run for sheriff?"

"That's all wonderful, Claudie, and of course your father and I are proud of you," she said, a bit offhandedly. "But you don't seem to be having much *fun*."

"You mean like getting wasted at weekend puke-fests? Going to concerts where freaks with Technicolor hair and dog collars play sound pollution that passes for music?"

"That's not what I mean at all!" *Thash*, she said, the glögg really kicking in for both of us. "You never talk about parties, or going out with friends for a pizza or movie. You never talk about dating."

Two deep breaths. "I *have* been dating. I just haven't mentioned it."

She flashed her world-class smile, the sparkling eyes and white, white teeth. "That's terrific, Claudie! But why the secrecy? What's his name? I want to know *everything*."

"Wrong gender. Her name is Helen."

Mother's smile froze and imploded. Instantly she looked ten years older. Usually she looked much younger than her age; people often took us for sisters. We had the same dark hair and gray eyes.

And for much longer than I preferred, you could have heard a fly fart.

"Surely you knew," I finally said.

"As a matter of fact I didn't." Her words were no longer

slurred, I noticed. "I thought you were . . . a late bloomer. A woman more comfortable with books than relationships, reclusive like your father. I assumed you'd find the right guy, in your own sweet time."

She drained her cup, and I took a generous sip from mine.

"You see," she continued, "I've known plenty of late bloomers. My college roommate, for one. She spent weekends reading Dickens or Thackeray to get a PhD in English literature and then move to Ohio. For years I didn't hear from her. Then, out of the blue, she invited me to her wedding, and I couldn't believe the change in her. She was so content!"

"Let me guess. She had seven children, discovered her inner nanny, and devoted herself to baking bread and canning tomatoes from her garden. She never read another novel in her life, and she routinely had multiple orgasms, and she lived happily ever after."

Usually I'm not so snotty. Must have been the glögg.

The next six hours (which were fueled by more glögg and cups of black coffee and English muffins to keep our stomachs from eroding) reminded me of my experiences with marijuana, moments of extraordinary clarity in a near-impenetrable haze. I remember her telling me how marriage reminded her of Churchill's description of democracy, flawed and barely workable until one considers the alternatives. I remember her asking me how I'd cope with the mean-spirited jokes and references to lezzies and bull-dykes. *Listen, Claudia, what happened to Matthew Shepard could have happened anywhere, and I don't mean just in frigging Wyoming.*

I remember telling her that I was who I was, and my sexual orientation was as much a part of me as my aptitude for math and science, my left-handedness, and my uncontrollable belching after Mexican food. I remember raising our voices (rare) and both of us crying at the same time (unprecedented).

We talked of other things, too, with exceptional candor. She told me about the UMASS philosophy professor's wife surprising them at their Cape Cod cottage and chasing her naked along the beach, swinging a golf club like a machete. I told her about making out with Louis Nelligan on the night of my senior prom, how I couldn't stop yawning, how, in the midst of a yawn, I snagged his upper lip on my orthodontia. How he bled profusely and then never talked to me again.

She asked if I'd ever had sex with a man. I told her I hadn't, and a hopeful flicker passed across her face. It wasn't hard to read her mind right then: *If only she finds the right one, she'll get over this.*

. . .

There are over twenty kinds of non-Hodgkin's lymphoma. Mother had one of the worst ones, the anaplastic large-cell type.

Her first symptoms were typically vague. Fatigue, poor appetite, low-grade fever. Discomfort in her flank, which she blamed on overdoing it in yoga class. Night sweats, which she blamed on menopause. She did her best to ignore the signs until the day she couldn't get out of bed. By then she'd lost twenty pounds, and the discomfort in her flank had become a lacerating ache.

Nothing worked. Radiation and chemo gave fewer benefits than side effects, from hair loss to anemia to diarrhea.

Nausea and vomiting made it hard for her to keep down tea and toast. As her disease worsened from week to week and day to day, she turned into a crone before our eyes. They diagnosed her in June and she died the next May, a week after her fifty-first birthday.

I was twenty-four. After completing my master's, I had my first good job, as a microbiologist at a local hospital. I had my own apartment overlooking a park, and I drove a maroon Mustang. The year before, I'd gone to Cancun, the year before that to London. Now should've been the best part of my life. But the only part of it I remember was Mother's dying.

Despite her bodily deterioration, her mind stayed clear. Aware of her impending death, she made many of the arrangements herself. Cremation, not burial. Bach and Brahms at the service—*I can't stand that insipid churchy music!* Even the catering at a reception to be held afterward. *Don't forget the scallops wrapped with bacon. Your father loves them.*

Does the word *controlling* have some relevance here?

To spend more time with her I took a leave of absence from my job and moved back home. I cooked meals, changed her sweat-soaked sheets, and gave her medications. But mostly I sat by her bed and we talked.

We talked of books, especially the novels of Kurt Vonnegut, patron saint of her youth and her favorite author. Of baseball. She'd grown up near Boston, loved the Red Sox, had gone to Fenway Park as often as possible. Of my father and brother. *They'll take this harder than you will, Claudie. Have patience with them, even when they're being jerks.* And we talked about her imminent demise. She had no obvious fear about it. *I'm not devout, but I do believe that there's a guiding spirit in the universe. My hunch is, it's benign.*

She grilled me about the woman I was seeing, a waitress/ aspiring actress whom she didn't like at all. *She's pretentious and as shallow as a saucer. She'd turn on you in a heartbeat. If you* have *to be gay, you can do much better.*

Two days before she died, she asked me, "Do you remember when you told me about your, uh, preference?"

"How could I forget it?"

"I asked if you'd slept with a man. You hadn't."

"I still haven't."

"So I figured." She signaled for me to hand her a glass of water from the nightstand. A few sips and she resumed. "I want you to. Once."

"Mother!"

"Come now, Claudia." She tried to sound disdainful, but her frailty made this hard. "I'm not asking you to take on the New England Patriots. Having sex with a man, just once, would it kill you?"

"That's not the point! You make it sound like turning a switch. *Tonight I think I'll be heterosexual!*"

She ignored me, her voice weak but unyielding. "A week, a month, a year from now, it doesn't matter. You'll know when. Think of it as—"

"As something to add to my book of life experiences."

"Precisely."

. . .

My closest friend at the hospital was Bruce Kellner, a pediatric nurse. Among his virtues were a sly sense of humor and booming laugh, a quick intelligence, and a gentle disposition. Pretty obviously gay but not a flaming queen. Twenty-eight.

He lived with a hairstylist named Lester. I suppose it would be possible to dislike Bruce, but you'd have to work at it.

I approached him at the nurses' station one afternoon, the October after Mother's death. "May I buy you a beer after work?"

"Sure. What's the occasion?"

"I need you as a sounding board for something."

He appraised me through rimless glasses. "This should be interesting." I smiled mysteriously and sauntered off.

Three hours later, we were sitting in a booth at the Cornerstone, a bar favored by off-duty staff. A few minutes of small talk and hospital gossip, and the waiter came back with our orders, an Anchor Steam for him and a zinfandel for me. Bruce chewed a pretzel and washed it down with beer. "So, what's up, sugarplum?"

"This is—I'm not sure where to start. You know my mother died last spring."

He gave my hand a pat.

"Mother never accepted my being a lesbian. It's complicated. She did and she didn't." I summed up her vaunted open-mindedness, her 1960s zeitgeist. Then, just as he was swallowing a gulp of beer, I told him about her last request, and he inhaled another mouthful.

"This is seriously bizarre," he said after he stopped coughing.

"No shit."

"It's also unfair. Did she think it was that simple?"

"Of course not. We're talking about a woman who scored 1500 on her SATs, as she'd be quick to tell you. A woman who graduated from college in three years, *cum laude*. Notwithstanding marijuana, booze, and fuckathons." I sipped some zin. "But it's tough to ignore a deathbed request from someone you love, fair or not. Imagine yourself in my situation."

"That isn't hard. I get the same message from my parents. *If only you meet a nice enough girl, everything will work out.* In my case there's this, too: I'm an only child. Their only shot for grandchildren."

"Out of curiosity, were you ever . . . with a woman?"

"I was once, believe it or not. I was seventeen. A teenage boy will have sex with a Chihuahua if there's nothing else around."

"How was it?"

"Unreal. Do you know anything about boxing? Sugar Ray Leonard was this really cute boxer. I kept fantasizing about him." He looked alarmed. "What are you asking? You weren't thinking—"

"Don't worry. I wouldn't risk a good friendship. I guess I just wanted to . . . well, get your ideas about some candidates."

He laughed, obviously relieved. "No offense, Claudia—you're an attractive woman. If I had those inclinations, I'd happily oblige. You'll have no trouble finding someone."

"I'm not so sure. Men don't exactly nip at my heels. Either they know, or I don't give off the right pheromones."

He finished his Anchor Steam and I signaled for another round. Suddenly I felt embarrassed and annoyed. "I'm sorry," I said. "It was an unfair thing for her to ask of me, and it was unfair of me to bring you into it."

"Relax, Claudie. I'm glad to help if I can." He pressed two fingers against his forehead, concentrating. "Let's brainstorm and see who we can come up with. There's Victor Chen."

"Works in pathology?"

Bruce nodded. "Affable, I always thought. Handsome, in a sexy Amerasian way."

Victor, a slender man of about six feet, had Asian features dramatically offset by light eyes close to amber. A few times we'd had lunch, as part of a group in the cafeteria. The beginning and end of our contact.

"The thing is," I said, "we've barely said more than hello to each other. Besides, there's always that whiff of death about him. You haven't noticed?"

Bruce's face brightened with incredulity. "He works in a *morgue*! What's he supposed to smell like, bay rum? Besides, he might even take a shower beforehand if you ask him nice."

We fell silent as the waiter brought our second round.

"What about Malachi Shaw?" Bruce continued. "Malachi's my favorite of the residents in pediatrics. The timing would be good, too. He just broke up with someone."

"For God's sake, Bruce!"

"For God's sake, what? What's wrong with *him*?"

"In the first place, he can't be more than four feet ten. If we did it standing up, he'd need a soapbox."

Bruce rolled his eyes. "You exaggerate. He's five-six easily."

"Plus, I hate that beard of his." Malachi had a reddish goatee I found singularly unattractive. "It's satanic. A satanic, height-challenged guy on the rebound. If that doesn't sound like a nightmare, I don't know what does."

Bruce sighed. "This may be harder than I thought. Well, what about Scott Edgarton?"

Scott, an X-ray technician in his early thirties, had brooding eyes, curly brown hair, and an aquiline nose. "Hmm.

Perhaps a contender," I said. Scott's body was that of a man who watched what he ate but didn't make a fetish of dieting. A pleasant smile. Well-spoken, if somewhat enamored of his own voice.

"I think he'd be perfect for your purposes," Bruce said. "In fact, I wouldn't mind having a go at him myself."

"Keep your hands off my man, you bitch!"

Bruce laughed. As usual his laughter had a rich trombone-like quality to it.

"How well do you know him?" he asked.

"Not very. He seems okay, though. And we have some things in common. We both played tennis in college. We both read a lot of crime fiction, and we like some of the same authors. Michael Connelly, Tony Hillerman, Nevada Barr."

"Well, then. It's meant to be."

Bruce drank down more and dabbed his lips with a paper napkin.

"But how," he asked, "do you propose to go about this?"

"I don't know," I said. "Guess I'll figure it out as I go along."

• • •

I'm not forward by nature, but I approached Scott in the cafeteria with determined eyes and resolute stride, a woman on a mission. My opening gambit, I decided, would be tennis.

He was sitting alone drinking coffee. "Hey, Scott," I said breezily.

"How're you doing, Claudia?"

He remembered your name, I thought. "Okay," I said. "May I sit down? I'd like to ask you something."

"Sure." He pointed to the chair across from him.

I sat and cupped my chin in my hands in a way intended to emphasize my high cheekbones, which, people had told me, were among my best features. "I know you've played a lot of tennis. Do you still?"

He nodded. "At least twice a week."

"Well, I haven't for over a year, and I want to get back to it before I lose my game entirely. What I'd like to know is, where do you play?"

"At the A-1 Racquet and Fitness Club on West Truman. The people who work there are friendly, and it isn't too expensive. I recommend it highly."

He bestowed his warm, attractive smile on me. He had good teeth too. Not as good as Mother's, but no one's were.

"We could play there if you'd like," he said, almost offhandedly. "You could come as my guest, try it before signing up."

We made a date to play the following Sunday afternoon.

• • •

I cleaned my apartment Saturday in case he came over afterward. If it got that far, would we go to my place or his? How did these things get decided? What was the protocol? How did I signal my availability without appearing wanton? Who brought condoms? I felt hopelessly naïve.

Every so often it occurred to me, *This is absurd. It's above and beyond a daughter's duty. You are who you are.* And, inevitably, the image came back to me. Of my mother dying, too weak to get a glass of water for herself, her body old before its time but her mind as adroit and irreverent as always. My mother, whom I loved above all people and things, more than my father and brother and the small collection of my lovers. My mother, who'd made this last ridiculous request.

I resumed cleaning my apartment. Then I went to Walgreens to buy condoms. Then I went to a seedy little shop called Personal Pleasures. To buy porn.

I'd never seen an erect penis. I hadn't seen a lot of flaccid ones, for that matter. Once in a while I saw my brother relieving himself when we were children (unimpressive). And in my ninth-grade human development text I'd seen diagrammatic renderings of them that passed them off as being as benign as pussy willows. I needed to prepare myself for the genuine article.

Ambling through rows of vanilla- and strawberry-flavored massage oil, crotchless faux-leopard underwear, cock rings, rubber suits, and leather harnesses, I made my way to the magazines. I grabbed three at random.

At home, I spread them out on my kitchen table, opened a beer, and studied them with particular attention to male organs. A veritable cavalcade of penises, every race represented, circumcised and unimproved. They came in two sizes, large and larger. If size truly mattered, these were some of the most important men in the world.

Near the penises, unclad women appeared to coo ecstatically as they prepared to pay homage to them. The more enthusiastic ones paid homage to two of them simultaneously.

My first reaction, I must admit, was disbelief. Do men, in

fact, possess such things? They must—cameras don't lie. Or were they digitally enhanced?

Other questions came to me. Surely these were not the norm, or were they? Do straight women *really* find them attractive? What happens if erections occur at awkward times, in the wrong places? Taking communion, for instance, when the communicant receives the host and suddenly the front of his pants forms a tent. Or going through customs at JFK. *"Do you have anything to declare?" "You betcha!"* After 9/11, would TSA pat down a guy who'd gotten all geared up for whatever reason?

More than anything, I found them freakish. It was good, I thought, that men had them tucked between their legs instead of protruding from someplace else, like say the back of their necks.

Erections struck me as freakish, but let's be honest here, they are imposing.

Possessed of a certain *je ne sais quoi.*

The truth was, I didn't know what to make of them.

Sunday afternoon exceeded expectations. Despite my layoff, I gave Scott a run for his money. He was fast but so was I, and both of us covered the court well. He had a powerful serve and a sneaky backhand with strong topspin, but I adjusted. My game was consistent, my placement and shot selection clever. He won both sets six to two, but we played more evenly than the score indicated.

Since he wouldn't let me pay the guest fee, I invited him for a drink and a bite to eat afterward. We both liked Japanese, so we went to a place called Yakumo. Upon arrival we had two beers each, and we accompanied our sushi with a carafe of sake. Conversation flowed easily.

"This was fun," I said as we were leaving.

"We could do it again. With or without the tennis." I felt the pressure of his arm against my elbow as we headed to the door.

"I'd like that. And I definitely want a rematch. I'm gonna join that place, and once I knock the rust off my game, I'll really make it worth your while."

We stood outside. A beautiful night, with a bright moon not quite full. A cloudless star-filled sky. Neither of us spoke. I thought about inviting him to my apartment but couldn't do it, Mother's edict notwithstanding. I just couldn't. If one of us made a move, it would have to be him.

"Well," he said, "we could go to my place for a drink."

I tried to sound nonchalant. "Sounds fine. Should I follow you?"

We sat on a couch in Scott's condo. I drank beer, and he'd switched to single malt scotch. He seemed less at ease than before, as if something weighed on him but he wasn't ready to divulge it.

"Can I ask you a question, Claudia?" he finally asked.

"Sure."

"I'm wondering . . . I guess I'm wondering what you're doing here." He was blushing.

"What do you mean?" I asked innocently. "You invited me for a drink, and I took you up on it."

He drank more scotch, his blush deepening. "There are rumors around the hospital that you're, uh . . . a lesbian."

I considered options. Denial. *Don't believe everything you hear, you silly goose. Now fix me a drinky-poo. Something girly, like a cosmopolitan.* Affirmation. *Yes, indeed, I can muff-dive with the best of them. By the way, sonny, d'you mind if I smoke a cigar in here?* Or I could tell him the real agenda. *I am, but I'd like to have sex with you anyway, because my dying mother said I should.*

Instead I asked him—calmly and neutrally—"What if I am?"

And I have to admit, I enjoyed watching him blush.

He finished off the scotch in a single gulp. A shame, the stuff must have cost fifty bucks a bottle. Words failed him, so I took him off the hook. "Don't make too much of it, Scott. It's okay for straights and gays to be friends now. What I told you in the cafeteria was true, about wanting to get back to tennis. It happened that I enjoyed your company afterward. I assumed that you enjoyed mine too."

"I did, of course I did—"

"Besides," I interrupted, "haven't you heard of bisexuals?"

He ignored the question and stood up. "I think I'll pour myself another drink. Can I get you something from the kitchen?"

"No, thanks." Sake and three beers had sufficed. (I weigh only 120.)

The blush was gone when he returned. "I'm sorry I got so flustered," he said. "I don't know why I did. Sexual preference doesn't matter to me. I have a gay cousin. He's great, and we get along fine. I guess it's just that I've never known a lesbian, at least not well."

"I'm sure you've known plenty of them. You simply didn't know you did."

With that, conversation became less self-conscious and more open. We spoke of earlier relationships, his broken engagement to the manager of a Pier 1 and my newly ended time with Annemarie, the waitress/actress. We discussed gay marriage. We talked about a play he'd seen based on the Matthew Shepard case; he'd been moved to tears by it. He went back to sipping scotch instead of gulping it as I drank Perrier.

A few times I saw him beholding me with elements of lust, bemusement, affection, wariness, and curiosity.

Then he said, "You're very pretty."

"Thank you. You're not hard to look at either." I felt as if I were trying out for a part in a soap opera, a part I would likely not get.

And then he kissed me, the first male to do so since Louis Novak. Remembering poor Louis and his bloodied lip, I reminded myself not to yawn. I shut my eyes and felt myself drifting. Grabbing the arm of the couch with my hand, I sought to tether myself, as though I'd float away if I didn't. The brush of his lips against mine was not unpleasant, nor was the brush of his hands against my breasts. Occasionally I thought of Annemarie, who had creamy skin and red hair, whose tongue flicked like a snake's. I couldn't decide if images of her would help or hurt.

Scott brought me to my feet and guided me to the bedroom. His speech, unlike his wavering gait, gave away no sign of his drinking. In the bedroom there were more kisses, a wandering of hands, a sense that neither of us was rushing. It was empowering and exciting (more empowering than exciting) to take note of his heightened arousal, the rapid breathing and growing bulge that pressed against my crotch. My eyes formed slits that made me think of cats as he unbuttoned my blouse, unzipped my culottes, unhooked my bra. Then, at the age of twenty-five, I stood naked in front of a man for the first time.

He began to undress himself. I liked his solid shoulders, firm chest, and the tapered lines of his belly. Wouldn't it be a hoot if this turned out to be enjoyable?

Then he took off his underwear. His penis, neither erect nor flaccid, dipped laxly below the horizontal. It was half as big as the ones in the magazines. He looked down, and even in the darkened room I couldn't fail to miss his pained expression. *Houston, we have a problem.*

I gave it my best shot, I swear I did. I tried everything I saw depicted in the magazines and even improvised a few things of my own. The more I tried, the more it shrank and softened, a sullen trifle.

Finally, we reached a tacit agreement to give up. "It's the motherfuckin' BDs," he muttered.

"The what?"

"The BDs. The booze droops. I should have quit after the sake."

"It's okay, Scott."

And it *was* okay; after all, this project wasn't *my* idea. Besides, the tennis had been fun, the sushi delicious.

We dressed in silence and returned to the living room. "I'm sorry, Claudia," he said finally. "That doesn't happen to me very often."

"It's okay, honestly," I repeated. "I just hope we can do it again. The tennis, I mean."

"Of course we can." But his face said something altogether different. *Never will you see me away from the hospital, and you won't see me there if I can help it.*

I kissed him on the cheek and helped myself out.

• • •

Driving home then, I made a decision. My next candidate would have no connection to the hospital. The mission would or wouldn't be successful, but either way I'd have no later dealings with the guy at my workplace.

In my apartment I tried to come up with other names. Stan Tyler, my cat's vet? Aaron Weiss, my accountant? Wanting to keep my business and personal life separate, I vetoed both. My second cousin, Harold Brooks? A congenial man, decent-looking, too, but I thought it best to stay outside the family.

And then it came to me, the obvious nominee, the one I should have asked in the first place: my brother's best friend, D. G. Mirabelli.

Dante Giancarlo Mirabelli and Eric had been inseparable since kindergarten. His parents worked long hours in their Italian restaurant, and he'd practically lived at our house. Through the years he'd joked with me, teased me—never meanly—and played kickball and computer games with me. If he viewed me as his best friend's pesky little sister, he didn't show it. When my breasts and hips rounded out, we engaged in a bit of lightweight flirtation, but we understood it would go nowhere.

One Saturday afternoon when both he and Eric were home from college, he dropped by my parents' to see Eric, but Eric was out running errands. My parents had left town for the weekend, so we had the place to ourselves. I'd just turned seventeen.

We sat at the kitchen table drinking Cokes and eating tortilla chips, and I told him I was gay.

Not batting an eye, he chomped on a chip.

"You okay with it?" he asked, and I nodded.

"Me too, then," he said. End of discussion.

The college he'd gone to was in California. After graduating, he'd stayed on to earn an MBA there. Still, we'd see him fairly often. He had a large, close family (four sibs, a slew of uncles, aunts, and cousins), and he'd often come back to visit. He'd been the best man at Eric's wedding, and he'd sat in our pew at Mother's funeral. Unmarried.

And he not only knew that I was gay, he'd also known my mother.

Meaning I wouldn't have to explain so much.

• • •

Hi, D. G., it's Claudia, I said to his answering machine. *Nothing urgent, but please give me a buzz. Are you coming home for Thanksgiving? Hope so.*

It was now November 11. He called two hours later. "Hey, Claudie, good to hear your voice. How are you?" He was the only one outside the family who called me Claudie except for my friend Bruce.

"I'm fine, D. G. How 'bout you?"

"Everything's great."

We exchanged news of jobs and family, and then I asked, "So, are you coming home for Thanksgiving?"

"Are you kidding? If Clara Mirabelli's your mother, you *come home* for holidays. It isn't open for discussion." Clara, a short woman with a bosom comprising half her body weight, was famous for her ten-thousand-calorie holiday extravaganzas. For Thanksgiving she made two complete meals, traditional and Italian. Corn chowder and antipasto, roast turkey and lasagna, pumpkin pie and tiramisu.

"Good, because I really want to see you."

"I want to see you, too."

"I really, *really* want to see you."

"Is something wrong?"

"No, but I want to ask a favor of you that's slightly out of the ordinary." It was feeling easier to ask him than I'd anticipated, so I went right ahead and did it: "My mom was insistent, too. About me having sex with a man once before I die. She asked me to when she was going downhill fast. So, well, I was wondering if you'd like to be the lucky man."

D. G. took his time before responding "I imagine this is a big deal to you," he eventually said. "And I'm flattered that you're asking me. But are you sure you're . . . *com*fortable with it?"

"Relatively speaking, yes. I'd be more so with you than with anyone else."

His skepticism lingered. "I mean, there's something incestuous about it, isn't there? You're like another sister to me."

"Think of it as sisterhood with benefits."

He laughed. "I admit, I *did* use to have lustful thoughts about you."

"I sensed that."

He paused again. I heard him pacing.

"To tell the truth, I'd love to," he finally said. "But before we do, I want you to think about it really carefully, okay?"

"There's still more than two weeks," I said. "I'm sure I'll be thinking about it plenty."

• • •

We sat in my apartment, D. G. on the couch, me in an armchair. I'd cleaned the apartment as if on speed, vacuuming and washing windows and polishing surfaces. You could have used my kitchen table for a heart transplant.

We drank Michelobs. I only had four bottles in my fridge; after the Scott Edgarton fiasco, I meant to keep D. G. on a short leash booze-wise.

"I must say, Claudie, I'm having a hard time processing this."

"You seem relaxed enough." He'd kicked off his loafers and semi-sprawled across my couch, stocking feet behind his knees.

"I am," he said. "I've always been relaxed with you. But we still have our clothes on." He cleared his throat then, and said, "I have to tell you something," and I thought, *Oh, God, here it comes. He has chlamydia or worse. Or wants me to pee on him first.*

I braced myself. "Go on."

He chose his words beyond carefully. "I'm not very good at sex. I don't have much experience, to begin with. You could write the names of all my partners on a postcard and still have room for more than one address. My longest relationship lasted four months. I'm also self-conscious about my body."

"What's wrong with your body? It always looked good to me." Back when we were young he'd hang around my parents' pool, and I'd seen him in a swimming suit a hundred times.

"I'm fat," he said now. "I have a hairy back. My bellybutton sticks out like a ping-pong ball." He drained the Michelob. "I'm very tense about the whole thing. Sex, I mean.

Sometimes I wish it would go away, but I want a wife and kids someday." He smiled wryly. "You could say it's an area of conflict."

"Isn't it for most of us? The easy hookups, the Internet porn, it's all a bit misleading. If sex was so straightforward, we wouldn't have a million books about it, or all those experts on the talk shows, it wouldn't be such a hot potato in the courts and legislatures."

I stood up, walked over to him, and held his hand.

"Listen, D. G.," I said, doing my best to sound confident. "This could work out for both of us. You help me fulfill my mother's absurd request, and I help you feel better about yourself."

"Maybe."

I helped him to his feet and steered him toward the bedroom. He hugged me as we stood together.

"Hold on," I said, and I pulled away to light the candles I'd bought for the occasion. When I returned to him, he held me so tightly that at times I found it a little hard to breathe. He kissed my lips, my cheeks, my eyes and neck. His inhalations became faster, jerkier. As his hands ran over me, I felt tremors in them. His palms were sweaty. I thought it best to undress myself.

And then we lay naked on top of my bed, I and this man I'd known for close to twenty years, this second brother to me. "Claudie, Claudie, Claudie . . ." That's all he said, a mantra. His breathing turned loud and staccato. My guess was, he hadn't been with a woman for months at least.

I ran a hand down his chest and belly and made my way downward. Urgency oozed from every pore. Way too much urgency, it turned out—as soon as I touched his penis, he ejaculated.

"Oh, God," he said. He swallowed hard. "I'm *so* sorry."

"It's okay. Honest." I kissed him, this time on the forehead. "I love you, D. G. I always will. Please, I beg of you, don't let what happened change things between us. If it does, I'll never forgive myself."

"It won't," he said. "I love you too."

Pulling my head against his chest and wrapping an arm around my shoulders, he began to relax. And I felt content right then, don't ask me why.

• • •

After D. G., I kept my mission in abeyance. I needed time to regroup. Besides, I had no timetable. Hadn't Mother told me so herself? *You'll know when the time is right.*

Although I still missed her fiercely, life was mainly good. Work fulfilled me, and my superiors always gave me rave reviews, several of the infectious disease docs urging me to go back to school and get a PhD. I spent time with my father, my brother, and my sister-in-law. And red-headed Annemarie, as fickle as she was stunning, had pranced her way back to me, although we didn't live together this time. I shared the apartment with my calico cat, and I'd made it clear I had no wish for further occupants, and she seemed to be fine with that.

Since my workday began at seven, I usually retired early. My friends knew this, so I got few late-night calls or visitors. I was therefore taken aback when my doorbell rang one evening at 10:30. I'd already gone to bed.

I threw on a robe and went to the door. "Who is it?"

"Bruce."

His voice sounded tight, close to choked. Opening the door, I was stunned by his appearance. Usually meticulously dressed and groomed, he wore jeans and a stained grayish sweatshirt. No coat, despite the December chill. He hadn't shaven for several days, and his thick blond hair was uncombed and unshampooed. (As a rule, every strand was in place and well-tended.) But the biggest change was in his eyes. Ordinarily lively and expressive, they were dull and reddened now. Above all else, they were unutterably sad.

"Jesus Christ," I said.

"Hello to you too," he said, and he tried to smile but failed.

I led him to the couch. "What happened?"

"Lester left."

He told the story in bits and pieces. Lester, the hairstylist he'd been living with for going on a year now, hadn't come home two nights ago. Bruce thought the guy had crashed with a friend after drinking too much—that had happened often. Lester already had a DUI, and a second one could've meant jail. When he'd come home the next morning, he'd told Bruce that they were through. And that he'd been seeing another man for three months, someone he'd met in a gay chat room. This after spending Thanksgiving with Bruce's family, after they'd made plans to go to Antigua in the spring.

"The thing is," he concluded, "I should have seen it coming. All the signs were there. The drifting off, the sexual apathy, picking fights over nothing. And he'd never been any good at commitment—his whole life! I knew that, but I thought he'd get better at it if *I* loved him enough. Oldest story in the book, right? The gay book, the straight book, every book there is."

"Can I get you a drink?" was all I could think to say. He did look powerfully in need of one. "I have Michelob, a decent Sauterne, and some Drambuie."

He shook his head. "I drank more in the past two days than in the last year. But I'll take orange juice if you have some."

I went to the kitchen, returned with juice for him and a diet Pepsi for myself. He looked less fragile now. "You met him a couple of times," he said. "What did you think of him?"

I considered how to answer. The truth was, Lester struck me as an arrogant, narcissistic waste of time, with a whining monotone and tinny laugh, and I'd always placed great stock in the quality of a person's laughter. If someone laughed as if they meant it, that cut a lot of ice with me, and Lester had laughed like a banker about to foreclose on you.

But despite my dislike of him, I decided to pull my punches. I figured that, no matter how anyone's lover wounds or enrages them, no one likes to hear other people trashing them.

"He struck me as self-absorbed," was how I replied, "and hard to trust. I thought he was unworthy of you." I stood, stepped over toward Bruce, rested my hand on his scruffy cheek. "I mean, you happen to be one of the two or three best people I've ever known."

He let that sink in. Then:

"What would I do without you, Claudie?"

"You'll never need to know unless I die on you."

Suddenly he looked drained of anger and disappointment. Drained of everything, really.

"Can I crash on your couch?" he asked. "I don't want to go back to my place."

"Of course. Stay where you are."

I went to my bedroom, came back with blankets, sheets, and a pillow, deciding, as I set down the heap of these things, that he needed me to take charge.

"Here's what you'll do," I said in my most authoritative tone. "You'll take a long hot shower while I make you a bed here. Hot showers work miracles. You can wear Annemarie's bathrobe when you're finished. Then I'll give you a Xanax. Tomorrow you can call in sick if necessary, but frankly I think you should go to work. The last thing you need is to spend the day alone brooding. You can live here with me as long as you want."

"Okay," he said. He wiped his eyes on the sleeve of his sweatshirt.

Later, back in bed, I found it hard to sleep. Just as I was finally drifting off, I opened my eyes and saw him, Bruce, standing in the doorway. It was strange to see a man in Annemarie's pink bathrobe. His eyes were fixed on the floor.

"I'm so ashamed," he said, his voice hardly above a whisper.

"Hurt and angry I can understand, but why ashamed?"

"Because I'm used to being the strong one. The caretaker. I like taking care of people. Why else would I go to nursing school—for the *money*? And now I feel incapable of caring for myself, much less a sick kid or anyone else. I hate the way I feel now, I'm ashamed of it."

I sat up in bed, smoothed my flannel nightgown, and drew my hands around my knees. "This will pass, as they say. A temporary aberration, nothing more. You'll go back to being the Bruce you usually are."

"I know that," he said. "I just don't happen to believe it."

"It *kills* me seeing you like this," I snapped. "I'd like to break that asshole's goddamn neck!"

He said nothing in response to that. And then—and I hadn't planned on doing it—I waved him to the bed.

"Get in here," I said. "You're sleeping with me tonight."

He stood there for a few seconds and folded his arms. Then he dropped them to his sides and walked over. He lay next to me beneath the covers, still wearing Annemarie's bathrobe. I drew him closer, noticing he smelled of my sandalwood soap.

"You'll be all right," I said, less a reassurance than an order.

And I've often tried to remember what happened next, but now, only snippets come back. His ice-cold hands reaching out to me. My attempts to warm them up by blowing on them. The sensation, as I touched his shoulder, of tension draining from his body. The brother-sister kisses becoming longer, growing less brotherly, less sisterly. The shock of feeling a stirring beneath Annemarie's bathrobe, the even greater shock of feeling myself responding in kind. And then he no longer wore the bathrobe, and I no longer wore the flannel nightgown.

And throughout, we didn't talk a lot. I do recall one thing he said, though. "This is *very* nice," he said, "but I can't guarantee I'll deliver a moment of truth."

"I can't either," was what I said. "But might it help if you think about Sugar Ray Leonard?"

"Okay," he said after he stopped laughing. "And you can think of me as Scarlett Johansson—equipped with a strap-on dildo."

• • •

Bruce and I were married in mid-June, just as I began my third trimester. A simple civil ceremony, my father, Eric and my sister-in-law, and Bruce's parents in attendance. There was no reception, but we did have a splendid meal afterward, at Brasserie Lyon, the finest restaurant in town; because my morning sickness had been long gone, I actually enjoyed the escargots, coq au vin, and profiteroles. And there was no lengthy honeymoon, but my father had pulled some strings at Delta and gotten us first-class tickets for a three-day weekend in Bermuda.

In September I gave birth to Violet Hope Kellner. She has dark hair like her mother and both of her grandmothers. She has her father's hazel eyes, and dimples worthy of a baby food ad. I am in love with her.

And to some people, I realize, Bruce and I have a marriage that makes no sense at all. What these people don't know, I imagine, is that our marriage works fine for us. We live together, remain best friends, and share the joy and exhaustion of raising Violet. We also share a bed in which we take comfort in the warmth of each other's bodies, and once in a while—a great, great while—we reenact our Sugar Ray/ Scarlett Johansson tryst. But mostly we only sleep there, in the same bed, too exhausted to stay awake for more than a few minutes after our heads touch the pillows.

Sometimes, when this happens, Bruce falls asleep before I

do, and I think about my mother, about how she believed there was a guiding spirit in the universe. In those moments before I lose consciousness myself, I'm never sure what to think about that—the existence of a guiding spirit—but I'm always sure that, without the memory of my candid, insistent mother, there would be no Violet, there would be no happiness of the kind only Bruce and I know, and for me, there'd be no sleep as deep as I often enjoy of late.

And during those several moments I'm still barely awake, I lie peacefully, savoring the wonderment.

CONTRIBUTORS' NOTES

DAVID BOROFKA'S first collection of stories, *Hints of His Mortality*, was selected by Oscar Hijuelos as the winner of the 1996 Iowa Award for Short Fiction. His most recent collection of stories, *A Longing for Impossible Things*, was published by Johns Hopkins University Press in 2022, and his novel *The End of Good Intentions* is forthcoming from Fomite Press. A member of the faculty at Reedley College from 1983 until his retirement in 2019, he now can be found most Saturday afternoons in the fall watching the television with the sound off so as not to jinx the Crimson Tide. His wife is suggesting therapy.

THE STORY BEHIND THE STORY: I finished writing a novel (well, to be honest, no novel is ever really finished; the best an author can do is surrender gracefully). Rather than feeling any kind of joy or relief, I felt only a gnawing anxiety that I was done. Nothing more about those characters, no more familiar situations, no more words. D-U-N.

In such a moment, you can drink or you can make a list of items and follow that old dictum, *Write what you know*. Or do all of the above. So, the list: a plaid sports jacket, a Roto Grip bowling ball, a George Foreman grill, a silk geranium, a sebaceous cyst. Get out the corkscrew, open the Pinot, and write a blended smoothie of a story.

I can't deny it: I once owned a jacket that no self-respecting used car salesman would ever wear. I also once owned a Roto Grip bowling ball, though in reality, it never lived up to the potential I gave it in "Attachment." On the other hand, the George Foreman grill was merely a by-product of repetitive advertising and an addiction to television I try to hide from polite company. In any case, those three objects became the ignition point for a story about gains and losses and the memories and emotions that become attached to things.

Unlike the narrator in "Attachment," I can't blame the pandemic or spring cleaning for the loss of items I've clung to over the years. My jacket of many colors vanished somewhere during my move from Tuscaloosa to Fresno. The bowling ball disappeared from the backseat of my '67 Rambler station wagon, along with a cassette tape deck and an AM/FM converter because I hadn't yet learned to lock the doors or roll up its windows, even in a rainstorm. Carelessness has a price: I have sorely missed both the jacket and bowling ball since 1982.

The silk geranium and the cyst remain in the closed and confidential medical records of the Borofka clan, intimations of mortality as well as evidence of survival.

As for the George Foreman grill, I still have designs on one, if only for the sake of manufactured nostalgia.

NIKKI DOLSON'S stories have appeared in *Best American Mystery and Suspense 2021*, *TriQuarterly*, *Tough*, *Thuglit*, and other publications. She is the author of the novel *All Things*

Violent and, most recently, the story collection *Love and Other Criminal Behavior.*

THE STORY BEHIND THE STORY: In 2011, a scene popped into my head: a girl in a cafeteria trading a pack of cigarettes with an older girl for . . . something. I didn't know what yet, but I knew everything about who Lucy was at that moment. She was determined and hopeful. I knew she was doing something she shouldn't be doing. I knew she was also doing what she thought she needed to do to become "someone" in her high school pocket universe. Within a day I had most of that scene worked out, but it wasn't a beginning, so I worked backward from there. I have been the girl who felt like she didn't belong, so I made Lucy my stand-in. All of my teenage insecurities were projected onto this girl, who also reminded me of my daughter. I added in my mother's butter yellow 1974 Subaru, then wrote and rewrote the story of Lucy off and on for eight years. No one wanted it. (Just checked—thirty-three rejections!) When I got the opportunity to publish a collection, I knew I wanted this story to be part of it, though I wasn't sure what that publisher's editor would think. But it worked out. "Lucy Lucy Lucy" was published, and it was then even excerpted in *TriQuarterly.* And it now lives on in *Coolest 2023.* I love Lucy and Therese and even the LaLas. I'm so glad to see them out in the world.

GERALD ELIAS leads a double life as an award-winning author and world-class musician. A former Boston Symphony violinist, he's been the music director of the popular Vivaldi by Candlelight concerts since 2004. His critically acclaimed Daniel Jacobus mystery series, which *Booklist* described as "brilliant and captivating on every level," is set in the dark corners of the classical music world. A longtime lover of Utah's desert wilderness, Elias has followed up his most recent Jacobus installment, *Cloudy with a Chance of Murder*, with his first Western mystery, *Roundtree Days*. He continues to expand his musical and literary horizons, dividing his time between the Berkshires and as a hands-on grandparent in Seattle.

THE STORY BEHIND THE STORY: Like so many millions of Americans in the era of Covid, my wife, Cecily, and I are on the Netflix and Amazon Prime bandwagon. Since I've been addicted to murder mysteries from the moment I learned how to read, in the past two years we've watched just about every mystery series our TV screen offered.

A few months ago, at the conclusion of yet another episode in which a detective finally figures out who the perp is two seconds before he or she was about to commit another heinous crime, Cecily asked me, "Wouldn't it be interesting if once in a while they nabbed the wrong guy and the real criminal got away scot-free?"

How much more of a light bulb does an author need than that?

I got to work the next day. I decided I didn't want the crime to be a murder because, in this day and age, I simply do not want to see a murderer elude law enforcement. So I chose a nonviolent crime and went from there. The story poured out, and then, after a few days of spit and polish, "A Scarab for Normandy" was ready to go. The question was, "Where?"

Underlying this question was the notion I've felt time and again in my fifty years as a professional musician: What good is a violin concerto if no one hears it? So with "A Scarab for Normandy" in hand, I clicked onto the Internet, scrolled down a list of publishers interested in short stories, and came across *Coolest*. I liked (a lot) what Mark and Elizabeth had to say about their mission, and it didn't hurt that their submission process was a piece of cake. I pressed SUBMIT, and it was done, except for the undying truth that when you submit fiction for publication, it's a lot like auditioning for a major symphony orchestra—it's a crapshoot. The competition is intense and daunting, and you do your best, hold your breath, and hope the gods will be beneficent; and if you win a few along the way, you consider yourself lucky.

In other words, I had confidence in my work, but my expectations were realistic. You have to be philosophical.

A couple weeks later, though, Mark and Elizabeth gave me the thumbs up. Even all these years into my careers in both writing and playing music, I was totally delighted. And why wouldn't I be? After all, the gods had come through.

NANCY J. FAGAN'S short stories have appeared in venues such as *Fiction International*, *NiftyLit*, and *The Garfield Lake Review*. She loves writing strong female protagonists in medical settings and digging through historical accounts and library archives. She is a registered nurse and has a BA in English from Mount Holyoke College and an MFA in writing from the Vermont College of Fine Arts. She lives with her husband and two ridiculous cats, Stan and Ollie, in Massachusetts. Joe DiMaggio once gave her a $20 tip. She is currently revising her debut novel, *Gin, The Imagined Life of Dr. Virginia Apgar*. Learn more at www.nancyjfagan.com.

THE STORY BEHIND THE STORY: "The Brick" came

to me as a package—an older woman, a drug addict son, and an innocent boy. I needed a way to connect them, and Legos, in my experience, are a toy most every child will play with. Full disclosure: My adult son is a software engineer for Lego, and all my kids played with Legos constantly; there are bins of them stored for future grandchildren in my cellar.

I don't think there are enough stories that involve protagonists older than sixty, and I believe there's power in characterizing them as more than fading souls. I worked on this piece in graduate school with an adviser who encouraged me to push it further with each revision. We talked about the more highbrow elements of storytelling, such as objective correlatives, but also about the nuts and bolts that make a story work, such as conflict, tension, and poignant losses.

As I wrote and revised "The Brick," I often thought about how life turns on itself, with no warning of what's ahead, sometimes leaving heartbreak in its path. For some of the story's plot points I used my own experiences; my observations of friends and family also helped me imagine a child unable to communicate easily with the world around him. More full disclosure: My software engineer son suffered in early childhood from a profound speech delay and learned to communicate with sign language and a picture board, so I knew of the speech therapy experience firsthand.

But I did not write about my son per se in this story, or about his specific problem. Instead, the drafting and revision of this story reminded me of what he and I had navigated years ago, and I reframed it. For the most part, I wrote about Jazzie's difficulties as if encountering him from outside his family and delved into how difficult it is to understand what others go through with problems as significant as his. As a nurse, I'd worked with several social workers and therapists, so I knew the system and its failures fairly well. The notion of a young child who was unable to relay with words what had occurred until the point he was found intrigued me personally, and as a writer I wanted to explore that.

ELIZABETH P. GLIXMAN is a mixed-media artist, a widely published poet, the former interview editor of the literary magazine *Eclectica*, and the author of four poetry chapbooks, the most recent of which is *I Am the Flame*, published by Finishing Line Press. She attended Boston University's School of Fine and Applied Arts and has a BFA in studio arts. As a visual artist she uses paint, ink, Cray-Pas, colored pencils, fabric, canvas, upholstery embellishments, sewing trims, cloth and gift ribbons, Styrofoam, craft paper, shiny glittery things, quilt batting, needles, thread, and old photos. As a writer she has pledged to use words, memories, and experiences—hers and those of others—to tell stories that remind readers of the power of the human spirit regardless of challenges or circumstances.

THE STORY BEHIND THE STORY: In 2003, I was diagnosed with chronic fatigue syndrome. This was a difficult time for me—I spent a lot of time lying on the couch, watching TV, and thinking about what in my life may have brought this awful existence upon me. I mulled over various decisions I'd made over the years, the demands of my upbringing, my relationships, and the culture that made me who I was. But one question recurred in my mind more than any other: Had I been pursuing what brought me contentment? Then my friend gave me an old Gateway computer, and best I could with the energy I had, I began writing stories based on situations I'd been through. My characters were not always people from my past but sometimes composites of them. My narrators had issues I was trying to work out, or issues other people I knew were struggling with. The primary issue in my own life remained *Why does my body have me spending so much time lying flat on my back?*—but I kept writing.

"Auras" poured out back then as a first draft I didn't revise and titled "A Sixties Story." The way I approached writing in those days was I never rewrote; when a story worked, it seemed like divine intervention, and when a story didn't work, I moved on to the next. I considered my aversion to revision an issue of mine, too, and even joined an online writers group to work on it—but instead ended up writing poetry for that group. Poetry made for an "easier" way for me to get to what I wanted to say, so for me in those years then and for quite a while afterward, poetry it was. Then, in 2022, I read "A Sixties Story" again and felt it was a story people could identify with, given all the bickering about gender and sexuality everywhere I turned. I was bothered by the fact that, now, all these years after the sixties (a time of acceptance and even celebration of sex and sexuality, in my experience), people in the U.S. were disagreeing about gender and sexuality to the point of anger and even hatred. For me in 2022, the Summer of Love was clearly not only over but also now forgotten and even discredited and bashed.

Still, for me, there was the memory of one girl I went to a New England all-girls high school with. And because she'd recently passed away, I wanted all the more to celebrate how fun she'd been—and how fun she'd made my coming of age. She was, in my mind back when I was a teenager and even more now, an admirable rebel: She painted her hamster with a nontoxic red dye and wore work boots and drove a jeep to school. The character Muffy in "A Sixties Story" had been somewhat of a composite of her and another girl who'd quit school in her junior or senior year to marry a man who was much older than she. Both these girls I'd known in high school had been nonconformists, women who today would be strong and respected by many. So when I heard about *Coolest American Stories*, I thought: Well, let's see how cool the publishers and editors of this anthology are. I submitted "A Sixties Story" to them, and they accepted it, editing it to make it a stronger statement about how, whether you're young or old or any age, sexuality is a complex, unique, sometimes troubling but always potentially exciting gift. Yes, Mark Wish's and Elizabeth Coffey's edits removed some of my favorite passages and changed the title, but by working with them, I came up with a story that flowed more smoothly and, again, twenty years after I wrote its rough draft, will remind readers to choose the experiences that affirm them and bring them joy.

R. C. GOODWIN grew up in Springfield, Illinois, and graduated from Yale with a degree in history. After medical school in Dublin, he completed an internship in New Haven and a psychiatric residency in Hartford. His published writing includes thirteen short stories, most with a medical/psychiatric slant, three of which won literary competitions. His debut book, *The Stephen Hawking Death Row Fan Club*, a prison-centric collection of six stories and a novella, was published in 2015. It was selected as a *Kirkus* Indie Notable Book. In 2018 his novel *Model Child* was published by the SideStreet Press in Chicago. His most recent project is a memoir, *Mak-*

ing God Laugh, to be published by Blydyn Square Books in 2024. That title was inspired by the proverb "Do you know how to make God laugh? Tell Him your plans." R.C. is also working on a novel, *Estella's Story*, based on the female protagonist of Charles Dickens's *Great Expectations*.

THE STORY BEHIND THE STORY: "A Mother's Last Request" is based (very loosely) on a conversation I had with a woman who'd recently learned that her only daughter was gay. She approved of her daughter's lesbianism in principle, but the actuality of it was something else. "A Mother's Last Request" itself is a twisting of facts and imagination in the name of poetic license; it's essentially a lie. It's also dedicated to my wife, Judy Goodwin, who, through the years, has been my staunchest supporter and most implacable critic.

NATHAN ALLING LONG grew up in a log cabin in rural Appalachia, worked on a queer commune in Tennessee, practiced meditation in a Thai monastery, and now lives in Philadelphia. Their work appears on NPR and in more than one hundred publications, including *Electric Lit*, *Master's Review*, *Witness*, and *The Sun*. *The Origin of Doubt*, a collection of fifty short fictions, was a 2019 Lambda Award finalist. Nathan's second book-length manuscript, *The Empty Garden*, was an Iowa Fiction Award Semi-finalist. Other distinctions include a Truman Capote Literary Scholarship, a Mellon Foundation grant, four Pushcart nominations, and scholarships to Bread Loaf and Sewanee writers' conferences.

THE STORY BEHIND THE STORY: I wrote "The Dog" the second year of my MFA program at Virginia Commonwealth University. I'd written a series of stories that all seemed similar—around four thousand words, about a young college educated man living in a city with a domestic conflict and an issue with his father. I recognized the pattern and was bored with it, even though each story had a different plot.

I wanted to write a story that was larger, in scope, in characters, in setting, in words, and in intention. I'd lived all over the U.S. and had traveled the country about twenty times—hitchhiking, by bus, by train, by plane, and by driving a car with friends—and I wanted a story that would try to capture the America I had experienced from my travels.

At the time, I was living with my sister, who'd spent a summer picking apples on a large orchard in Washington, and after hearing details about her work there, I decided to center the story around an orchard. The two main characters—Ray and Bill—came to me quickly, with their divergent tastes: hitchhiking and drinking versus riding "the Dog" and smoking pot.

As I wrote, I decided to incorporate as many states as I could—there are references to about twenty-five. And though I'm not Christian, biblical images seemed to rise up, from the apples to Eden, to being a carpenter, though I wasn't trying to send any religious message.

One of my writing teachers shared with us a writing technique that entails telling little stories within your story, suggesting that they acted "like little engines" that helped move your story along, so I tried that technique, filling this story with stories about America I'd experienced or heard about from friends and other travelers. The Flagstaff guy's dialogue was nearly word for word from what someone I met at a bus stop said, as was what the guy in Grand Junction says.

I worked on "The Dog" steadily for about a week. During breaks, as I walked my dog or headed to class, I'd think of some other encounter I'd had in my travels and figure out a way to work it into the story.

It was clear from the start that Ray would never get Susie, but I wanted to put in the scene that happened at night in the back of the bus because I didn't want the story to be completely a straight story. I'm always interested in writing about relationships between men that can't be considered entirely straight or gay, connections that fall in between. I think this is why, in the end, "The Dog" is more about Ray and Bill, their connection, and Ray realizing what he had in his friendship with Bill, than it is about what he might have had with Susie.

PATRICIA GARCÍA LUJÁN'S stories have been published in *Blackbird*, *Atticus Review*, *The Rumpus*, and *Lost Balloon*. She is a former culture writer at *Vogue* and graduated as a James Michener Fellow from the University of Miami's MFA program. She lives in Miami with her family, where she's currently at work on a short story collection. On her birthday, you will always find her swimming in the ocean.

THE STORY BEHIND THE STORY: I started writing "Views" during a trip to Los Angeles in 2021. Whenever I went out, I'd play a strange game where I'd imagine backstories for each person walking down the street. The dog walker once wanted to be a rock star. The Amazon delivery man had auditioned for over a hundred soap operas. The barista was a failed contestant for *The Bachelor*, while the bartender was still trying his best to break out on Instagram. During that trip, I quickly realized I considered L.A. a city made up of mostly broken dreams—the perfect setting to start my next short story.

As a Venezuelan writer, I center most of my work around the country's devastating recent diaspora, which has displaced over a fifth of the country's population, sending them to various locations around the world. For "Views," I decided to follow a couple, from each of their different points of view, who move to L.A. in hopes of finding something better than the life they left behind in Caracas. I wanted to explore what happens when one of them stops believing in the promise of the American Dream while the other desperately clings to its allure of easy fame, money, and success. It's as much of a story about immigration as it is about America's waning sheen.

ALEX PICKETT is the author of a novel, *The Restaurant Inspector* (University of Wisconsin Press), which Padgett Powell called, "A kind of *Fargo* on terra firma that may make a real movie." His short stories have appeared in journals such as *The Southern Review*, *Subtropics*, *The Rupture*, and *Passages North*. He received his MFA from the University of Florida and currently lives in London, England, with his partner and a cranky old bichon frise named Milo. Most recently, he taught creative writing to undocumented refugees and asylum seekers for the British Red Cross. More at rapickett.com.

THE STORY BEHIND THE STORY: Back when I started thinking about what turned out to be "Practice," I was determined to write a story about a football coach. I enjoy writing about people I feel I have permission to pick on, and then finding something redeeming in them, if they deserve it. Mediocre guys who consider themselves "leaders of young men" are easy targets, especially when they are directing boys on how to play a game. In general, I find sports to be a boring subject for fiction, but petty men who get their kicks from bossing around children will always be hilarious and fascinating to me.

I was also rereading Donald Barthelme at the time. My favorite Barthelme stories have wonderful penalty-oriented premises that mirror and heighten real-world anxieties, and I took cues on how Barthelme controlled and executed his narratives. I wanted to explore punishment that did not result in grace or rehabilitation. (This isn't exactly true: While writing "Practice," I simply wanted to craft a funny story, but in retrospect this "grace or rehabilitation" idea is probably what drove me to stick with it.) From the beginning, I knew the coach would merely become enamored of power and the boys would learn nothing that would alter their behavior on the football field.

Earlier versions of the story had the coach administering mundane abuses. For a while, I thought the story lay in the coach's reaction to wielding significant power for the first time. When I realized the punishment meted out was the crux of the story, I made myself take a walk and not return home until I figured out a ridiculous punishment that was also legit enough to have made me fall in line when I was a freshman in high school. I was near the Marks & Spencer in South End Green, a few blocks from my old flat, when the idea of the coach texting the players' fathers came to mind—and I laughed out loud, so I knew it was right. After that, the story came quickly.

One other note: Eric Duoss was a good friend of mine in high school, and he generously gave me permission to use his name in the story. He pointed out that the Eric Duoss character in the story couldn't possibly be based on him because the Eric Duoss in the story is good at catching a football. But like the Duoss in the story, the real Duoss was and is smart—I believe he's now a scientist doing something with 3D printing that's above my head. He also mentioned that the coach in the story doesn't resemble our high school coach, since our coach spit when he yelled and wasn't creative with his punishments.

GEORGIA SMITH was born and raised in Atlanta, Georgia. She attended Elon University in North Carolina, where she earned her BA in literature and served as an editor for two literary magazines. In 2019, she received a New Voices Fellowship for fiction at the inaugural Emerging Writers Festival in Alexandria, Virginia. Still a resident of Atlanta, she was *not* named after her home state but after her grandmother Georgia, a quilter and artist who often taught her the value of creativity and "coloring outside the lines."

THE STORY BEHIND THE STORY: For a while now, I've been frightened by how social media has eroded the boundaries between stars and their fans, making accomplished artists both more powerful and more vulnerable than ever. Tweets and Instagram posts from teenagers declaring this celebrity or that as "the only thing that can make me happy" or "the reason I'm still alive today" recently led me to wonder: What could be missing from our own lives that leaves us searching for meaning in the lives and stories of people we don't know? And what happens when an escapist infatuation with a celebrity crosses the threshold into reality?

So I began writing "Meet and Greet," and as its plot developed, the character of its narrator, Kat, did, too. I knew I was telling a story about a teenager who places much of her hope in a TV show actor, and whose motivations begin as sympathetic but escalate into something disturbing. Inspired by Raymond Carver's "Fat" (one of my favorite stories), I drafted and revised Kat's narration so she'd sound as if she were talking to a friend plainly and bluntly. It felt right, then, that her first line of dialogue was "Shut up"—that is, the line moments before she did what she did to get the $400 she wanted. While writing that scene in her Aunt Allison's driveway, I felt Kat become much more than just a lovesick teenage girl—she became a person who has learned that to get what she wants she must play games, and that sometimes games played for money can require toughness and a sharp tongue.

As I wrote about the meet and greet itself, I tried to imagine how such an event might feel from the point of view of the celebrity: looking out at hundreds of strangers who've sacrificed their money and time for a few words from you spoken to them "personally" and maybe a flash of eye contact with you. Would you, as the celebrity, feel happy or more disconnected than ever? It occurred to me, the more I developed and revised that scene, that a meet and greet might be more emblematic of contemporary human interaction than I or the readers of this story might like to admit: often staged, often loaded with expectations (of fulfillment, validation, money, love, or who knows!), often therefore prompting the people involved to say things that aren't true. Did this realization make me happy? Not in the least. Still, the story compelled me to write it.

MORGAN TALTY is a citizen of the Penobscot Indian Nation where he grew up. He is the author of the story collection *Night of the Living Rez* (Tin House Books, 2022), and his stories have appeared in *Granta*, *The Georgia Review*, *Narrative Magazine*, and elsewhere. He's won the 2021 Narrative Prize, and his work has been supported by the Elizabeth George Foundation and National Endowment for the Arts (2022). He's an assistant professor of English at the University of Maine, Orono, and also serves on the faculty at the Stonecoast MFA program in creative writing and the Institute of American Indian Arts. A prose editor for *The Massachusetts Review*, he lives in Levant, Maine, where he can be found picking up cat toys.

THE STORY BEHIND THE STORY: "A Thin Line Rises" was my attempt to expand a roughly eight-hundred-word story I'd written back in 2011 called "The Dark Room." It was largely autobiographical and was a glimpse into the room I'd stayed in when I'd visited my father during summers growing up. My father, in real life, had blown up his room with his oxygen tanks. Luckily nobody was hurt! If you'd have asked him if he'd been smoking when that explosion happened, he'd have denied it.

Some years back I had the urge to push "The Dark Room"—to open it up, so to speak. My father passed away in 2012 from a heart attack, and I thought "The Dark Room," if I could revisit it, might help me deal with the way he and I had left things. Much of the father's behavior in "A Thin Line Rises" is in actuality the way my father had behaved the summer my wife and I visited him, before we departed for Costa Rica—only for that trip to be cut short because my father had passed away.

I decided to use fiction as a means to get at this relationship, to try and find some way to come to terms with what I wish had happened. My biggest hope is that readers come away from this story knowing how hard it is to love difficult people, but that we should never quit on them, in the same way that, as writers, we should never quit on our projects, no matter how difficult they seem. I can't even begin to describe the amount of struggle I encountered with this story. Let's just say the entire process—expanding "The Dark Room," revision, revision, revision, editing, revision, and so on—took place at a literal workbench where I was surrounded by tools. This was a tough story to put together, and I felt like that setting was a perfect metaphor for what I needed.

Funny what place and its surroundings can do for you!

FRANCISCO URIBE is a 2018 PEN America Emerging Voices Fellow, a Pushcart nominee, and a finalist for the John Steinbeck Award in Fiction. His work has been published in *BULL*, *Reed Magazine*, *Huizache*, *Crab Orchard Review*, *[PANK]*, *Aquifer: The Florida Review Online*, and several other literary venues. He currently lives in Long Beach, California.

THE STORY BEHIND THE STORY: Some years ago, I was going through a life transition. And as one does in such situations, I began reorganizing my living space, moving around furniture, and deep cleaning. In the back of my closet, buried under clothes I hadn't worn in a very long time, I came across a Def Leppard shirt that had belonged to an ex-girlfriend. Finding the shirt felt like a bomb. I froze on the spot as I was flooded with all these memories. That's what got me started on "You Don't Have Very Far to Go."

As I began writing the story, it was very difficult to get going. At first, the character, like me, was a Latino man living in Southern California pining over his Latina girlfriend, who had just left him. The problem was that those earlier drafts were much more sentimental and lacked humor. Things clicked once the main character changed. That happened when a friend of mine, all credit to him, Sean Moor, was telling me how he had been at a bar watching the fourth fight between Juan Manuel Márquez and Manny Pacquiao, a boxing match where the unexpected happened: The much-favored Pacquiao lost the fight via a knockout. Sean had just gone through a difficult breakup, and his forlornness at the bar was attributed to a bad bet he'd placed. I used bits of his story in my story, and in doing so, new life was brought into mine.

Once I found the right voice, the story just poured out of me. The voice became much inspired by Larry Brown and other Southern writers that I so much enjoy reading. Writers like Barry Hannah, Harry Crews, as well as Jim Harrison. Of course, I worried about writing from the POV of someone whose race, ethnicity, and upbringing was different from my own. But that voice gave me the distance I needed to be able to tell the story I wanted to tell.

As a Latinx/Chicano writer, I always feel the pressure to tell "our" stories. Every Person of Color feels this pressure—how to best represent "our people." It is a pressure that white folk don't seem to have. They seem to be able to tell their stories, and let them be just that, their stories. Historically, they could also veer off and tell stories from a Black perspective, a Latino perspective, an Asian perspective, or so on. So

I thought it was due time for a POC to tell a story from a white perspective.

Many thanks to Jim Krusoe at Santa Monica College and Ben Loory and Lou Mathews at UCLA Extension, who read earlier drafts and made great suggestions.

But the best suggestions were made by Mark and Elizabeth at *Coolest*. They requested that I lengthen the story. In the original draft, the one I submitted to *Coolest* at first, the story ended with Larry at the bar surrounded by the kindness of the people around him, including his friend Tito, who happened also to be drinking Larry's beer. It was an ending that left Larry with a sense of false hope, and with little room for growth and redemption. *Coolest* was very patient and helpful and generous with their notes, suggestions, and edits. Much love to Mark and Elizabeth both, because the new ending, I feel, now leaves room for the possibility that Larry has learned a hard lesson but also has changed for the better.

T. E. WILDERSON is an African American, New Orleans-born writer currently living in Minneapolis. An avid figure skater and traveler, by day she is an editor and educator. Her short stories have appeared in *Crack the Spine Anthology XVII*, *The Louisville Review*, *Tishman Review*, *Notre Dame Review*, *F(r)iction*, *Still: The Journal*, *Cobalt Weekly*, and *The Account: A Journal of Prose, Poetry, and Thought*, among others. Wilderson's work has been nominated for the Pushcart Prize and recommended by a literary magazine editor for *The Best American Short Stories*. She holds an MFA in writing from Spalding University and was a 2019 McKnight Foundation Writing Fellow.

THE STORY BEHIND THE STORY: Unfathomable family situations and their complex dynamics have been a theme in my writing for some time now. Add to this that interracial relationships also often find their way into my stories. I grew up in Minneapolis in the 1970s. Although the Twin Cities at that time were largely white, interracial relationships and biracial ("mixed") children were not uncommon. My biracial friends had a different experience with race than I did, one that was more intricate than mine as a Black with New Orleans Creole roots, and that difference has always intrigued me. How these biracial friends self-identified—as Black, white, or "mixed"—depended on so many factors that I couldn't parse. Coming from a place where I know my identity unquestionably, I write to understand what it would be like if it weren't so clear-cut.

Enter Veronica, the white main character of "The Only Way." She's in a position that's of her own doing and choosing. Her pregnancies may have been accidental, but she's making the most out of her situation. And, given her own difficult childhood, she's determined to put family first, which is why she takes in her cousin's kids. This is a challenge for her, but she makes it work. Until she gets pregnant again. The difference this time is that she really loves the baby's father, who happens to be Black. While the baby's color is not an issue for Veronica, neither she nor the father are in a position to care for yet another child.

For me while writing "The Only Way," it was important to show that *both* Veronica and the baby's father had their hands tied, and that the decision Veronica ultimately makes feels like it's indeed the only way. It was important that the father be as heartbroken and helpless as Veronica—if not more so—over giving up their baby. Having him be the one she would've liked to raise kids with was key to the narrative working emotionally. Otherwise, the issue of the baby's race might have rendered Veronica's decision as at a minimum self-serving or, even worse, racist. This is how I came to the opening line of the story. The rest was living up to that truth.

ABOUT THE EDITORS

MARK WISH has seen more than 125 of his short stories published in print venues such as *The Best American Short Stories*, *The Georgia Review*, *TriQuarterly*, *American Short Fiction*, *The Antioch Review*, *Crazyhorse*, *The Gettysburg Review*, *The Southern Review*, *New England Review*, *Virginia Quarterly Review*, *The Yale Review*, *The Sun*, *The Missouri Review*, *Paris Transcontinental*, and *Fiction International*. His short stories have also won a Tobias Wolff Award, a Kay Cattarulla Award, an Isherwood Fellowship, and a Pushcart Prize. Mark served as the fiction editor of *California Quarterly*, was the founding fiction editor of *New York Stories* and a contributing editor for *Pushcart*, and has long been known as the freelance editor who has revised the fiction of many once-struggling writers, leading to its publication in dozens of respected venues, including *The Atlantic*, *Tin House*, *The Kenyon Review*, *Michigan Quarterly Review*, *The Antioch Review*, *The Hudson Review*, and *The Best American Short Stories*. His third novel, *Watch Me Go*, was praised by Daniel Woodrell and Rebecca Makkai and published by Putnam. His fourth novel, *Necessary Deeds*, will be published by Regal House in 2024.

ELIZABETH COFFEY is an award-winning design director at Random House, where she has designed book interiors for Barack Obama's *A Promised Land*, Michelle Obama's *Becoming* and *The Light We Carry*, Glennon Doyle's *Untamed*, and numerous other bestselling titles. She dabbled in poetry in the nineties and published in several small magazines. She is working on her first novel, a mystery about estranged sisters. Her pen name is a tribute to her beloved great-grandmother Johanna Coffey. Elizabeth has been Mark's go-to editor for virtually all of his published short stories and *Watch Me Go*.